The black owl appeared.

Huge, malevolent and horrific, it dropped from the flame-lit sky. At its awful screech Syagrius' war-horse reared. Not even its training could hold the beast steady in the face of such eldritch terror. The horse threw its rider and bolted. The consul fell heavily.

The black owl rushed down on him with another ear-splitting scream. Its wings were black brooms, thirty feet from tip to tip, that drove the summer air in gusts. Its eyes flamed yellow. Its beak was stretched wide for cracking bones while its feet flexed like twin arrays of metal hooks. Other war-horses scattered in blind fear before it.

Cormac's sword was in his hand without his conscious thought. He slashed at the monster—and felt gooseflesh when his sword passed through its body to no effect. It glared, gathered sinewy legs beneath it, and made a hopping spring at the Gael. He went down beneath it. . . .

WHEN DEATH BIRDS FLY

WHEN DEATH BIRDS FLY

ANDREW J. OFFUTT
KEITH TAYLOR

SF
ace books
A Division of Charter Communications Inc.
A GROSSET & DUNLAP COMPANY
51 Madison Avenue
New York, New York 10010

WHEN DEATH BIRDS FLY

Copyright © 1980 by Andrew Offutt and Keith Taylor

An ACE Book

First Ace printing: November 1980
Published Simultaneously in Canada

Table of Contents

"The Roman empire is beheaded; in the one City, the whole world dies. . . . All things are doomed to die . . . every work of man is destroyed by age . . . but who would have believed that Rome would crumble, at once the mother and tomb of her children. She who enslaved . . . is herself a slave."

—St. Jerome, A.D. 415

"Gaul was lost to the Empire. If the ruling class of Auvergne held out against Euric the Visigoth . . . it was for the sake of the new-won independence rather than from loyalty to Rome. Further north, Syagrius, son of Aegidius, animated by the same spirit, became a de facto 'king' of Gaul between the Somme and the Loire."

—Larousse Encyclopedia of Ancient and Medieval History

Prologue:
The Black Owl

"For these are the birds of death; the Owl, a predator of the night, and the Raven, presider over battlefields."
—Alexandros of Chios

Sorcerous evil swooped above Nantes on broad black wings. Hate and Evil slept fitfully in the nighted city below. Those two dark forces called to each other as land to restless sea. Black wings slanted downward, riding the wind. The warm summer's night seemed to shiver around the ragged edges of swooping night-wings spreading broader than a man's height.

Sigebert of Metz, more lately called Sigebert One-ear, stirred in his bed and muttered. Much strong wine without water had gone down his throat earlier this evening, more than one cup drugged by his physician, a man tight-lipped against his patient's cursing. The wine brought Sigebert no peace, him most men would have said deserved no peace.

A recent sword cut had caught and torn one corner of his sensuous mouth, plowed messily along his cheek, and shorn off the ear on that side of his head. The raw pain of it came into his dreams even through the fiery fumes of drugs and drunkenness. Even so, in Sigebert the hate was stronger than the pain. Through his villainous

1

brain burned visions of a sinewy, tigerish Gael of
Eirrin and a huge ax-wielding Dane.

"Death for them," he mumbled, and he panted.
"By Death itself—death, death for them! Death
slow and awful! Death!"

Sigebert awoke to the drumbeat of his pain.

His skin was cold with fevered, nightmare-
induced sweat. The coverings of his bed pressed
suffocatingly on his limbs and athletic form. Was
difficult for him to be certain whether he slept or
woke, and in truth Sigebert hardly cared. He lay
gasping and sweating, hating.

Of a sudden he went rigidly still. Eyes invaded
his chamber. Eyes—yellow as topaz, lambent,
blazing—were fixed on him from the foot of his
bed. Something—not someone—was there, staring.

Am I awake? Surely this too is dream . . .

His horror-stricken gaze could discern no more
than a blocky and indistinct shape that was like a
short thick log, or a man's head and limbless torso. Black as the heart of midnight it was, indistinct in the darkness of Sigebert's draped night-
chamber. Yet it gave a strong, foul impression of
deformity and distortion; or perhaps that was in
Sigebert One-ear's mind, weighted by pain and
alcohol.

In his terror he thought that some goblin or
hellish fiend had come for his soul, which was
admittedly damned.

The thing moved. Grotesquely, it seemed to
shrug and expand. Vast wings flexed and their
tips reached nigh from wall to wall. Their spread
was more broad than the height of a tall man.
Black feathers ruffled.

The thing spoke . . . or did it speak? Sigebert heard words . . . or did he *feel* them?

Do not cry out, Sigebert of Metz. An you do, I shall be gone, the which will be to your detriment. I bring news of your enemies.

Night-spirit, Sigebert thought wildly. Some demon in the form of a gigantic *bird . . .*

"Who are you?" he said, and heard his own voice croak.

I am the soul of Lucanor Magus the Physician. Far—

Something surged in Sigebert. Relief, preternaturally sent? Blinking and with sudden hope he said, "Physician?"

Aye. And mage, Sigebert of Metz, and mage!

"You—have you come to help me in my agony?"

Sigebert received an impression of mirth, which angered him even while it despoiled his shaky foundation of hope. *Against your enemies,* he was told. *Is not your hatred for them as much a part of your agony as your physical hurts?*

This time Sigebert was unable to speak, and the bird continued, voicelessly.

Far to the south, in a village of the seafaring Basques, my fleshly body sleeps. All of me that is significant has winged hither, to aid you to destroy those you hate whom I also hate—yea, and for greater reasons than yours! Yet it is known to me aforetime that you will not heed my advice . . . this time. On the morrow, in day's bright light, you will believe this was merely a dream, gendered by your hate and pain. You will ignore it.

Sigebert's thoughts moved in slow, murky

channels. Already he had gone from fear to disbelief to fear to hope to shattered hope and
wonderment—and curiosity. Half drugged and
but partly wakeful, he yet put a shrewd question.

"You know this? Then why trouble to come to
me, physician, mage . . . creature?"

*For reasons that you will learn from your folly,
and heed me when again I come to you. You know
those enemies I refer to; you well know them and
their inhuman prowess and luck! They are Cormac mac Art and Wulfhere the Skull-splitter of
the Danes—those bloody devils of the sea!*

At those names Sigebert came wide awake, and
hatred pulsed in him more strongly than the pain
that rode his heartbeat. "Ah."

*They live, and thrive. They have taken refuge in
the Suevic kingdom, ruled by Veremund the Tall,*
that whispery voice went on, that was not a voice.
*He now employs them. Even now they prepare to
leave Hispania, those bloody pirates. They un-
dertake a mission to the land of the Danes for this
same Veremund. Once I served him. I, Lucanor
Magus, served him, and served him well. Now he
has exiled me and, could he lay hands on me,
would have me die slowly. They are to thank for
this—Cormac mac Art and Wulfhere the Dane of
their ship Raven. May they be accursed and accursed to world's end and Chaos to come, and the
Black Gods of R'lyeh devour them!*

Sigebert One-ear laughed hoarsely. "I know
not your gods, mage. But I share your wish!"

*Then attend. Three days from this, these pirates
leave the port of Brigantium in Galicia, and will
sail east. For a short time they will lie to in a
sheltered bay below the Pyrenees. Though they*

know it not, I await them in that same region. I shall incite my . . . hosts to slaughter them, for these Basques are a folk who love outsiders not at all.

An I am successful in this, you will not set eyes on me again, Sigebert One-ear, for I shall have no need of you. Should the Basques fail me, these pirate scum will doubtless run by night up the western coast of Gaul. Past Burdigala, past the Saxon settlements—and past your own city of Nantes. Beyond that lies Armorica, called Lesser Britain. There they two have friends and can find a measure of safety. An you are vigilant, you may entrap them ere they reach that haven. In your hands will it lie then, agent of Kings!

Sigebert strained to pierce the darkness with his stare. It seemed to him that the creature crowding his bedchamber with its presence was an immense, malefic owl. God's Death! The musty stench of its feathers was choking him!

Yes, an owl. He could distinguish the bizarre shape of its evilly wise head, the blazing eyes and hooked beak. Though he saw them not, he sensed too the taloned feet, ready to drive inward-curving claws with merciless power through live flesh. An owl; a black owl! The bird of Athena. Silent-winged predator of night. Terror of those more timid night-creatures it fed upon. Emblem of death and occult wisdom from ancient days. And vaster than an eagle, this one!

So. A wizard's soul gone out from the body in tangible form.

In the dim Frankish forests, Sigebert's people knew of such things, for despite his Latin education and manners, Sigebert One-ear of Metz was a

German: a Frank. His own people called this sort of sorcerous messenger Sendings, or *fylgja*. He could not doubt that this owl was real; Lucanor's *fylgja*.

Lucanor.

The name was strange to him. Greek, was it not? No matter; the names of Cormac mac Art and Wulfhere Skull-splitter were very, very familiar indeed. Pirates. Too recently, whilst they sought to dispose of their sword-won gains ashore, Sigebert had acted in his official capacity as representative of the king. He sought to take them into deserved custody. Was then that a sword in the hand of one of their men had butchered his face.

"Be sure that I will act," he promised, who had been called the Favoured, for his good looks, since he was first able to walk. No more.

Laughter?

I am sure that you will not! In the light of day you will believe that none of this occurred, and put it from your mind. You are not the Count of Nantes, nor will you go to him with a tale so doubtful. The more fool you!

Sigebert gritted his teeth and his nostrils flared in an angry breath. He'd like to meet this Lucanor as a man, and see how sneery he was then!

His visitor saw. Despite its haughty tone, the thing that was Lucanor knew well that it might need this Frank for an ally. As chief customs assessor of Nantes, Sigebert held some power, and was well informed of all goings and comings within the city. More, he hated the huge Danish pirate and his dark henchman even as Lucanor did. Yet Lucanor's physical body lay far indeed from northward Nantes. It had not been possible for him to travel so far, swiftly enow to give Sigebert this warning in the flesh. Nor would he place himself physically in the power of this clever villain until he had shown the Frank his value.

Besides, his spirit double, his Sending or *fylgja* as the barbarians called it, must return to his body ere dawn, for the sun's direct light could destroy it. They were no friends, Sendings and sunlight.

You will remember, the black owl said, or whispered, or thought harshly. *You will not believe, Sigebert One-ear, Frank, of Metz and now of Nantes . . . but you will remember, and in my time I will come to you again.*

With a horripilating rustle the great fell bird hopped to the window and was gone on spectral wings. Sigebert felt the air stir. The thing's shadow was an evil splotch that flowed over buildings and dark streets of Nantes. Watchdogs and alley curs across the city cringed and whimpered softly at its passing. None dared bark.

1

The Raven

"*The temporary rescue of Italy entailed the permanent ruin of Gaul. A vast horde of Vandals, Suebi and Alanas, escaping from the central European domination of the Huns, crossed the ill-defended Rhine, and fanned out across the interior provinces, threatening to invade Britain. Italy was powerless to help, and the British proclaimed a native emperor. . . . He crossed to Gaul, and expelled the invaders; but they withdrew the wrong way, not back across the Rhine, but across the Pyrenees into Spain. There most of them stayed. The (Suevi) . . . descendants still inhabit northwestern Spain; the Vandals passed on, to leave their name in Andalusia, ultimately to found a stable kingdom in what had been Roman Africa.*"
—John Morris, The Age of Arthur

That same purple night of summer lay on another coast far to the south and west; on Brigantium in the Suevic kingdom. Here in northern Hispania the night was graciously warm and all but cloudless. The spacious harbour with its triple bays sighed and surged with the tide.

In a richly tapestried chamber, five men conferred 'neath the beams of a low ceiling. At the head of the smooth-topped oaken table sat Veremund the Tall, king of this land. Though his long legs were stretched out he was not the tallest of this extraordinary gathering. At his right hand sat his kinsman and advisor, tawny-moustached Irnic Break-ax in his tunic of blue with its crossed sets of yellow stripes; Zarabdas the mage, once a priest of Bel in Syria and now among the Suevic king's most valued servants, was at his left. His dusky skin, forked jet-black beard and expressive dark eyes, no less than his eastern robes among the fair, Germanic Suevi, gave him an air of strangeness and alien mystery that Zarabdas was not ashamed to exploit. No charlatan, this dark mage among people whose hair ranged in hue from nigh white to a medium brown, and seldom that dark. His powers and learning were real. So too were the theatrical instincts he had cultivated, along with his impressive robes.

"Wisdom alone," Zarabdas had told his king, "will not gain one a hearing."

They three dominated and ruled the Sueves who dominated northwestern Spain. They three sat at table's head, and did not dominate that gathering.

The other men at the stained and battered table were more memorable still. Neither Germans nor Easterners nor even Celts were these twain, neither members of royal family nor wizards—in the usual sense. They did possess a certain wizardry at tactics, and at relieving laden ships of their cargoes. And at the bloody work of sharpened steel. Indeed one of them combined dark hair and dusky skin with pale Celtish eyes, though they were so deeply set in their slits as frequently to appear darker.

The one was an immense Dane with an immense red beard. His physique seemed to crowd the low room, compressing the others into corners. When he lowered his voice others were put in mind of distant thunder; when he raised it, of thunder bursting directly above their heads. Was a voice that had long led men, had competed with sea-storm and battle-din to be heard, and never could accommodate itself long to more polite indoor tones. The chest whence it emanated bulged like twin shields and gold armlets and ornaments flashed on the giant.

The fifth man of that gathering went clean-shaven as if to flaunt his scars of past combats. He was without ornaments though his black tunic was bordered with gold. His square-cut black hair and dark, somber face made a setting of startling contrast for the cold, narrow eyes in their slitted niches. His rangy body bespoke and radiated a different sort of power from the massive Dane's; swifter and more compact. His hands, one of which gave pensive support to his chin while the other lay relaxed on the table before him, were long-fingered and sinewy with tendons prominent on their backs. The right had been scarred, as had his face, more than twice. With weapons or unaided, those hands knew all there was to know about the business of killing.

King Veremund, and his brother Irnic, and his mage Zarabdas. And their two . . . guests. At this moment dreams of these latter two troubled the sleep of a Frank named Sigebert One-ear. Only days agone, they and their crew of reivers, sea-raiders, had done the Suevic king a high service. Now they spoke of matters more mundane, though of little less import.

They were Wulfhere Hausakluifr and Cormac mac Art of Connacht in Eirrin.

"Trade!" King Veremund said, nigh exploding the word from under his droopy yellow-white moustache. "Shipping! I said once that it has been worse than poor these thirty years, and this supernatural terror that has haunted our shores all but destroyed it. Because of you, my friends, the terror is now destroyed . . . and yet that is only a beginning. There are other dangers."

"Pirates," Cormac said, without the sign of a smile.

"Foul bloody seagoing dogs who cannot be countenanced," Wulfhere added, and when he grinned his full beard moved like a fiery broom on his barrel of a chest.

Zarabdas the mage muttered, "Set a thief . . ."

"True, you and your reivers have done well," Veremund the Sueve went on. "You have also had your losses. Are there more than twoscore able men left to work your ship *Raven*—and to fight?" The question was rhetorical; Veremund knew there were not. "I would copy the Vandals. I would make my nation powerful on the sea, though we began as a race of horsemen far to the east—as they did. Meseems the best course were to employ renegade Vandals to make up your numbers, and shipwrights from the same source. Do you agree?"

Cormac mac Art frowned while Wulfhere impetuously answered at once, though with a brave effort to be tactful in a king's presence and conceal his disgust with such a suggestion.

"It's in no way the same, lord King. Look you:

these Vandals did begin as an inland horsefolk, like you Suevi. But they did not end their travels in this Hispania, as your own Sueves are doing. The Vandals crossed into Africa generations since, lest they be trapped and destroyed. At that they had to be given sea transport by some Romish lord in Carthage . . . What was the fool's name, Cormac?"

"Bonifacius," the Gael answered. "It was their aid he was wanting, against a Roman rival. Fool, indeed! He might as well have imported plague. There was another such fool, in Britain. It's Jutes and Saxons he is after inviting over his threshold. His name was Vortigern. Jutes and Saxons rule many gobbets of Britain now, men without the price of twenty cows calling themselves 'kings' and gaining land, followers—and more than twenty cows."

The latter words were spoken for the benefit of Irnic, Zarabdas and the king, to whom *Britannia* was only a word, same's *Eirrin* its neighbour, which they knew of as Hivernia or Hibernia, these Suevi. Wulfhere knew the story of Vortigern and his importation of Hengist; knew it as well as his Gaelic blood-brother. He should have done. Hengist the Jute was Wulfhere's greatest enemy. The Dane's blue eyes glittered coldly at thought of that burly Jutish tiger, but Hengist was far away in northern waters—the lying treacherous triple-dealing bastard.

But it was the Vandals that mattered, this far south.

"Aye, Bonifacius," Wulfhere said in his reson-ant rumble. "Well, he's dead now and no matter

his name save on Loki's list of Great Fools. The
Vandals took Carthage for themselves. Now
they've made themselves the greatest sea power
on the Mediterranean." He lurched forward, and
his elbow jarred down onto the table as he
pointed. "But what worth be there in that? The
Mediterranean is enclosed and tideless as a
washtub. Once it was Rome's lake and now it's the
Vandals'! Fine for children to go swimming in
. . . but lord King, it's a man's ocean ye have to
deal with here!"

Noting that everyone at table had leaned a bit
back from him, Wulfhere let his shoulders and his
voice drop a bit. "The Vandals still build their
ships to the Romish pattern. Believe me, that is
not suited to the wild Atlantic or the Bay of
Treachery yonder!" He waved a mighty arm,
thickly pelted with red hair, unerringly in the
direction of the sea off Brigantium. Wagging his
big head, Wulfhere leaned back and spoke as if he
were a Greek lecturing a class.

"None but the boldest of Vandal captains dares
venture past the Pillars of Heracles, as they call
'em, and up these Hispanic coasts. Those I and the
Wolf," he said, now indicating Cormac by banging a fist off the Gael's thigh, "have met—in their
blundering triremes—we have sailed merry circles around."

He paused, as if working out his own sentence
to be sure he'd stated what he intended. Wulfhere's command of his native tongue was hardly
a scholar's; his Latin was ghastly, and so most
men spoke, in this part of the world. At that it was
better than when he and Cormac had arrived here

awhile back, having fled the soldiery set on them by that Sigebert fellow whose pretty face they'd ruined.

"Rings around Romish triremes built by Vandals in Carthage," he said again, savouring the sound and thought of it. "I suppose ye'd wish your own navy to do the same."

Cormac mac Art's dark, sinister face showed some small tension about mouth and jaw. Only Zarabdas, by watching him closely, observed it.

"You suppose rightly, Captain," Veremund the Tall said. "I am answered."

Cormac relaxed as unobtrusively as he had tensed for trouble. Few kings indeed would accept such truculently declaimed outspokenness so mildly. Veremund, though, was like unto no other king Cormac had met—and was the first the Gael had found whom a man might respect and like. The Sueve knew the uses of forebearance without being weak—or even appearing so, to intelligent men of craft.

How are these Sueves after having got a good man as king, anyhow? Cormac mused. *Unique, Veremund is.*

While the Gael thought thus, it was Irnic Break-ax who spoke. "What of the Basques, then? They have been seamen from ancient times, and surely they know Treachery Bay as well as heart could hope for! I am told they build goodly ships."

Cormac was impressed even while his face went cold. From a commander of horse-warriors and kinsman of the king, it was a sound evaluation. Irnic spoke true. Basque shipwrights and sailors would be worth the having. Cormac did not like to disillusion the man with whom he'd developed camaraderie.

"True for yourself," he said. "It's better for the purpose the Basques are than Vandals would be—were there any getting them. But there is not. It's fiercely independent and clannish they are; more so than the Gaels of Eirrin, and that's saying much. In their time they held off the Romans from their mountain valleys, and they held off the Goths, and by the black gods!—they are fell toward outsiders. Never will they be lifting a hand for someone not of their own race, unless it has a weapon in't, and that for the spilling of blood and doing of red death." Cormac mac Art's sword-grey eyes looked broodingly back into his own past for a moment. "At base they be the same folk as the Silures of west Britain, and the Picts of Alba," he said low, "although the latter bred with another race in the long ago; a strange race, squat and apish, the signs of which can still be seen on them. Their breed and mine have an enmity older than the world."

Cormac, whom men called the Wolf, did not exaggerate. Older than the world was that feud, indeed . . . or older than the world as it now existed. Vague memories of former lives and other epochs stirred in his brain, tempting him to lose the present in that strange reverie others called 'the rememberings' that sometimes seized him without warning. Cormac rejected its lure with all his iron strength of will and focused on the visages of the two Suevi below their barbarically knotted hair.

"An ye doubt me, my lords," he said grimly, "send ambassadors to these people. Set beside the

northern Picts, it's the very flower of gentleness
they be—and even so ye'd do well to send men ye
can spare."

King Veremund doubted not, nor was he inclined to put Cormac's test to trial. The Basques of
the Pyrenees were far closer neighbours of his
than were the Vandals. He knew all about them.

"What of the Britons of Armorica?" Zarabdas
asked. "Are they not skilled in these arts?"

"They are so," Cormac admitted. "Their ancestors crossed the sea from Britain, most of them
from Cornwall. The pulse of the sea is after being
in their blood since long before Rome was a power. For the lure of your wealth, lord King, they
could be had, though it were better elsewise. It's
Celtic Britons those folk be, by blood and language. It's too fiery a mixture they'd be making
with Danes and Suevi." Cormac shook his head,
leaned back, and showed Veremund an implacable expression. "Nay, as we're to be replenishing
our crew and bring yourself the master-
shipwright ye desire, lord King, it's a longer voyage than that is called for."

Veremund blinked, started to speak, glanced at
Irnic. Wulfhere added to the case Cormac had
presented:

"Besides," he grunted, "Danes build ships better, and sail 'em better, every day of the year."

King Veremund's fine brow furrowed in
thought. He looked at his cousin Irnic, and though
he did not speak his mind Irnic was able to follow
its turning. The king much desired the service of
these men—needed them, in truth. He was loath
to send them excessively far beyond his reach.

"A longer voyage," the King of the Sueves repeated. "Even unto the land of the Danes?"

Wulfhere Skull-splitter chuckled. "It's there most Danish men are to be found."

,Wulfhere . . . plague take ye . . . Cormac thought, but the king and his two advisors showed no offense at the Dane's over-plain words. Veremund visibly considered. The thoughts moving in his head were as convoluted as the thick, barbaric knot of his hair; a twisted 8 atop the back of his skull.

"So be it," he made concession at last. "One does not ask aid of experts and then tell them how their work should be done. The Powers speed you on your journey and bring you safe back to Galicia. Rest easy that while you're away, your wounded shall have no less care than mine own hearth-companions."

Cormac smiled in sardonic appreciation of this gentle reminder: the king held hostages against any deceit or failure in what he doubtless saw as the reivers' duty. A low rumble of laughter filled Wulfhere's bull-throat.

The giant said, "The shipwright I have in mind is a man named Ketil, lord King. He is far-travelled. In his early youth he was apprentice to an itinerant boat-builder who helped Saxon families—and sometimes entire villages—cross the water to Britain. Since then he's lived among the Franks and the Frisians; aye, and those Armorican Britons too, in pursuit of his trade. What last I heard, he had settled to family life in Jutland."

"Then would he wish to leave them for our

service?" Veremund asked, with a hand at his brown beard. "It's a long journey to make for a promise."

"To found a sea-fleet for a king, I am thinking he'd be unable to resist! He is the master of his craft and has made it an art, and loves it as—as I do mine, by the Thunderer! Moreover, news of your wealth in silver will sweeten him greatly, King of Sueves! When we show him our offspring of your enchanted chain, lord King, there will be no sailing fast enow for Ketil!"

Half-smiling, Cormac thought on Veremund's wealth in silver. Wealth indeed!

In the king's treasure room lay a chain of massive links of silver, twelve of Wulfhere's stridey paces in length. Dwarves had forged it long aforetime, under the direction of their king Motsognir. It had the unique and most desirable property of growing new links when heated in fire, so that it could spawn new wealth forever, were its power not abused. Cormac and Wulfhere had earned five paces' length of such new growth. It was theirs, to take where they would—and it was silver indeed, and permanent. Yet, at Wulfhere's words Veremund's eyes narrowed a little at realization that they meant to take it out of Galicia.

And yet . . . it made little difference. They had earned the payment. Were they so short-sighted not to return to him, they were not the men he wanted, after all. The thought and concept had occurred to Zarabdas, though as yet it but toyed at the edge of the king's mind: wealth was power. Unending wealth could lead to absolute power. With a goodly fleet and good leaders of good weapon-men, along with clever merchants and diplomats—that chain could change the course of history and make Veremund the Tall master of Europe—and beyond.

"With your permission, lord King?"

Was the dry, scholarly voice of Zarabdas the mage. Veremund's gesture assured him of utter freedom.

"Cormac mac Art," the easterner began, and his dark eyes were intent as those of a ship's lookout in dangerous waters. "I know that naught will turn you from this voyage. Yet I foresee it will be filled with such danger, physical and else than physical as well, as even you have seldom confronted. Monsters and sorcerers loom dark athwart your path, and wraiths of haunted darkness flap among the shadows of the time-to-come on wings of death. Whether you will triumph, or they, I cannot know. In this only can I advise you hopefully: do you keep ever on your person the golden sigil that once you showed me. It will aid you."

Cormac's dark face remained impassive, despite his surprise. The object Zarabdas spoke of was an ancient golden pendant in the shape of a winged serpent. It had come to the Gael as most things of value come to a pirate: in the way of plunder. He had kept it, though mentally disavowing superstition. Even now it hung agleam against the black linen of his tunic. Mac Art's hand did not go to it at its mention as any other's would have done; this man was not like any other.

"Ye say so, mage? Ye're after telling me otherwise not long since, when ye named this pendant no more than a piece of jewellery."

"A blind," Zarabdas said, his expressive hands

making light of the matter. "A distraction. You were a foreigner come to our shores, with pirates and by night. I did not know you. Besides, I was not sure of the object's nature. Since then, I have found mention of it in my books, and one rude drawing. The winged serpent is an Egyptian sun-symbol, mac Art, and far older than the winged disc of Atun that the saintly if impractical Pharoah Akhenatun caused to be worshiped. Yea, older and more powerful as well."

"Why, that bauble almost wound up betwixt the breasts of a mere taverngirl of Nantes," Wulf-here said, forgetting that the young woman he mentioned was now quite close to the King of the Sueves of Galicia, whose wife had died in the service of Lucanor's god of ancient evil.

Zarabdas took no notice whatever of the Dane's blurted words. His dark gaze remained on mac Art, and intense. "I believe the sigil adorned the prow of one of the mystical boats of Ra, long and long agone, in which souls were ferried to the sun-god's paradise. Although," the mage urbanely added with a wave of his hand that rustled his robe's full sleeve, "you must know this, mac Art. You yourself spoke of its power to protect you, on the day we met."

"Aye," Cormac nodded brusquely. He had said something of the sort, to bluff Zarabdas and test his knowledge. Was not the first time a lie of expediency had enveloped a kernel of truth.

So far as Cormac knew, the Egyptian sigil had no more magical power than a stone he might pick up in the fields. *Could* wearing the turquoise, amid certain incantations, make one fearless? *Was* the aventurine the sacred power-stone of dead Atlantis? *Might* the amethyst as so many believed, heighten shrewdness, particularly in matters of trade and business? Zarabdas might now be attempting to befool him in return. He might even be both sincere and correct, though the likelihood of that seemed small. It scarcely mattered. Cormac had kept the sigil because it was after all gold, and of value. He would continue to wear the golden serpent beneath his mail on the off chance of its aiding him—though he'd not be depending on it. He put no faith in such trinkets.

"And should it fail you, Cormac," Irnic Break-ax said smiling, "your sword-arm must make good the lack!"

Cormac shrugged. "My wits and my sword are all I've ever trusted."

"Well then, my lords," Wulfhere said, pouring ale down his throat, "I sail with the Wolf here as soon as our ship is provisioned." He looked about at pleased expressions. "And if this settles all our business, I know where two eager wenches await me—and by Wotan, I'd be cruel did I keep them waiting longer!"

Veremund grinned, all strain off him. "By all means, Captain Wulfhere, go and join them," he said, doubtless thinking of the woman who was his own new interest.

"As for me," Zarabdas said, "I have studies to pursue."

Irnic Break-ax advised that he had promised himself a night-long drinking bout with the *comites* of his cousin's bodyguard, and asked Cormac if he would like to join them. The dark Gael shook his head.

"Perchance later. With thanks, Irnic."

He departed conference chamber and King-house, and took his thoughts and seat-stiffened limbs for a walk. He strolled through the nighted streets of Brigantium. A tall man, leanly muscled and powerful, moving lightly in his black, gold-bordered tunic. He was accustomed to the weight of link-mail over leather, but now, although he had sworn no oath of allegiance, he had become a king's man and enjoyed a king's favour. Such made a difference.

Even so, the scabbarded sword at his side thwacked his leg with each pace, and a long double-edged dirk was sheathed at his other hip. The habits of his violent outlaw life had begun firming of necessity when he was but fourteen. Mac Art was more comfortable armed.

Men looked at him strangely as he passed. Native Hispano-Romans with curly dark hair they were, for the most part considerably smaller than he. He was swift and deceptively powerful for one so rangy, as some of these knew. He was not much more like their Suevic overlords than he was like unto them. Many were but squatters in dilapidated houses, with little to do but loaf and stare. Only a tiny part of the legacy of Rome: detritus. The Roman-built city's population had declined since the great days of Empire.

Was not natural for mac Art to move unpurposefully through a darkened city without being approached by women, but so it was in Brigantium. He did receive a couple of smiles that might have been tentative invitations. He walked on.

Cormac came to the waterfront district, which was in even poorer state than the rest of the city.

Hardly a craft save fishing boats was moored at the long white docks. Uncrowded and unmanned, the boats looked lonely, stark. Seawater slapped on stone with a melancholy sound, as if lamenting Brigantium's past busy importance. The one Gael of Eirrin in all the land smelled the open sea, and longed to be under weigh.

Cormac knew well the reason for the harbour's lack of activity.

Of late months the sea had become a source of dread and eerie terror, round about Galicia's coasts. Ships had been destroyed by a nameless agency, and on nights otherwise gentle. Men's lives had been smothered out in the old Roman lighthouse tower where they tended Brigantium's fiery beacon. For long and long none knew what unnatural force slew them. Wreckers had been at work—but of no natural kind, nor with natural powers, nor from natural motives.

To this coast had Cormac and Wulfhere sailed, accomplishing the nigh impossible, and they had known none of the horror haunting their destination. Behind them they left treachery and blood and marine-loaded warships bent on their doom. And they had almost fallen the wreckers' victims when they approached Galicia in their long ship *Raven*, storm-driven and weary.

The Gael's grey eyes shifted within their slitted dens. Now the beacon-light burned bright and safely in the many-tiered tower that reared up immense at the harbour entrance. Cormac smiled his bleak, unhandsome smile at memory of the day he had first seen that structure, and at what he'd found therein. A tower of death it was then, and he had entered and ascended to discover the smothered, blood-drained corpses of men with horror in their glassy eyes. He recalled his first meeting with Veremund the Tall, King of the Suevi, and the pact they'd made between them. For sanctuary and reward of silver, Cormac and Wulfhere agreed to rid Brigantium of the mysterious horror that haunted it.

Ultimately that had cost Danish lives, and it had cost Galicia one of its physicians, and the king his own wife.

Cormac stared at the tower and remembered that desperate night when he'd abode there, awaiting that which came. Masses of moving, crawling kelp, either sentient or sent, came rustling and dripping up out of the dark sea. It climbed the tower like phantasmal ivy, with a thousand thousand tendrils and a thousand thousand leech-like mouths for the drinking of the blood of men.

Only Cormac's foresight, and the firewood and quicklime he had stored in the tower by day, allowed him and his companions to withstand the soulless onslaught. Had been a hideously near thing, even so.

Then had the Gael discovered the source and nature of the attacks. With his eyes he had seen the ancient, plague-evil minions of R'lyeh's black gods, horrors of another age and long dormant— or so it had been thought. He'd heard their hissing, croaking voices, and had fought them hand to . . . hand. Worst of all, he had discovered the hidden sect of humans and semi-humans that worshiped those ancient challengers of humankind, led by the king's own physician . . . and his ensorcelled queen.

Even the strife-scarred brain of Cormac mac Art preferred not to remember how that had ended.

Still, it had ended. The wide sea rolled quietly, holding naught now save its own normal dangers. They were entirely enough. Lucanor the physician, revealed as Lucanor the mage, Lucanor the traitor to more than his king—to his own humanity—had escaped with his life.

Doubtless fled the kingdom, the Gael mused. *Only the dark man-hating gods he worships know where that Romano-Greek dog cowers now!*

Cormac gave his head a jerk to clear it of what had been. He was not the sort of man to dwell in the past; were he so, he could not bear the memories of all his ugly yesterdays. The physical act and resolve changed his mood; the desire for solitude dropped from him like a funerary cloak.

He wheeled from the hissing, slapping plain of the sea. Surely Irnic and the *comites* would be deep in merry carouse by now! The Gael turned his steps again toward the king's hall and strove to forbid himself to think.

As he approached a stand of dark, pointed trees that sighed like surf in the night breeze, someone appeared. Muffled in a long, long cloak, someone stepped from between two pines, and beckoned him. Cormac's hand slid across his middle to the sword-hilt on his left hip while his slitted eyes warily searched the deeper shade behind the cloaked figure. Once already had men attempted to do murder on him in this land.

Then he recognized the stance, the way of moving, the poise of that small exquisite head. He spotted the glitter of jewels in high-piled hair. He knew Eurica, the king's younger sister. Cormac's teeth snapped together, biting into silence the curse that sprang to his lips. Though she was of age and technically a woman at fifteen or sixteen, Eurica had led a protected life and was very, very young—as Cormac had been an eerily older man, in terms of maturity, at that same age.

Clenched teeth ground. The princess was enamoured of him, or the glamour of him—or had been. How she felt now he neither knew nor over-much cared. Once she had come to his room at night. He had got her out of there posthaste. To him she was most attractive, aye—and a child, and . . . simply a blistering nuisance. And a danger to his life greater than any armed foe. Cormac had had it to the eye teeth with the daughters of kings. And Princess Eurica here . . . alone with him at night . . . even good men had been slain for less.

He greeted her civilly. That much circumstances forced him to do.

"Only in harpers' tales do kings' sisters walk out unattended, my lady, and with the most recognizable head in the land displayed. Who be watching over yourself, and from where?"

"You are brusque as ever, Cormac mac Art." Her girlish voice held displeasure. "There is— well, there is someone watching. That could not be avoided. Yet I promise you, she is my most trusted attendant, who nursed me when I was little. My attendant, not my royal brother's." Her voice dropped an octave, with ignorance of having reminded him of the very reason they must have no meeting, not even low-voiced converse. "She will not betray us, Cormac."

"Will she now?"

Cormac was considerably less trusting. He wished he could think of some way painlessly to make the point that there was no "us" to betray, and that without sounding finicking or priggish. None suggested itself. Peradventure she could be affrighted away . . .

"Royal persons have been stabbed in the back by attendants erenow, Eurica."

"Not by my Albofled!" the princess assured him, with impatience on her. "Oh, Cormac—she's out of earshot, and were she out of seeing-range as well, I'd be in your arms this instant!"

"And I'd be hanging from a gallows tomorrow," Cormac said stiffly, "or fleeing this land with blood of the king your brother's henchman on these hands."

"Be not foolish," she said indulgently, going royal. "How should he know? As for fleeing the land . . . Cormac, oh Cormac, I have heard you are about to do that in any case. Is it true?" Close by now, she looked up and her eyes shone.

"No, my lady." *Call her not by name,* he told himself. *Be not moved. Aye, it's attractive she is, and more than willing. It's also a silly and theatrical brat she is. Many her age are, but how to tell a king's sister so?*

"But there has been talk of a long and perilous voyage into the *north!*"

Eurica's eyes were large, aglisten in the starlight. To her, the north was a legendary place of floating mountains and cold grey seas, of fierce monsters and savage manslaying giants, where corpses walked and all men were Wulfhere's size—six and a half feet, unshod—and blood was drunk smoking. Aye, and truly, along with the ordinary business of living and tending crops in a land where winter was like unto an unwanted relative that came early and stayed late, all those things had been known to exist and to happen.

"You hear much," Cormac said, and damned himself for a weak, weak answer worthy of any boy.

"So I do," Eurica said smiling. Nor did she reveal that her source of the northbound rumour was one of the bed-wenches even now sporting with Wulfhere. Her smile suddenly vanished. "Cormac, you may not return for a *year!* You—you may not return at all! I beg you, remain here and be safe!"

Safe with you, he thought. *Safer battling him who sleeps in sunken R'lyeh, sister of a proud ruler!* "My lady," he said, striving to push his brain to choose words, "that I may not do. It's a mission for the king that Wulfhere and I'll be undertaking. We cannot now go back on our agreement and still keep his friendship—even did we wish to change our minds. Which I surely do not."

"Why?" Eurica looked anguished. "What is this mission that your life must be risked for it, who has already saved our land?"

"A matter of ships and shipbuilding that will bring new life to the kingdom, and perhaps more," Cormac said, and listened to her snort her scorn. "For me, my lady, a purpose. Aimless roving and plundering has been my lot since I went into exile from my own far Eirrin. A man Eirrin-born does not forget his green homeland. I'd not be complaining; a wild life and merry it has been, but now desire is on me for something more."

The instant the words left his mouth he knew his blunder. Desire was a word Eurica could relate only to herself. Eyes ashine, forgetting the watcher among the trees, she enwrapped Cormac with her arms and rose on the veriest tips of her toes to kiss him with passion.

He was not made of steel and ice. His sinewy arms gripped her hard, firm warm young flesh tight and fatless over patrician bones. He forgot calculation in the madness aroused by her soft body and sweetly moving tongue. She moaned with delight and strove to press herself through him.

"You will not go," Eurica said with assurance.

That aided him to break the brief spell. "After that, it's more convinced I am that I must go, lady Princess. For surely my need of the king your brother's favour is all the greater, now."

"Go then," Eurica whispered. "Each day you are gone will seem ten days, Cormac. When you return, there will be something more than aimless roving and plundering for you. I promise it, Cormac."

She kissed him once more, swiftly, and broke away to run for the dark trees, gathering her cloak about her as she flew.

Cormac stood moveless. At last his teeth showed in his grim, sardonical indication of a smile. What was the dear youngster thinking of? Her hand in marriage and half the kingdom, peradventure?

I promise it, she had said. Promises were cheap, and this one she had no power to keep. That power lay in her brother's hands, though she doubtless had no thought of dissemblance and meant what she said with such sweet heat.

The Gael's black brows drew together. *Aye now; there is that. Her brother.* Did he and Wulfhere build the navy King Veremund wanted, as Cormac knew they could do, then might the king indeed consent to his sister's marriage with an outlaw pirate? Cormac mac Art was *self*-exiled from Eirrin. He was not an outlaw in this land of Galicia, and when a king approved of what a man did, he was not then a pirate.

It would bring me position and power, on these new shores.

And do I want such, an it mean marriage?

Samaire, he thought, and though it was the Gaelic word for daybreak, it was not the sun's dawning he thought of.

These were questions for the future, he told himself firmly. A long voyage awaited him now, as did Irnic and the *comites* . . . and a woman Cormac mac Art had taken unto himself here, a woman who was no princess and no virgin, and whom a man could tumble with, with no thought of far-reaching consequences.

Alone in the darkness, Cormac laughed aloud, and forgot Eurica. With a wolf-like step the son of Eirrin continued on his way to the king's hall.

2

When Wizards Duel

"*The Basques . . . claim that they are the only unmixed descendants of the pre-Aryan inhabitants of the Iberian peninsula. This claim has some basis, for in 19 BC, when the Roman conquest of Spain had been completed, the Basques [Vascones] were already established and managed to maintain their independence. Their love of freedom and independence has characterized their entire history.*"

—J.S. Roucek

"*They formed a single cultural unit, reinforced by traditions, by a strong sense of racial homogeneity, and by the Basque language. . . .*"

—Encyclopedia Britannica

In the fishing village well to the east of Galicia, people rejoiced. True, fishing villages seldom knew rejoicing when pirate ships came down on them, and three such were drawn up on the fine yellow sand of their bay. But villagers and pirates alike were Basques, or *Vascones* as the Latin had it, as the sea the Romans called Vazcaya was Basquaya to these folk who had named it, or Bascaya sometimes called Biscaya. To them who had so long known it, that sea of ever-shifting winds was not the Bay of Treachery that strangers named it.

A driftwood fire roared and crackled, hurling sparks high into the purple dark and mingling its scent with that of the salt sea. Other tempting aromas filled the nostrils of the pirate chieftain: wine and roasting whale meat and blubber yielding its oil in cauldrons.

Lithe this man Usconvets was, with his fine musculature well displayed: for he wore only a leather kilt. With his dark skin, lean, straight-featured face and black eyes, Usconvets quite resembled a former king of the British Picts named Bran Mak Morn, who had lived some two hundred and eighty years before. Usconvets did not know of that likeness. He would never know it, and had he known would have deemed it a matter for no particular interest or comment. The Basques had never at any time chosen a king or suffered one, or divided themselves into commoners and aristocrats. Nor had another people ever succeeded in imposing a king on the Basques. The Roman Empire had tried, and failed, and the Gothic Empire after it.

Neither had the Picts of far-off Britain bowed to Rome. Their racial kinship with the Basques was recognizable now only in the lines of the Pictish chiefs. Their followers amid the Caledonian heather had otherwise become a grotesque, distorted image of the race that produced them. Of this Usconvets did know, though only by rumour and hearsay.

Such matters were of minimal interest to him. Usconvets the pirate was interested in his immediate people; Usconvets was interested in Usconvets.

Now he bit deeply into succulent whale steak. Its juices flowed down his throat to strengthen him. Immediately his stomach cried out for more.

Usconvets was a hungry man. He had earned this eating. Had been his spear that slew the whale, far out on the blue sea. The village would feast on this catch for days!

Watching his black-haired rovers disport themselves, he grinned. Some, paired with girls of the fishing village, danced with all the violent energy of the flames that limned them black and gold. Others had gone from the firelight with chosen partners. Yet others ate and drank, talked and sang with the high exuberant animation of their race.

"Usconvets."

He looked at Tenil, daughter of the village headman—the "first among equals" in the phrasing of the thrice-proud Basques. Usconvets had married her a year agone, and so far as he was concerned she had no equal. Just now his strapping woman Tenil sweated profusely from the heat of the rendering kettles, and she smelled of the whale oil, and the pirate leader wanted to pull her down beside him and embrace her here and now. Overwhelmed by sight and smell of her and unaccustomed to resisting whims, he did so.

"Wait! Trouble!" Tenil gasped, fending him off. Such was not her wont at all, and Usconvets frowned his surprise. "Hear me, Usconvets . . . there is trouble abrewing. Kuicho thinks the same. We have been talking—see, there he comes."

Aye, there Kuicho came. Usconvets's hands remained where they were on his woman, one clutching, but the fingers ceased moving. Trouble? He watched Kuicho without enthusiasm. Taller the man was than the pirate by a little, and far thinner, and so much older that Kuicho's hair and beard had no right to remain so black. He stood straight as a wand. Strange were his eyes; he looked into distances that had naught to do with mundane horizons. He could read omens in the wind, Kuicho could, and in the flight of birds and the crash of surf, and he could foretell the weather. The pirate leader had learned to listen to this far-seer who had sailed with him for years.

"Tenil speaks of trouble," Usconvets said, releasing his woman with a reluctance he showed by keeping a dark hand on her thigh.

"Worse than trouble," the older man told him darkly. He hunkered down and bent his head close. "It is evil blacker than the secret pits of the sea. A stranger is here in the village; a Roman."

Usconvets felt lazy with food and drink and preferred to remain so. Besides, he wanted Tenil in his arms again. Carelessly he said, "Even Romans are not that bad, Kuicho. They are no longer so much trouble! Why did the people suffer him to stay on?"

"Suffer him to—" Tenil clenched formidable fists in bitter fury. "My brothers strove to drive him away with sticks. When he stared at them and spoke to them, they stumbled and fell down and could not get up—like babes learning to walk! He bade them keep their distance else he do worse."

"He has our tongue?"

"Latin only, I think," Tenil said, looking uneasy. "His meaning was plain without a shared language. Still, you have Latin and it is you he wishes to speak with. He said your name."

"Orko!" the pirate swore, springing to his feet.

"All this—and from the time we landed, not a word to me? Not even from you?"

"None dared say! You arrived in such jubilation! I came to tell you, just now."

"None dared say because your brothers tripped over their own feet! Where is this . . . *terrifying stranger?*"

"In yonder hut, alone," Kuicho said somberly, and he pointed with a bony arm. "I am told he has abode there for two days, neither eating nor drinking. Such has the sound of a sorcerer's fast. Those who dared approach the hut turned back pale and shuddering ere they reached it. I know something of such things, and I tell you that they were wise. Already the place smells of darkness and the abyss, and him here so brief a time."

"It is only a hut," Usconvets growled.

Yet he rubbed his lean jaw reflectively and stared about at the fisher-folk with new eyes. Of a sudden it seemed to him that their revels were too intense, as if they would deny a brooding fear that haunted them all. Darkness and the abyss, was it—and the demon-prowled pits of the sea!

"He would speak with me? Then he shall, and he'll not enjoy it! By Orko," the pirate swore, invoking for the second time his Basque thunder god, for even his ship was named *Odots*: thunder. "I'll drag him forth by the heels!"

Tenil's hand closed hard on his arm and he felt the bite of the ring she wore; he'd taken it off an imperial ship two years agone. At feel of the harsh tension in her body he stared at her, astonished. She was not looking at him. She stared at something else, away on his left. Something tickled at

Usconvets's armpits as he turned his head in that direction and, for some reason he could not name, he felt cold.

A man stood at the edge of the leaping firelight.

This was the dread Stranger who invoked such fear and low-voiced talk?

He did not look so awesome. Once magnificent, his body-enveloping green robe was filthy from hard travel and neglect. Too, it fitted less well than once. The man had lost flesh in his journeying. Nor had two days' complete fasting helped him regain it. Nor was he tall. All this Usconvets saw at once, and that the fellow's greasy black hair and beard had become as unkempt as the rest of him in his days of hard traveling.

Hmp. Had he any noteworthy feature at all, it was the black eyes that smouldered above a nose like a blade. *Rara avis in terris!*

"Who are you?" the pirate demanded, in Latin. "What do you here?"

"*Nomen mea Lucanorem est,*" the stranger said in a quiet voice: "My name is Lucanor. I seek the sea-chieftain Usconvets."

"Behold him! Mine this village is! A woman of it I have married. Trouble here you have caused, and you not of my people."

"Not so, chieftain. I protest that I have done no harm, and none I intend. Naught have I taken, beyond space to rest. I have not eaten of your food, though I had power to demand it. Now only to talk I wish."

Kuicho muttered in his own language that the man was an unctuous liar. Usconvets motioned the tall man to silence. Kuicho would not heed: "He has not eaten because he is about some sorcery or divination that required fast!" he blurted in Eskuara, the language of the Basques; Kuicho, who affected to have no Latin. "I tell you, this man brings evil!"

Usconvets grinned, for he was a pirate and long since had trained himself to show only confidence, or rage. "Then best he should not see us quarrel! Fret yourself not, friend. I am about to listen to him, not grant his every whim. Surely there is about him no appearance of a man of great power."

At Usconvets's satirical tone Kuicho lapsed into a silence that compressed his lips. His stare remained baleful nonetheless, and it never left the stranger called Lucanor.

"Talk, then," Usconvets said, again in Latin.

Lucanor eyed him calculatingly with that odd burning gaze. "Your race is ancient, seachieftain," he said, so quietly. "The Vascones have been great sailors and builders of ships since the world began. Are you pleased with the way the world wags nowadays?"

"*Bascones vivent, Roma fuit,*" Usconvets said with wicked simplicity; "The Basques exist; Rome has perished."

"You are bold."

The pirate's dark eyes narrowed to stare into those darker ones. "What then shall I complain of?"

Lucanor, mage of Antioch, made an expansive Oriental gesture that flapped the sleeve of his robe. "The Saxon sea-rovers, perchance? The Heruli? The Armorican corsairs? Even the men of Hivernia, who sometimes raid this far from home? Once it could be said, and truly, that the Canta-

brian Sea belonged to the Vascones. Now every
wave of it is contested by others."

Usconvets laughed. "You mean that every wave
flings up their drowned corpses on the strand!
Others may dare the sea yonder, Lucanor; we, and
only we, *know* it. The Cantabrian Sea belongs to
us because we belong to it. My people will still be
here when the Saxons, the Heruli and those others
are a *memory!*"

So softly Lucanor said, "What of the Suevi?"

Those he named were a Germanic tribe, like the
stronger Vandals; they were Suebi to the Basques.
They had come into Spain with the Vandals and
had stayed behind when the Vandals under their
ruthless, crafty king crossed the strait to Africa.
Now the Suevi held the northwest of Hispania for
their own, despite the Goths who raided the rest of
the peninsula—except, of course, for the demesne
of the Basques.

"What of them? We will be here long after they
have gone, also! Besides, we are speaking of the
sea. The Suebi do not fare asea. They are lands-
men utterly."

"*Praemonitus, praemunitus,*" Lucanor said.
"Their king plans to make them a sea power." The
man's sunken eyes flamed with a consuming
hatred; Usconvets noted. "He has hired men to
help him do so. The Vandals did as much, remember, under a strong king who knew what he
was about! And in the end the Vandals sacked
Rome. The Suevi are first cousins to the Vandals."

Usconvets nodded slowly. "Forewarned," he
said, "is as you said forearmed. What men has he
hired, this first among the Sueves?"

Shivering with the force of his enmity, Lucanor said, "Wulfhere Splitter of Skulls, and Cormac mac Art."

"Ahh . . ."

Usconvets well knew those names. No man plying the pirate's trade along the western shores of Gaul could fail to know them. The Suevic king's plans had seemed laughable, at first. Now the firelight danced on Usconvets's face to show its concern, and Lucanor noted.

"Were you to slay them," the dark-faced mage said, "the matter would end aborning. I can aid you to do this thing." His eyes were *black*. They pierced.

Tenil swore hotly. "My man, will you listen to this trouble-maker? He hates the Dane and the Hivernian, that's clear, and would make you the tool of his spite. Could be no plainer! What be his squabbles to us?"

"Naught," Usconvets said nodding, and shortly. "Naught in any way, woman. Yet an he speaks the truth in these other matters . . . aye, I will listen."

"You are in error," Kuicho warned him.

"By the Sun above me! I will decide that! Continue, stranger."

Lucanor's *I have him!* was a fleeting smirk. "These red swine are sailing from Brigantium, in quest of shipbuilders for King Veremund. They will find them. Unless . . . They will befoul these waters with their accursed presence within five days at most. Best it would be for yourself and all Vascones, sea-chieftain, did they never leave them. And is not Cormac mac Art's race the an-

cient enemy of your own? The man is a Gael of
Hivernia. Blood of Atlantis and Cimmeria runs in
his body—"

"Not of Atlantis!" Kuicho snapped, bristling,
betraying his understanding of Latin. "We are the
race of sunken Atlantis, we and no others."

This Kuicho believed, for it was the tradition of
his people. Lucanor knew better. The Basque race
had its origin in the Pictish Isles west of Atlantis,
in those ancient days before two awful cataclysms
had changed the shape of the world. It did not
astonish, that millenia of word-of-mouth repeti-
tion had confused the Pictish Isles with Atlantis
itself.

"So you say," the mage said sharply. "None the
less, were Cimmerians and Picts as brothers in the
long ago? Were the Gaels and Basques as brothers,
here in Hispania? Is not the blood debt between
them and you ancient, and heavy, and scarlet?
The Danish Skull-splitter and Cormac mac Art are
coming here, with one ship and scarce forty men!
Slay them all, sea-chieftain, for the sake of what
was and to prevent what may be!"

Lucanor stopped himself. Though he panted
with passion, his cunning told him he had said
enow. To harangue the pirate further would be to
lose so proud and willful a man. He stood and
watched, thinking hatred, while Usconvets considered the scheme without making reply.

Usconvets was tempted by the prospect of a
good rousing fight, and who knew what rich
plunder might be aboard the Raven of the Skull-
splitter and mac Art? Besides, it was certainly true
that he did not wish the Suevic kingdom to grow
powerful asea. Yet—Tenil and Kuicho had much

of right with them, too. Usconvets neither liked
this stranger nor cared to be used in his machinations.

"Now I will speak!" Kuicho cried. "I know you,
Lucanor, you who worship the Black Gods of
R'lyeh, accursed and banished since before there
were men! I know also this man you speak of, aye
who he is and who he *was* as well, this Cormac
mac Art. I too have my powers, lackey of Cthulhu,
and ways of knowing what other men cannot. In
former lives he was friend to my people, this un-
dying *ka* that is presently Cormac mac Art. In
times to come he will be our friend again."

Usconvets, like Lucanor, stared at his old companion Kuicho, and when he felt Tenil's hand slip
into his he was not loath to press it.

"Once he was King Kull of Valusia," Kuicho
was saying, his eyes seeming to flash like
polished gems in the firelight. "Then his war-
companion and blood-brother was Brule the
Spear-slayer and his ally the chieftain Ka-nu. His
ancestor in the body he now habits was Cormac,
Prince of Connacht, ally in battle to Bran Mak
Morn who was the last great king of the British
Picts. I see; I know. Kull is Kormak the Kelt!"

For a moment later Kuicho stared at Lucanor,
and then he rounded on Usconvets. "And this too
I see! Follow the counsels of this man and he will
lead you to disaster, Usconvets!"

The pirate was troubled, and showed it. "Well,
you say one thing, old friend. This . . . Luke says
another. You both claim powers common men do
not have. Suppose you strive together? I shall be
guided by the advice of the victor."

Although he spoke it slowly, as a thought said

aloud and a suggestion only, the savage laughter
in his eyes belied that. Both Lucanor and Kuicho
knew that refusing was not among their choices.
Usconvets *ruled*, by being Usconvets. He
amplified that fact by making a sweeping gesture
that said it plain: *Get ye at it, both!*

Basque and Graeco-Roman faced each other;
the tall lean man in the unkempt robe and the tall
stringy one in nothing much; a stark figure of
humankind with roots running back thousands of
years—and full consciousness of those ties to past
times and lives.

They faced each other in the firelight, and that
swiftly it began.

The Basque diviner seemed inhumanly tall and
straight, his leanly muscled lines nigh unbroken
by clothing and the firelight playing upon him.
Yet about the other man's rumpled, insignificant
figure the shadows thickened and swirled. Only
the sounds of the surf disrupted the stillness—
and *something* seemed to perch on Lucanor's
shoulders or to erupt from his body. Partially
merged with that robed form, a part of him, it
seemed to ruffle vast black wings. Tenil's face
paled, and it was from the grip of Usconvets's
fingers on her hand. They stared, and she was of
no mind to beg for release. Usconvets would have
taken his oath that the stranger's eyes blazed yellow as candle-fire or the stone called topaz. The
pirate's bold heart chilled within him. Tenil
turned her face away from Lucanor, into her
man's bulgey chest.

The villagers were silent. Many had surreptitiously fled or slipped away into the darkness.
Fearsome sorcery hovered over their village, and

the air was laden with a miasma of the preternatural.

All knew that forces strove just as had there
been the clash of steel on iron and wood and the
grunt of striving warriors. Two stares met and
clashed and challenged. Kuicho's eyes, stretched
wide in his masklike face, mirrored the stars that
seemed to stumble as they were called on to feed
the power that mage turned on mage. Lucanor's
eyes had narrowed. Their abnormal, xanthic,
lambent glow might have been some trick of the
firelight . . . but Usconvets did not believe it.

He *felt* it, palpable as heavy fog or low clouds:
mighty forces surged between these two and no
two weapon-men ever strove the harder with
sharpened steel.

Both men's faces gleamed and then they were
sweating huge drops, though they stood motionless. They strove mightily, without moving from
where they stood and without so much as raising
their arms. Kuicho's bare long limbs could be seen
to tremble with effort, with focused energies.

The very air between the moveless combatants
sang and vibrated with unseen forces. Usconvets
knew that he watched war, eerie and of the
shadow-world with powers drawn from the
minds and those breathless gulfs between the
stars, and that combat was no less than the striving one against the other of two enemy ships on
stormy waters. Did he know doubts then, at having pitted his old companion against the newcomer whose appearance was obviously deceiv-
ing, as a long, lean rangy man could be strong as
one with muscles like stones?

He had cause to be. As abruptly as it had begun,

it ended. Kuicho shrieked, shook and twitched like an aspen in a gale, clutched at his eyes—and crumpled to the sand.

Instantly Lucanor reeled as with release of some mighty tension, and the illusion of the great winged thing surmounting and sharing his body vanished. Yet he fell not. Too, he no longer seemed aught save a most ordinary man. Breathing in great gasps, he stared at Usconvets.

"Vici," he croaked; *I conquered.*

Usconvets swallowed again so that his voice emerged strong. "What of Kuicho? Is he dead? By Orko, if he has died our bargain is void—and your life as well, stranger among Basques!"

"He lives," Lucanor said thickly; another short Latin word. "He will . . . be ill for many days, however. He . . . drained himself . . . as the conflict has cost me hard. Ah! *Cthulhu fhtagn!* Give me meat and wine!"

He seemed to fall to his haunches. Squatting shapelessly, he bowed his head.

Usconvets waved a hand to indicate that the Antiochite be given what he wanted. Out of a certain morbid curiosity he asked, "Have you no further need to fast?"

"My need is for strength," the mage mumbled. He received meat, and began to eat. "Does our bargain stand, sea-chieftain?"

"Aye," the Basque said, almost unwillingly. "Usconvets is loyal to his word. Show me the ship *Raven* and I fall upon it with all my strength."

"That is good hearing," Lucanor said, past a steaming mouthful of whale meat. Delight as much as exhaustion fed his tremors now. "I have

time, not immensities of time, but it suffices . . .
to regain my strength, and then to fast for another
day, and to perform certain divinations . . . yes.
When they appear, you will know, lord. You will
know."

None failed to note that of a sudden Lucanor
had become curiously servile. Mayhap because of
the expenditure of so much energy, and strength?
Whatever the reason, Usconvets took cue from it
at once.

He nodded curtly. "Then eat," he said. "It has
long been my thought that Wulfhere Skull-
splitter—the great oaf!—ought to have stayed in
his cold northern waters. Now he shall learn it
himself, by the Sun above me!"

3

When Dead Men Attack

"In a world where the old-time skill of the Roman swordsman is almost forgotten, Cormac mac Art is well-nigh invincible. He is cool and deadly as the wolf for which he is named; yet at times, in the fury of battle, a madness comes upon him that transcends the frenzy of the Berserk. At such times he is more terrible than Wulfhere, and men who would face the Dane flee before the bloodlust of the Gael."

—Conal the minstrel, of Britain

Dusk had begun to shadow the blue water. Red as fiery copper, the sun of Behl sank lower in the direction of Galicia, which Raven had now left eight days' sailing to westward. Behind the bay where Cormac and Wulfhere had rested their crew for a day and a night, the foothills of the Pyrenees rose dark against the sky. Beyond them shouldered up the great mountain peaks in mauve and scarlet and burnt gold, brilliant yet in the last of the light.

Coppery dusk illumined too the pirate galley's swelling sail as Raven put to sea. The sail was new, of Galician manufacture; blue stripped with green. The ship slid forth silent as a crafty predator—which it was. This time Raven was on no piratical mission.

Wulfhere, standing immense by the shield-rail,

breathed the twilight air with pleasure. His crimson beard fell to spread in untrimmed exuberance over his scale-mail corselet. Over his shoulder he bore the overlarge long-hafted ax that was never far from him. Braces of gold and brass flashed like fire on his arms, which were big as most men's thighs. The mighty Dane made a picture of rampant barbarism not easily forgotten; and just now, of a contented man.

The barbarian loomed over the world Rome had conquered, and ruled, and lost. Unlike so many, this one was not interested in scrabbling over the truncated corpse of empire; Wulfhere Hausakluifr was content to live and to fight and to laugh.

"Ha, Cormac," he rumbled, "this be more to my liking! By the Thunderer, I had begun to feel choked in that cramping harbour of Brigantium! Was well enow for yourself; ye be at home with kingly intrigues and politics. Not I."

Cormac smiled faintly without making answer. The Skull-splitter had voiced some such comment on each day of their voyage thus far. Nor would the Gael be disagreeing with him. Cormac mac Art was not so much at home with matters political that he didn't savour this challenge. Asea, he and Wulfhere were their own masters, and the kings of the earth could do no more than gnash their teeth over the fact.

Once again Cormac wore his black mail of chain mesh. Its reassuring familiar weight covered him from throat to mid-thigh, clinking. Above it his dark, scarred face well suited the war-shirt's implications. His black mane, not long, was bare to the wind. Beside him on a vacant rowing bench rested his plain helmet. Its crest of flowing white horsehair stirred a little with the breeze of *Raven's* movement. At one hip rode his straight, double-edge sword in its sheath; on the other hip he wore a Saxon fighting knife.

Planting a foot on the rowing bench beside his helmet, mac Art set his two hands on that knee and inhaled salt air while listening to the sound of water furling past in a hiss, and the thunk of oars accompanied by the grunts of those pulling them. Just now *Raven's* unmanned oars were over-many. Threescore men made her full crew, fifty to row and ten to handle steerboard, sail, and lines. Now here they were, he and Wulfhere, roving the sea with but twoscore.

Still, mac Art of Eirrin did not fret over that for which there was no help. They'd been under-manned aforenow. They had prevailed. They lived.

Well they knew this western coast of Gaul. Here, in these waters where Gallia and Hispania met, heavy swells were common. In crashing gouts of foam they broke dangerously near sunken rocks even where the water was deep. Farther north, off the River Garonne and the Saxon islands, tidal streams ran tricky and inconsistent as though designed by hunt-wise foxes. To run up this coast by night required not only men who knew what they were about but bold ones besides. Necessity bred boldness as kings did conflict. The night did offer cover, and western Gaul was stiff with the reivers' foes.

Big brusque Guntram, the Gothic Count of Burdigala that would be Burgundy, craved their bodies for exhibition on a gibbet to placate his master King Alaric. Athanagild Beric's son, who commanded the royal Garonne fleet for Alaric, yearned even more to capture them.

More enemies were the Saxons settled in the Charente region and the large islands nearby. They knew the reivers; they knew Cormac had not come by his Seax-knife—Saxon dagger—through amiable trade.

Nor was it likely that Sigebert the Frank, now chief customs assessor of Nantes, would have forgotten them. He'd set a cunning trap for Cormac and Wulfhere not two months previously—and failed to take them though he had them at swords' points. He'd lost an ear for his trouble.

Ah, half the world was set against the self-exiled Gael of far green Eirrin, and he was not even taking Lucanor into account.

His reflections were most rudely interrupted. "Three ships on the steerboard side!" the lookout bawled. "They come fast under oar, from astern!"

Three! Cormac snatched up his helmet and went swiftly aft while he settled it on his head. Ordlaf the steersman greeted him with a nod.

"Yonder, I'd guess," he grunted. "I see naught as yet."

Cormac stared into the deep-blue gloaming. Three shapes emerged. Cloven water hissed white at their bows. Each was smaller than *Raven* but seaworthy and fast in the highest degree. Aye, Cormac knew them and for him a glance sufficed: Basque ships. They neared, well-rowed.

"*Wotan!*" Ordlaf burst out, in a voice of incredulous horror such as Cormac had not previously heard from the stolid Dane. "*What phantoms be these?*"

"Phantoms?" Cormac stared in puzzlement.

"What is it ye mean, man? It's ships I see on the breast of the sea, and men on them bent on a fight. Bad enough that is—what's this of phantoms?"

Ordlaf looked at him as if he were mad while Ordlaf's were the wild eyes of madness. From the crew's sudden braying of panicky invocations of Wotan, Aegir and other gods, Cormac understood that something was badly wrong. Were his own eyes failing him? He squinted at the oncoming ships. *Raven* was undermanned and pursued, badly outnumbered, aye and undeniably. But it would take more than that to shake this crew of battle-hungry demons Wulfhere and he led. What then? *What?*

Wulfhere Skull-splitter himself burst through the uproar on knotty legs, seeking advice from the man on whose crafty counsel he depended. Cormac saw that his eyes, too, were wide aghast.

"Wolf! Do ye see them? Surely it's from Nastrand itself those demons have voyaged to find us!"

"Nastrand?" Still not comprehending, Cormac heard his friend name the cold barren shore of Hell, where the corpses of cowards and perjurers were eaten by monsters till the end of time and breath. "Blood of the gods! Nastra—Wulfhere? *What see ye there?*"

For the second time Cormac received from eyes less than rational a look that questioned his sanity. "See? What is there to see? Rotted ships of death, crewed by liches!" Hearing himself, Wulfhere gathered up the reins of his own runaway control. "But we'll soon cause the sea to cover those corpses—again!"

Again Cormac looked at the approaching trio of ships. He saw ships crewed by staring weapon-men. *Is that the way of it*, he thought. *Illusion and seeming—and I immune!*

He wasted no time in attempt to convince his fellows that what they saw was unreal. What mattered was to make them fight. An they were still the men he knew, they'd do so. He raised strong voice.

"All who row not, string your bows!" he commanded. "Swiftly, swiftly! Teeth of Fenris, be ye children to quake at sorcerous illusion? Ivarr—come man, feather me thatun standing by the mast! Those are men, *men!*"

The three strange vessels were swiftly overtaking *Raven*. White water furled back past what all save Cormac saw as skeletal ships: naked wooden ribs, grown over with mussels and barnacles and trailing masses of dismal kelp like ragged nets. Sails blew aflutter in rotting rags from the yards. The oars that rose and dipped were decayed or broken. Yet in spite of all, the death-ships moved across the sea at a better pace than *Raven*.

Aye, and to all but the Gael their crews were men long since drowned.

Wulfhere saw horrid white eyes, that had rolled up to stare blankly like those of landed fishes. Blue-grey were their skins and slick with corruption, like wet slate. Sea-lice had eaten them here and there to form hideous patchwork. Such men were *dead*—and they rowed.

Those not naked wore garments that seemed only rotting sackcloth and leather; that hung in tattered ribbons from their ghastly bodies. In dreadful silence they brandished weapons yet able to bite, though corroded by brine.

With coldness like drift ice in his stomach, Ivarr obeyed Cormac's order. Oh, he had no misgivings about his ability to hit his ghastly target. What the Dane dreaded and half expected was to see it continue standing with his arrow betwixt its visible ribs. What could an arrow be, to something dead and rotting that yet moved and challenged the living?

The bowstring said *thunng* and Ivarr's barbed shaft keened out over the water accompanied by his curse—and prayer. The arrow skewered the shape by the mast. Through the belly it took him, and Ivarr saw the creature tumble and fall down, kicking. So saw the other archers, and so did Cormac mac Art, though what *he* saw topple was a living human, an armourless Basque.

"Well done!" Cormac called, as if 'twere an accomplishment more than standard, for the need for encouragement was obvious to him. He knew how to motivate men, by praise and threat, by shaming and challenge. "What ails the rest of yet, that ye gape and delay? Shoot for the rowers!"

Heartened at the falling of the supposed lich in the manner of an ordinary sailor of blood and flesh, they loosed their arrows in flights of ten. Speeding angry bees seemed to hum shrilly over the sea.

The Danes were marksmen, who made the finest bows and produced the most deadly archers in all the lands about the Baltic. Oarsmen in the foremost of the attacking vessels began to suffer.

"Ye see?" Wulfhere bellowed. "Weapons can destroy them—WE can destroy them! Hard about!

To portside now, and ram that weed-grown
hulk!"

Oars increased stroke on the same side of Raven
as its great steering-paddle; those opposite were
raised but not shipped. The slender pirate craft
came about hurling white water in a close circle.
The foremost Basque ship continued to plow in.
Raven's coppery beak was now directed at the
broad side of the attacker. The Danes bent to their
oars with renewed will and a savage enthusiasm.

Unlike her enemies, Raven was fitted for ram-
ming. Her bows had been strengthened and
braced within, sheathed in scales of hammered
copper without. Her dragon's head laughed savagely the while she bore down on the enemy. And
now the Basques saw what was intended, even as
they saw their prey's speed increase.

The Basques strained mightily to avoid the impact. They succeeded only partly.

Raven's deadly beak, driving fiercely through
the water, did not bite amidships; instead it
smashed one of the Basque's long steering-
sweeps with a terrible grinding popping crack—
and with a crash, half-shattered the stern. A
splinter of wood thick as his arm and longer than
he drove through a Basque's body as if it had been
a hurled spear. His ship lurched violently over
while he gurgled death. Crew and marines flew
through the air like hurled toys to plop-plop into
the water like so many clods of dirt.

Cormac's sword glittered bare. The glitter in his
sword-grey eyes was no softer and his lips drew
back from his teeth in a wolfish snarl. The dark
Gaelic rage was upon him. Reason shrank and
battle-frenzy ruled his brain and body. He only

just remembered to snatch up his shield.

"HAAAA!" he yelled earsplittingly. "Sunder them!"

He sprang to *Raven's* shield-rail as though he knew no encumbrance of sword and ten-pound helm of steel over sponge and forty-pound mail-coat and heavy buckler of wood and iron; and thence he pounced down into the Basque ship. Another ugly feral cry tore from him.

His round shield, thrust ahead of him into snarling black-bearded faces, deflected two spear-heads while breaking off another it happened to meet squarely. Basques went down under this mad assailant's greater weight, sore surprised and disconcerted by a man who used seventeen pounds of buckler as an offensive weapon.

Cormac swung that lindenwood shield more, in a bone-breaking arc this time, to gain space for himself. Springing fully erect, he ruthlessly stamped the head of a man downed by his leap. An ax banged on his shield and his own elbow was driven into his side, mail against mail in a rasp of steel links. His sword replied. The point ran into a man's side; a man Cormac never saw. More surprise for the enemy: Cormac mac Art was fond of using his point. He yanked it free in a sluicing spurt of blood and slashed sidewise without ever looking at the foe whose arm he destroyed.

The attackers were attacked by a madman. The raging Gael cut his way forward without looking back to see whether any comrades followed him.

Half a dozen did. Despite the horror of what

they thought they saw, they noted too that Cormac was fearless and that hideous corpses fell before his one-man charge. The Danish pirates were not backward about discovering that what they perceived as living dead could die again, and fall like men. Leggings and arms were splashed warmly. Crimson runnels spilled over the ship's timbers.

Wulfhere's instincts were to plunge after his blood-brother. But Wulfhere commanded *Raven*. He cursed and cheered Cormac equally and without bias, while knowing he durst not follow into the blade-reddening action he loved. His archers were still speeding volleys onto the two remaining Basque ships. Close upon them now, those vessels were bearing down in foam-sided furrows white as new samite.

"Belay that!" Wulfhere roared in a voice like an ocean-storm. "Bend to rowing, ye geldings! Would ye be cracked like a nut betwixt tongs? Lay alongside that one, the nearer—we'll grapple to her! Ugly bastards, aren't they! Best we aid them along to Ran's arms where they belong, lads!"

His broad face darkened with passion above his flaming beard. Ax upraised, his immense height increased nearly to seven feet by his horned helmet, Wulfhere Skull-splitter was a fearsome sight. The bitter necessity of leaving mac Art fighting for his life made the giant's rage greater, if such were possible. He loosed another hideous bellowing cry that froze Basque blood into marrow and whitened dark faces. He gnashed his teeth and foam speckled his vast beard like white-hot flame amid red.

Glaring, he brandished his terrible ax and raved

threats against the ship he had designated for assault. He cursed each moment that passed ere the first grappling hook could fly.

To Wulfhere—as to all left aboard Raven—they moved against a vessel of unnatural life-in-death. All too recently he had coped asea with foes otherworldly and inhuman. Now his eyes assured him that death's head liches stared at him from sockets like thumb-gouged holes, and thirsted for his blood. Yet he never hesitated, nor did his men.

Grappling hooks flew gleaming like dragon's teeth. Some bit into wooden strakes while others missed because the ship's structure was not what they saw it to be. Those men reeled in and tried again even as feverish fishermen, the while Raven drew closer by means of those lines that had found purchase. Wood creaked and water hissed and gurgled as the two craft swung close.

Wulfhere Hausakluifr was first over the side, in a flying leap that should not have been possible to a man of such size. Like those of a mad giant his big feet crashed to the deck of the other vessel. Behind him swarmed his men, yelling in the way of wolves or berserks. They rattled onto the Basque craft, tall fair men all agleam in armour of glittering bosses or lapping scales sewn to byrnies of boiled leather.

Counting their leader, the Danes numbered five-and-thirty. While their arrows had left about that many Basques to face them, the Danes in general were bigger men, and armoured besides.

Faces of corrupting death leered at them. Weapons hacked and stabbed in fists with tattered grey flesh raveling around knuckles of bare white bone. The northerners' noses were deceived, too, for the stink of death was as of an old burial-barrow torn open. Yet their very revulsion nerved the Danes to fight with transcendent fury.

Axes and swords swung and hacked, flashing like lightning bolts playing about the deck, and where they struck crimson sprang up. Basques went down. Attackers had been attacked; attack became massacre.

Wulfhere strode raving through the melée. His ax rose and fell, chopping and streaming, in a racket of cloven bone and metal. In his mighty arms it described huge horizontal eight-figures in air, the interlocked circles formed of a scarlet-dotted blur of grey, so swiftly did he swing his ax. A sword rushed at him and the shield of the man just behind Wulfhere rushed forward. It did not stop, and a seemingly half-decayed face shattered around the iron boss. Teeth clattered onto the deck. Wulfhere plunged on. He disdained a shield; he had his ax. *Thus!* and a head flew from ragged shoulders. *Thus!* and blackened stinking bowels burst from a belly that had appeared swollen tight with putrefaction.

The third ship wavered. Its oars contradicted one another. Then it turned about and fled the battle become massacre. It vanished into the blue dusk and was seen no more.

Usconvets, aboard the ship Wulfhere and his men were rapidly making into a slaughter-yard afloat, saw it happen. From behind the grisly magical illusion that masked his face, the Basque pirate cried out in despair.

"Cut free! Part those grappling ropes and break off the fight!"

His men rallied, fired by desperation and the

example he showed them.

Yet still they did not fight as they ought, and could. The illusion encompassed the vision of *all* save Cormac. What the Basques saw bracing the Danes was not their chief, but a foully animate corpse. It did not inspire them, though it shouted in a voice that was nearly Usconvets's. Had Wulfhere not seen how things stood, and been content for his own reasons to let the "liches" depart, his Danes would have surely devastated the ship from end to end. They had almost done so in any case.

"Let them go!" Wulfhere thundered. "By the Hammer! Whatever landfall they can make is welcome to them! Back aboard *Raven*, ye blood-hungry dogs! Cormac's needing us!"

His voice blared above the din of the fighting like one of the Romans' big *buccina* horns. When men did not obey him swiftly enow, he whacked them lightly—by his standards—with the flat of his gore-dripping ax and shoved them to the rail with his other hand, big as a foot. And ever he roared at them to move, move, and cursed their tardiness.

They tumbled into *Raven* and pushed off, leaving the Basques to go where they could.

4

No Crown of Laurel

Usconvets's command was reduced to a reeking shambles where dead and dying men lay about while barely a dozen stood on their feet to receive his orders. He glared wildly about at them. All, all had the semblance of things come slinking hideously from a salt grave, both the upright and the prone. The Basque pirate felt a nigh-irresistible urge to draw his dagger and stab himself through the heart.

A leader of men, he mastered himself. And from egregious defeat and despair and near-madness was born a blazing anger.

The stranger, Lucanor. He caused this.

"Into the sea with the bodies," Usconvets commanded, and watched without tears while it was done. "Now pull, pull for home. We have a reckoning to exact, there!"

"What of the others?" a man asked. He was unrecognizable, as were they all.

His leader turned what appeared to be empty eye-sockets on the third of their ships, which *Raven* was nearing fast. He asked wearily, "What can we do?"

Usconvets asked it of no one, and none answered.

Raven came alongside her prey with a grinding of timber. "Ho, Wolf!" her captain bawled. "Be not greedy and hoggish, man—leave some for us!"

The Gael showed teeth and answered with one short word.

Of the six Danes who had followed him onto the ship of enemies, three remained alive and one of those was down with a spear through his thigh. He kept murmuring "Gudrid," which Cormac felt was at least better than the "Mother" he'd heard too many times. Nevertheless the downed man fought on. He dragged a Basque down beside him, even while he groaned. When the fellow attacked him with a dagger the Dane gained a wrestling lock on his arm, snapped it with a stomach-turning sound, and soon was grimly strangling the Basquish weight with a forearm across the throat. His thigh pumped red.

Cormac and the others of his shipmates stood together, holding the deck by plying swords and ax till their arms were weary to the bone and breath was a rasping torment. Yet they had held, and held still. Now came salvation in the form of more than thirty raging comrades with Wulfhere Hausakluifr at their head.

Of forty Basques, Danish arrows and Cormac's hand-to-hand fury had left three-and-twenty. They lasted not long. In a horrid joyless orgy of blood, the Danes showed them no quarter but cut them down to a man.

In horridly short order all lay lifeless in a welter of red that rose and rose in the bailing well—but not to Danish senses, for they saw blood that was curdled, stinking and black; and flowed not copiously, because it came from bodies already dead. The prodigious ax of Wulfhere broke the timbers of that unclean craft, and they left it to sink.

"Hah!" he grunted, cleaning that ax that had slain so many men and now a ship as well. "Cormac . . . saw ye the like of those fish-eaten dead men ever afore? I wonder what they can have wanted with us?"

Cormac said unsmiling, "Listen, bush-face, it's no attempt I'm making to give ye the lie, but what I saw was not fish-eaten corpses. Basque fighting ships I saw, and Basque weapon-men acrewing them. What's more, all lived and were hale."

"Wha'?" Wulfhere stared. "It cannot be!"

"It is—or was," Cormac told him. "Illusion, Wulfhere. One of us was deceived. Let us not be arguing which, for the present. Come—where else of late are we after meeting with false appearances asea?"

Wulfhere stared blinking. "Who could forget? In Galicia! I see where this breeze blows. Was that Lucanor's work, there! And Lucanor escaped and is alive, alive—and with no love for us."

"Aye."

Both men reflected in silence for a space.

They'd had to face a supernatural barge made all of white fretted bones, a fell impossibility that rode the waters nonetheless, and bore a false guide-light to lure ships to their destruction. Nine pale, pale sea-women had graced its deck, seeming to lounge while they worked their magic. Nor had it been easy to attack and slash such opponents. With their Danes and some of King Veremund's Sueves, Cormac and Wulfhere had done—and discovered the eerie beauty of those women to be a lie. When their true forms had been revealed, hardened pirates had shuddered to see them. Sea-spawn, and not human. Worship of Cthulhu, the monstrous tentacle-faced god who slept in drowned R'lyeh, had been at the heart of the business, and all the cultists in Galicia had sought to do was bring up that humanity-hating god and make him supreme.

Aye, and the cult's priest had been Lucanor of Antioch, formerly physician to the king's wife, poor dead woman.

"Lucanor," Wulfhere said. "*He* incited these . . . Basques? To attack us? Cormac, they were Basques, and mortal men? Ye be certain of this?"

"It's what I'm after seeing. My guess would be that Lucanor is after casting that foul illusion over them to affright us and make us easy prey. The greater fool he."

"Aye! Right!" Wulfhere grinned broadly. "He must ha' forgot we've dealt with such glamours afore."

Cormac finished his careful cleansing of his sword and set aside the torn short-cloak he had of a dead foeman. "The Basques had not, Wulfhere. They cannot have liked it. Methinks they saw each other just as you saw them. By the blood of the gods! It would be shaking any man's nerve, to see his battle-companions all mouldering corpses! It wonders me not that the last ship turned back without fighting, and the other fled when it could! The mage blundered badly there. Three ships against our one! All might have gone differently had he restrained himself from his tricks, or played with the sea, or wind, or something."

"I am grieved," Wulfhere said bleakly, "that I cannot have that blackbird between these hands."

Cormac shrugged and clapped him on the shoulder. "Would it were so! Well, mayhap the Basques who fled yonder will do to him all that ye've a wish to, and more. They'll not be loving him for what happed there to-day."

"A good thought." And Wulfhere showed his big teeth again.

He moved forward then, shouting orders. What ailed them? The sea-fight was over, and they had this perdurable Gaulish coast to put behind them. Was it their wish to fight Goths and Saxons as well?

It was not. Seven Danes had died in that red shambles. He with the transfixed thigh joined them in the night, muttering the name of his Gudrid, because too much blood had run out of him. For the crew, it was so much pirates' work. Cormac and Wulfhere, who commanded between them, felt darkness touch their spirits, although neither spoke of it.

We began with forty men. Now it's two-and-thirty we have, and ten of those wounded, and a long journey yet to make.

Wulfhere did not seem to wonder why Cormac alone had seen the Basques in their true appearnace. To the Gael, meticulously scrubbing and picking cruor from his chaincoat, it was a question that called disquietingly for an answer—and he had none. Unless . . . unless it was the golden sigil he wore beneath his armour? The Egyptian amulet.

Had Zarabdas's advice been sound after all, and his words truthful?

Lucanor too had a long journey to go. For him there was no ship. His divinations warned him of what was in store, for Cormac had been right about the mood of the surviving Basques. A stranger had come among them, crushed and done face-loss on their trusted diviner, and persuaded them to action—which had been only disaster; all loss and no gain.

Lucanor only just escaped into Gaul with his life. Hungry, weary and destitute, with many leagues between him and the city of Nantes, he cursed his evil fortune. In one of his rare moments of clear sight, he cursed himself for not planning the affair better.

For a brief while there he had triumphed. The Basques had been eager to do all that he wished. Had he been content to leave its execution to them . . . had he not used sorcery to lend them an aspect of ghoulish terror that somehow had not frozen the marrow of those damned Danes after all . . .

Past, past and done. Nor was Lucanor capable of further sorcery now. He dared not risk the exhaustion such would entail.

So Lucanor traveled north as the lowliest peasant traveled, footsore in the dust and heat of summer and by no means sure he would reach his destination without succumbing to illness—or having his throat cut by robbers so ill-advised as to accost a man with nothing.

His self-pity increased as he walked.

His face worked and worked, and his high opinion of himself returned. He bethought him of Sigebert of Nantes; Sigebert One-ear, and Lucanor's face worked. A German. A loutish barbarian was that one, under his polished manners, and a pretentious man, in truth was Sigebert. Far from so civilized as Lucanor thought himself—or so wise.

Still . . . Lucanor was forced to make an admission, even to his arrogant self. *The Frank is a crafty planner. The two of us should make a team for the reckoning with.* Walking alone in his filthy robe, Lucanor nodded sagely. *Aye!*

If only my legs and this left calf and my stomach hold out. If only I can reach the fellow. . . .

5

When Kings Plot War

"The Franks, a strong, violent people, who had remained loyal to their Germanic weapon, the light single-edged Francisca [Frankiska] or missile-ax, was still far from being united. Clovis, a minor king of the Salian Franks of Tournoi, was obliged to resort to killing his rivals before being eliminated himself, and had to take advantage of every chance he could get."

—Larousse Encyclopedia of Ancient and Medieval History

"Wheels turn beside wheels, within wheels, and all do their work whilst only a few grind one on the other."

—Athaninus

The boarhounds bayed clamourously and the thicket burst open. There, snorting, stood the quarry on his four cloven hooves, one ear torn to a scarlet rag. Scarlet dripped too from below his mouth, and that blood was not his. One hound at least would never hunt again.

Even in his summer coat, the boar was big. For a heartbeat or twain he glared before him from tiny eyes. Then he charged. His sharp little feet hurled up bits of forest mould.

"Ha!" grunted the young man in leather vest and leggings the colour of aging copper. Coolly, he grounded the butt of his heavy spear and

66

guided the broad point just under the brute's chest as it hurtled at him—*so!*

A slamming impact jarred him to the heels as the boar impaled itself. Eyes like little red coals glared into a pair pale as winter ice. Froth from the champing tushes fell on the young hunter's hands. It was pink froth. He smelled it, felt the beast's breath, its rage.

Its foaming tushes gleamed white as ivory. The larger two, drawing the eye by their size and curve, were harmless. They existed only to hone the short straight pair, the killing pair, and this the hunter well knew. Braced and straining, he held his spear-haft with strong big hands.

Madly, the beast thrust against the spear. Without the stout crosspiece just behind the spearhead to hold it, the enraged boar had charged up the impaling shaft to rip the bowels out of its slayer and die atop him.

One last shuddering attempt the beast made, and fell dead.

The young man drew a nasal breath of mingled relief and satisfaction. He maintained his grip on the spear-haft whilst he backed a pace, warily. Tall and rawboned he was, with ruddy skin and yellow hair flowing loose and long. Grace was not one of his qualities. He moved with a loose-jointed gangle on feet too large—as were his hands. His long face with its drooping moustaches had an equine look. Yet was he known for his strength, and it took a bold man to meet the stare of his eyes. His name was Clovis, and he was quite young, and he was a king.

Other men rushed into the glade now, with a crackling of acorn-hulls underfoot. First among them were his cousins, Ragnachar and Ricchar, brother-kings of Cambrai. Their hunting party followed. Chararic, also a king and Clovis's cousin, hung tardily back in his red-barred green vest. That was like Chararic. Clovis's pale eyes narrowed with the suspicion that came so naturally when a man belonged to the Frankish royal family.

Had it been chance that he'd found himself isolated, and had to deal with the boar alone? Much could happen tragically to mar a day's hunting!

Aye, and especially had it been planned . . .

"Oh, bravely done, my lord!" ·

"A worthy bit of work, cousin!"

Ignoring the shower of congratulations, Clovis accepted a wine-flask from the hands of a man he trusted. The youthful king swigged deeply. Rays of the late afternoon sunlight that slanted through the glade gilded his yellow moustaches and fell vividly on the blood of the slain boar. All around the Franks and their dead quarry—and the whining, still excited dogs—stretched a vast tangle of oak and birch and beech, threaded by game trails but impenetrable else. This was the forest called *Arduenna Silva* in the Latin so many still spoke and wrote; a fine place to hunt. It was also a fine place for the insuring of privacy whiles one conferred with one's cousins.

That night, in a leather tent erected by servants in those Ardenne Woods, Clovis did so. Lamplight brought a ripe wheaten sheen to the hair they all wore long and flowing as a mark of royal rank. Lamplight wavered on the faces, too,

of the four kings. Somehow it accentuated faults
and weaknesses.

The shifty eyes of straight-browed Chararic
seemed less trustworthy than ever. The signs of
debauch were marked in Ragnachar's heavy features; although he had yet his youth, with
strength and energy, that jowly king was going
quickly and badly to seed. His brother Ricchar
was less fond of wining and wenching and eating,
more steady—and duller. He followed where
Ragnachar led, and Clovis was convinced that the
latter thought with his gut and his genitals.

Nothing of weakness showed in the face of
young King Clovis. If faults there were, such as
cruelty, treachery and ruthlessness, they were not
the sort of faults that held a man back from the
path of ambition. Twenty years old, Clovis had
been a king for a quarter of his life. He dominated
the group.

"Ha, that boar-sticking of yours today!" Ragnachar cried with a wagging of his jowls. "Glad
am I that I saw it! Now I cannot let you have all the
honour, cousin. If luck sends us a bear or a wild
bull, it is mine!" He ducked his chin, doubling it,
and emitted a sound that was part hiccough and
part belch.

Clovis shrugged. "Boars are well enow, cousin.
It pleases me to leave bears to you! Have them and
welcome, and have too the wild bulls! As for
me—it is a stag I would hunt." His voice became
low and intense and his round pale eyes pierced.
"A stag of Rome, d'you hear me? A royal stag with
twelve tines to his crest . . . and by name Syagrius."

Syagrius . . .

The name rustled about the tent. Officially he was their lord, the last consul of Roman Gaul, successor to Aetius and Aegidius, his father. Gothic barbarians ruled south of the Loire, Celtic Britons in Armorica that was Little Britain or Brittany. Only the realm of Syagrius remained Roman in more than name. To such had shrunk Empire.

Chararic blurted, "War?"

"War!" Clovis echoed, almost in a whisper that held ten times more drama than would a shout. "War, my lords. War against the Roman king, Syagrius! I put my battle-host in motion ere the moon is new again. Are you with me?"

As swiftly and bluntly as that, it was put to them. The Frank Clovis meant to move on and overthrow the last Roman ruler; to end what Roman Julius had begun 500 years agone. They gazed upon him, and the lamplight danced on eyes of grey and blue.

Ragnachar of Cambrai grinned. "I awaited this. The time is ripe. As for the Roman kingdom . . . it is falling-ripe! It wants only knocking from the tired old tree. None of us could take it alone. In concert, though—I am with you, cousin."

Ricchar spoke not, but inclined his head in agreement.

Chararic, eyes shifting and hooded, scratched nervously in his armpit. "This is rash talk. Syagrius is the Emperor's man."

Clovis snorted. "The Emperor! Zeno rules afar, in Constantinople! He can do naught here. If we do not take Soissons, some others will, and leave us with empty hands. I say strike now."

"And I say nay! The Goths would welcome the

excuse to crush us in the Emperor's name and he'd give them his sanction with a joyful heart. I shall have no part in this."

Now it was Ragnachar's turn to snort, while Clovis stared, looking implacably grim. Ricchar remained silent and seemingly impassive.

All three knew well that Chararic was not so pitifully timid as he wished them to believe. The Goths under their present weakling monarch were no threat. Chararic knew that. Emperor Zeno could send his distant subordinate no aid that mattered. Chararic knew that. No; Chararic's real motives were plain. He wanted his cousins to take the risks of waging war, and bear the losses. Were they defeated, and did the Roman King Syagrius drive them back into Frankish domains, Chararic would be waiting to complete their destruction, to his own lasting profit. Should they win—

"Think again, Chararic," Clovis said softly. "Think of the loot of Soissons! Think of the glory we four will share." His eyes stared hard.

Stubbornly Chararic shook his head. "You will break your strength on Syagrius's legions, and the earth will cover you, Clovis."

Ricchar spoke at last. "Syagrius's legions!" he mocked. "Standstill fighters! We will mince his horsemen, and then our axes will smash his legions flat and trample them!"

"Bah. You talk a great victory, cousin; but I think not."

"Enough," Clovis said, showing his impatience. "My lord Chararic, you have answered us so that we are left in no doubt. Let it be so."

Something in the younger man's pale, deadly eyes and whetstone voice froze King Chararic to

his treacherous soul. Instinct told him—too late—
that here sat his master in double-dealing, in war,
and indeed in all things; here was one who would
remove him the moment it was convenient. What
made Chararic so certain of this he could not have
said. He knew. Clovis had uttered no threat,
veiled or open. He had simply looked at his craft-
iest cousin. And Chararic was hideously sure. A
death sentence had just been passed.

Feeling a sudden urgent need of wine, Chararic
poured himself a tot with an unsteady hand.

"We waste time," Clovis said, softly, so softly;
butter sliding along the whetstone. Somehow,
Chararic had been excluded from further talk.
"My lords, we must raise our forces, combine
them and march as soon as may be. Who shall lead
them?"

"Why, the three of us jointly!" Ragnachar said.
"Are we to arm a host and then give it to you to use
as you please? Ha! Would you do such a thing for
us?"

"I would not," Clovis said grimly. "Nor was I
proposing that you should. It is my dearest wish
that one of you accompany me to this war, and
lead his own warriors. Aye. Both, however, were
neither needful nor wise. One should remain at
home and guard the kingdom."

His meaning was clear. Clovis did not trust
Chararic, were he left unwatched behind their
backs to be at the making of mischief. Likely he
did not trust his allies overmuch either, and
wished to separate them. Besides, the twenty-
year-old king of five years had shrewdly guessed
that Ragnachar did not altogether trust his own
brother Ricchar. In that case Ragnachar would be

certain to bring to war every able-bodied man, lest
Ricchar prepare for him a stronger triumphal welcome than he wanted. When one was a Frankish
king, one did not leave a knife even in the hand of
a brother while one turned one's back.

They talked.

Clovis used all his harsh powers of persuasion
to get his way, and had it at last. Ragnachar agreed
to leave Ricchar in charge of Cambrai, whilst he
and Clovis led their combined forces against the
Roman kingdom.

They parted next day in bright sunlight of no
boding. Watching Chararic and his hunting party
take their own road, Ragnachar smiled bleakly.

"We had better win our war, cousin," he told
Clovis. "I'll not relish having 'hararic at our backs,
an we should fail." He scratched the back of his
scalp, under his mass of corn-hued hair.

"Failure is not part of our plan," Clovis said.
"We will succeed—and even then, we will be
better off without yon snake-eyed daggerman.
When we return in the splendour of victory, my
lord cousin, I will see to that myself."

"You seem very sure of winning," Ricchar
grunted, and received hard looks from Clovis and
his brother. He traded them glower for glower. "I
should be pleased to know why." And never for
Chararic.

"Why, you sluggard? Are we not Franks?"

"Easy, Ragnachar," Clovis advised, with a tiny
smile. "Ricchar may be more subtle than you
grant, for there are other reasons why I be sure of
victory."

The two brothers stared at the young king.

"I've had spies at the court of Soissons for some

time," Clovis said with a completely open face. "One master agent in particular. Think you I rose one bright dawn and said, 'Would be a fine thing were I and my kinsmen to conquer Soissons! I shall put the matter to them and discover whether they agree!' "

Despite his slowness of thought, Ricchar was not easily swayed from a point. "This agent of yours . . ."

"A courtier. He has worked with great care to suborn the men who lead the Frankish auxiliaries in Syagrius's army. I chose him well! He has been discreet and successful. When Syagrius marches against us, my lord cousins, his Frankish contingents will desert him and fight with us, which is fitting. You will see why I had no wish to talk of this whilst Chararic was with us, and him uncommitted."

Ricchar considered that, and smiled broadly. "Good! Good!"

"There is more," Clovis said coolly, hardly basking in this praise. "Know ye the Bishop of Reims?"

"I have met the man," Ragnachar said, looking intent while he scratched his outer thigh.

"As have I. So too has my spy. My lord Bishop is a most practical churchman who also desires my conversion to his god. On my spy's advice, I made him offers in the guise of interest in his faith, to gain some notion of how he might respond to conquest. No fool he! He sees as surely as I that the Roman kingdom cannot last many years longer, and that we are the most likely ones to seize it. I can get along with him. Will be needful, you know. We can conquer the Roman kingdom methinks, but lacking the Church's aid, cousins, we should find it difficult to *hold*."

Ragnachar laughed shortly. "And shall we make submission in name to the Emperor at Constantinople?"

"Aye," Clovis said most seriously indeed, "and mayhap receive the cloak and purple robe each, proclaiming us consul. Why not?"

There was one whelming reason why not. In each man's mind was a picture of himself as Consul of Gaul officially and king in fact, and no thought of sharing the honour. What was more, each of them knew that the other thought thus.

Ricchar asked, "What of this spy of yours now?"

The younger king's eyes narrowed. "One cannot be sure," he admitted slowly. "I believe Syagrius began to wonder about him. Not suspect him; merely wonder. Had it been more than that, Syagrius would surely have had him slain rather than sending him from the court. The fellow was given a post in Metz, and he'd no choice save to accept it. It is there he now abides. I have heard that he met with misfortune at the hands of robbers, but his hurts were not mortal. I shall reward him for his services after we have conquered Soissons."

This rang true because for the most part it was true. Clovis had lied only about the city to which his agent had been dispatched by the Roman king. Was Nantes, not Metz, and the post he had been given there was that of customs assessor for the district. The wight's name was Sigebert. Misfortune had been his indeed, although many said it was richly deserved, and now referred to him as Sigebert One-ear. He had been so unwise as to lay trap and cross swords with the pirates Wulfhere the red-beard and Cormac mac Art.

Sigebert's fate had been maiming and disfigurement at the hands of one of their men, Clovis had been informed, and he remembered.

Sigebert, too, remembered.

Yet none of this really mattered to Clovis or Chlovis or Chlodwig or Hlovis or—Roman-style—Chlodovechus, King of the Salian Franks. It mattered to Sigebert, and to the two pirates. Even now the fact was drawing Wulfhere and his black haired, blue eyed Gaelic partner to the grimy fringes of Clovis's plan to conquer Soissons.

6

Prince of Corsairs

"The withdrawal of Rome from what had been Empire left a vacuum in the world. Pirates rushed to fill it."
— Ricart of Lyons

Tricky and hard to navigate were the coasts of Armorica, now called Lesser Britain or Brittany. Many a granite reef lurked offshore and the tides could be deadlier than any sea monsters invented by human minds. Dwellers in Armorica must of necessity be superb seamen, or not go to sea at all.

Raven came along those coasts in full daylight and weather clear as a child's eyes. The ship's blue-and-green sail was a broad banner above gentle waves.

"Show a white shield at the masthead, Halfdan," Wulfhere ordered. "Else these Celts be like to shudder and faint at sight of us."

"Ye will not, o'course, be saying such a thing to their faces," Cormac said. "The time's ill chosen to provoke a slaughter."

"Ah, nag me not, Wolf! 'Tis not as if these runaways from Saxon invaders be your own people—Britons out of Britain are they, all. And them calling themselves *corsairs* and squabbling like gulls over the scraps we leave! 'Tis pitiful— but I'll spare your feelings. Mayhap there be pig-

farmers amongst 'em, eh? Eh? Kindred souls!"
And Wulfhere laughed.

The white shield that signified Raven's peaceful intent was swiftly lashed to the masthead. The
galley's sail had already been lowered, so that
dipping oars moved her smoothly toward the narrow strait. The oars threw crystal sparkles into the
air and a bit of white foam rolled back past Raven's stern.

On the western side of the strait, rearing gigan-
tically from the gorse, broom and heather that
covered the thin soil, stood a menhir of astound-
ing size. More than ten times taller than great
Wulfhere's height it lofted, weighing hundreds of
tons. The lost years of time had been sealed within
its pitted surface as honey in the comb. The first
Caesar, Caius Julius, had seen it. From this spot, it
was said, he had watched his fleet put defeat on
the Veneti, and even then the menhir had been
ancient out of memory.

"Rider on our steerboard side, coming down to
the beach," Makki Grey-gull called out.

Cormac's head swiveled. Aye, the horseman
was there, coming swiftly with the sun blazing
behind him. His mount's hooves threw up pale
spurts of sand. Richly as he glittered with golden
adornment, the horse glittered no less. A magnificent purple plaide blew about him. No, no; was a
Romish cloak he wore, not a Celtic plaid.

He drew rein at the water's edge in the way that
his grey horse was flung back almost on its
haunches. Water surged in foam about its fet-
locks. From a mouth stretched wide between
moustaches the colour of a wheat harvest, the
rider bawled challenge in . . . Latin!

"Who may ye be that in a warship you armed
have come across the sea? The shield of peace at
your masthead I see; still, consent or permission
to land here you have not asked of my lord Howel,
Prince of Bro Erech. Tell me your names and your
purpose ere further you go, or as enemies be
cried!"

Wulfhere bristled. Cormac grinned wolfishly
and clapped a restraining hand on the giant's
shoulder. To the coast-watcher of Armorica he
replied ashout, and not in the Roman tongue.

"It's failing your eyes be, Garin son of Teregud
Hundred-hands, for I know ye though I must look
into Behl's eye to see ye there! Sure and it's a
strange pass things are come to, an I not welcome
to your lord Howel, whether announced or unan-
nounced! Cormac mac Art of Eirrin am I. Your
prince will be remembering the day we fought the
Saxons off Cornwall."

Raven was forging foamily through the tiny
strait now, not slowing her pace. Cormac had on
him a cloak that billowed behind. His helmet's
horsetail crest danced in air the while he stood
gazing shoreward, wearing a smile and deigning
to touch nothing save the planking under his feet.

"*Cormac!*" Garin cried from shore. "Och man,
it's welcome ye be to me also! It is in peace ye
come? Ye speak for your shipmates?"

"My head upon it."

Garin brandished his silver-mounted spear in
acknowledgment. There would be no braying of
horns, no signal-smokes to bring forth Prince
Howel's weapon-men with blades bared. Had
Raven borne the menace of hostile crew, they'd
naturally have slain Garin with arrows upon

being challenged. The deed would not have gone unwitnessed and arms would have been raised posthaste. Little comfort would Garin have gained from that! For its danger, his position as coast-watcher was held in honour.

Raven left the strait astern. Before her spread the Mor-bihan, the Little Sea, some hundred square miles of sunlit water shading with depth from green to amethystine purple. Many islands it contained, though some were no more than sandbars. They disappeared occasionally or regularly with the tides, Cormac mac Art knew well. When the tide ebbed, some of them linked together in ship-biting barriers barely visible. Threading a way among these natural traps could be difficult or worse. Cormac watched close; so did others.

"By Wotan," Wulfhere muttered, scratching at brine within his beard where it was wont to crust. "This be like trying to navigate in a wash-tub. Slow, slower there with the stroke! An we run aground in this Bretonish pond the shame will be crimson, and I'll flay someone!"

Slowly, slowly they oared past a brackish lagoon whose white sand beaches were swept by the tails of tiny lizards. Rushes, marram grass and sea-thistles clung along its shores.

Then *Raven* received the blessing of deeper water once more.

The hall of Prince Howel was builded on the largest island in the Mor-bihan, one of the few that was never submerged. Circular in plan, the keep lay within a complex of ditches, earthworks, and dry-stone fortifications. Thus the hall was proof against all and aught save a determined assault by great numbers of seasoned fighting men.

The problem of taking it did not interest Cormac or Wulfhere, save as a problem for amusement. It seemed unlikely that a force sufficiently mighty would find cause for the expense of coming against such a place. Mac Art was passing happy to arrive here as friend.

Raven's herringbone of oars backed water briefly. Her two iron anchors went out with great splashes. The ship lay still upon the sea. Despite the sign of peace she displayed, peasant folk were running for shelter within the isle's fortification. Mothers snatched desperately at their children and Cormac shook his head at the jumbled mix of Celtic and Romish clothing.

"Blood of the gods! Best we be going ashore and content them."

"Aye," Wulfhere agreed, turning to his steersman. "Ordlaf: ye will command until we return. Enforce their behavior, I care not how." And he let his cool gaze pass over the rest of the crew.

Ordlaf Skel's son grinned. "They will behave, Captain."

Wulfhere and Cormac waded ashore shieldless. Wulfhere bore his huge-headed ax as a matter of course, and Cormac's sword in its metal-chaped scabbard lay across his shoulders, against the splashing of his companion's enormous feet. Out of the water, he buckled it normally about his hips.

Up the shelving beach they strode, and gained the firmer footing of the path to Prince Howel's hall. Ere they had covered the third part of the distance, they were met by a bard of middle rank, in company with two warriors.

The bard, a red-haired young man freckled in extreme degree, gave them formal greeting.

"My lords! I am Oswy . . . the prince sits in judgment this forenoon, else he'd have met ye on the shore, and he has charged me to say so. In the mean time, it is his command that all ye wish be done."

"And that be fine of the Prince Howel," Wulfhere rumbled. "For the present, all I want is for my men to come ashore and beach my ship. And when they've done that, to stretch their legs a little. And for myself—about three vats of ale."

By the look Oswy gave the northerner, attempting to take in his vast dimensions at a distance of four feet and failing, he half believed that so much would be required. He said "Naught in that exceeds my authority, God knows! And yourself, my lord?"

"One vat will suffice me," the dark-armoured Gael said.

With sea-salt astringent on their skins and the taste of it itching in their throats, they two came to the open grassy space outside the prince's hall. Crowded the area was, with the bright retinues of the two chieftains here present for litigation, and with Howel's own retinue as well as lookers-on.

In a chair draped with rich fabric sat Howel himself, Prince of these Britons become Bretons. Howel was a strongly built man whose moustaches were long and reddish. His wife, the Lady Morfydd, had seated herself on the grass beside his chair. Her green-skirted legs were curled neatly under her in disregard of her own high rank and station. Yet she was no fool, this woman. Despite her youth her long black hair was stranded with grey, and it was said that her eyes could see into the human heart or into the time-to-come.

Howel was hearing a case and pleas, and the proprieties of giving them attention took precedence over those of greeting visitors. Thus he did not glance at the approaching weapon-men from the sea, and Cormac understood. His hospitable intent was manifested by serving wenches, who brought the pirates a jack each of honey-coloured ale. Wulfhere did not so much as drink his as breathe it in with one long inhalation.

"Another," he said, hardly gasping, and sat to pull off his sea-wetted footgear.

"And for me," Cormac said. "It's gone this will be by the time ye're after returning." And he too sat, and removed his boots.

The girls exchanged a look and departed; Cormac and Wulfhere also looked at each other, nodded in appreciation, and gave attention to the proceedings.

The case being heard seemed to involve clientship. One of the Armorican chieftains wanted to attach a man to his retinue. The man's kin were impugning the proffered contract because they would lose by it. The matter took some time to settle, and twice loud angry voices had to be quelled.

Cormac yawned, thinking that there were advantages even to being an outlaw. When someone wished to join one's crew, and one was willing to have him, the newcomer simply sprang aboard. After that, did he talk or shout out of turn, one bade him shut his face. If he did not, one dealt with the problem most directly. That necessity did not arise, under Cormac and Wulfhere. The Gael did oft proclaim that one should not kill unless it was necessary—and was wont to add, and prove, that all too often it was necessary. Wulfhere made no such ridiculous statement in the first place. Nor did crewmen wish to tangle with a captain who looked as if he could handle a Frost Giant or two—or might have been sired by one—and on a passing large human mother, at that.

The proceedings ended eventually. By then, lounging bootless in the sun and with ale warming his innards, Cormac paid no mind as to the prince's decision and did not see where went the individual desired by a chieftain. Howel's duty to his people was done for the nonce; he could greet an old acquaintance.

"By Morgan the sea-queen!" he swore, gripping Cormac by the hand while the gathering disintegrated in all directions with a buzz as of bees at their springtime swarming. "Cormac mac Art, ye be welcome here as a Saxon's death, I vow! Ah . . . no offense, Wulfhere."

The Dane was puzzled. Luckily, it did not occur to him that he could be confused with a Saxon. Prince Howel stood smiling while the two shod themselves. The three passed within his hall then dim and cool under its thatch. Under their soles fresh rushes rustled on an earthen floor that many feet had stamped iron-hard, over the years. A double circle of pillars of red yew-wood upheld the roof, while brilliant tapestries adorned the walls. A servant hurried to spread furs and soft leather cushions over the marble steps of the hall's dais, speckled like bird's eggs.

"Cormac," the Armorican ruler said, "wonder's been on me whether ye yet lived; we received word of that business in Nantes, and that ye'd escaped whole. Afterwards came naught but rumors. The tale that seemed most likely was the least pleasant; that ye'd attempted crossing the Sea of Treachery to Hispanic coasts, and had been swallowed by the waters."

"Attempt!" Wulfhere said, with indignation. "We did it, and the seas thrice as high as the mast and raging. Oh, it tried to swallow us, right enough!"

"Aye, was a feat though I say so," Cormac put in smoothly, channeling the talk lest Wulfhere give away too much. "And little it—"

"Ye two crossed that hellpit the Basques call Bay of Biscaya?"

Cormac nodded. "And little it—"

"A feat indeed!" Howel said, and his moustachioes streamed in the air as he gave his head an impressed jerk. "Drink that ale yourselves and bring wine for me and my guests!"

Cormac waited a moment longer, but Howel was looking expectantly at him and seemed not disposed to break in again. "And little the feat profited us," the Gael said, rather hurriedly. He went on normally, "At Garonne-mouth we're after making the finest haul I've yet seen, and in Nantes we lost it to a prancing customs man, as ye've seemingly heard. We lost a man there also—Black Thorfinn, and a good man too. Two choices the Roman warships left us, to cross the sea of Treachery or be taken. So far off course were we blown that we nigh missed Hispania's coast altogether! Last of all we had to fight our way clear of some angry Basques as we were returning north. It's sore depleted our crew is, Howel. It is on us to return to Dane-mark, for more men."

Cormac leaned back on his elbows on the dais-become-couch.

"Aye," Wulfhere said, absently or so pretending, while he looked after the servant who'd gone to fetch them wine. Following the lead of his blood-brother of Eirrin, he did not attempt to tell of the things Cormac had left out of the account. No mention had he made of their service with King Veremund the Tall. Best leave it so. This Breton should not be encouraged to speculate that Raven might hold more than hard tack, smoked salmon and salt fish, and some thin ale. He was, after all, part of the legacy of Rome: a pirate.

Easy will that be, Wulfhere thought. *Even our own men do not suspect!*

Five yards of heavy chain they had with them—pure silver, Veremund's payment for their lifting his seaward curse. And well they deserved it, both men thought. Had been Cormac *ancliuin's* idea to tarnish it black to resemble plain iron, after which they'd used it to replace a portion of Raven's anchor chain.

Ah, that crafty brain of his, Wulfhere thought, smiling now as he saw the returning servant, pleasantly laden. *What better hiding place?*

Was not that Raven's commanders mistrusted their own men. Was merely that two might keep a secret, whereas twoscore never could. Meanwhile, Wulfhere thought further, Cormac seemed to trust this Howel. But . . . keep the secret! He scratched meditatively under his eagle's nest of a beard, where sea-salt was crusted on his jaw.

The two, Briton and Eirrish, knew each other of old, from the days when Cormac had led a crew of Eirrin's reivers in many a fight. They had shared ventures and danger and loot, for Howel was *corsair* as these folk called it. Yet would be foolish to tell him what they had elected not to tell their own crew. He was, after all, a pirate.

Morfydd joined in the talk with the freedom of a Celtic woman.

"Will you wonder if misfortune dogs you?" she asked, her strange hazel eyes all shifting depths and glimmers. "You have nowhere to go with your successes. When you have no home but the wide sea, the wide sea drinks all that you have. Meseems you should seek a secure base of your own. Cormac; sea-chieftain Wulfhere—have ye never thought of taking service with some great lord? Many must there be who would welcome your prowess and experience, and make ye both rich!"

Wulfhere grinned broadly. Cormac, expressionless of dark scarred face, said, "Mayhap it's a sound notion ye have, Lady Morfydd."

"Aye!" his partner laughed. "The hard part were to find one great lord who'd not have us cut down on sight, on our reputations alone! Well and well . . . who knows but that we can do even that? Mayhap we will be attempting it! We have need of building up our crew though, lady. It is why we make for my land of the Danes again." He swigged his wine with contentment. "Prince Howel: might we be making some ship's repair on this your shore?"

"Indeed! More, all supplies ye have need of are to be yours. A comrade of Cormac mac Art may ask and have aught short of my right arm—or Morfydd!" Howel seized her in his arms and kissed her fiercely.

The talk turned then to old times that Wulfhere Skull-splitter had not shared, and a board game beloved of the former companions. Bored, he broke in at last:

"Why make ye your home on this island, Prince? Surely all things save victuals must be fetched from the mainland, and likely some of that."

"Aye true," Howel said, a bit absently as he was busy at setting up the pieces for the game between him and Cormac. "Ye forget that I look to the sea, Wulfhere. It brings me tribute, and plunder. Besides, I care not for the stone walls of Vannes, or to have the Church droning in my ear night and day. Bishop Paternus has his see in the town. Ha! Paternus croaks that the corsair trade is mortal sin, but I've yet to see him refuse a gift I gained by the plying of it!"

"A charming preacher of the slave religion!" Cormac pushed a game-piece forward.

Howell was truculent: "Look at me. See you a slave?"

Cormac's smile was thin as heifer's milk. "No, Howel—and I see on ye the neck-torc of your ancestors. And there be no cross upon your person."

All fell silent. Cormac was out of step with the times. The Church of the cross-worshipers—a Roman execution symbol to him, and no more—

was not for him. It had weeded up in the east
somewhere, to spread through Rome's Empire
and become its church. Aye, and into Eirrin,
where a black-robed priest had done treachery on
his father, and on him. Of its tenets he could make
neither head nor tail . . . nor alpha nor omega.
The "Friends" as they'd begun, or "Saints" as
they later styled themselves; Cross-worshipers, or
"Christ-ians"—these seemed all to agree that the
founder of their belief had been crucified by the
Romans as the rabble-rouser he was, and then
risen from his very tomb—a borrowed tomb, at
that. In most other things they were fanatically
and often sanguinely at odds. Some said he had
been a man. Some maintained that he was a god.
Some said both at once, a god sort of masquerading as a man. Some avowed that he was neither,
but a different order of being. Some claimed that
he had always existed, others that he had not. No
matter what their claim or belief, these saints were
prepared to kill everybody who disagreed with
them. The cult thrived on death. Its symbol, fittingly, was a gallows of Rome. Knowing that they
believed all was going to be wonderful for
everyone once they had died, Cormac mac Art
wished them speedy attainment of such happiness.

Now the Christians held power in all the lands
that had once been part of Rome's empire. Their
enclaves strengthened in Persia and Arabia. They
had "converted" the Ethiopians, and too the in-
vading Goths and Vandals. They were likely to do
the same to the Franks within a generation. Their
numbers grew in otherwise uninvaded Eirrin it-

self; the Irish seemed to take seriously their
pacifist preaching and grew isle-bound and un-
ambitiously pacific.

Cormac loved the Christians as he loved the
wasting leprosy.

"Talking of cities," Wulfhere said, seeking to
break his comrade's dark reflections and slice
through the tension among old friends, "I would
be asking questions in Nantes, Prince." Moving
restlessly, he tested a spear from the wall for balance and heft, found it good, and nodded praise
to Howel. "'Tis but two days' sailing distant.
Questions concerning that Frankish dog Sigebert, who slew Thorfinn! Mayhap ye can be telling me. Be Sigebert there yet, or did he die of the
wound our comrade Black Thorfinn dealt him ere
he was himself cut down?"

Howel of Bro Erech appeared troubled. He
moved a piece on the game-board and affected not
to hear. His wife shook her head.

"It will not be solved in that fashion, my lord,"
Morfydd told him quietly. "Cormac will be learning for himself, an you do not tell him. Silence can
achieve naught, save maybe to mar your friendship."

"Aye." Howel gnawed his moustache and his
fingers drummed silently on his thigh. "Thorfinn
did not die that night, Cormac—or until three
nights later."

Behind the corsair prince, Wulfhere's bulk stiffened. He grounded the spear he held. His knuckles paled on the stout shaft he gripped. He
waited.

Cormac had grown very still. He forgot the
move he'd been about to make as he forgot the

bone game-piece he held in sinewy fingers. He said tonelessly, "Tell me the rest."

"It could not have been!" Wulfhere snarled. "By the All-Father! I saw a Frankish soldier's ax sink into Thorfinn's very side, and after that Sigebert put sword through his belly. I say I saw it! We'd never have left him while we escaped, else!"

Cormac watched Howel.

"True," Howel said in a subdued voice. "He should have died then and there. Was Sigebert's doing that he did not. He had physicians brought in at once, and Sigebert had them tend Black Thorfinn to prolong his life all they could. Not to save him, you understand? The man was beyond saving, with his guts pierced and a lobe of his lung torn open. No, Sigebert had it done so that Thorfinn would linger in pain, while the Frank drank heavily to numb his own pain to face and ear—and saw that Thorfinn had no such aid. He is a fiend from Hell, that one, and whate'er the pit that spawned him, it should take him back!"

"May it be so," Morfydd murmured.

"As for Thorfinn," her husband said on, "he was a strong man. He survived longer than any could have believed. In two days the rot was in his belly and half Nantes could hear his screaming. The tale is that those sounds of agony eased Sigebert for the pain of his gashed face more than wine or drugs—which he downed in quantity— and that he cursed for disappointment when Black Thorfinn was silent at last."

For a heartbeat of the silence of grimness, naught happened in that room of Howel's hall. Naught—save that the whalebone game-piece in

Cormac's fingers cracked across, and blood oozed from under his thumbnail, and Wulfhere's massy muscles quivered with stress and the butt-end of the spear he held was impossibly driven deep into the hard-trodden earth of Howel's floor. Neither man noticed what he had done. Wulfhere's hand dropped from the spearshaft, and it stood there, and Morfydd stared in some awe.

"Blood of the gods!" Cormac snarled, snapping to his feet and his face awrithe with passion. The black link-mail of his body chimed harshly. "The filthy dog! The gods-bereft alley scavenger— Sigebert shall *die!* Were he Emperor of Rome, were he High-king of Eirrin, he would *die* for this!"

"Aye," Wulfhere said, and his voice was that of a mean old hound as he leaned forward over the point of the spear. His bristling beard covered the leaf-shaped head. Hot, volcanic flames burned in his eyes and his voice quivered in rage. "I'll cut the blood eagle on that trollspawn, with my own hands. It's a thing I never did afore to any man. I never hated any enough. Yet I swear—Sigebert *shall have that death."*

Morfydd had turned pale, and for another long while there was only silence.

Howel said, "Then if ye'd not heard that, I have word of another enemy to ye both that perchance ye've not heard either. Hengist is abroad."

7

When Sea-wolves Plot

"Hengist!"

The startled echo of that name came from Wulf-here the Dane. He stared, and Howel of Bro Erech saw how the name alone drove thoughts of vengeance on Sigebert One-ear from Wulfhere's mind. He took his hand from the spear—which stood, noted by all but him—to pace closer with his deep interest in his eyes. He thrust his massive head forward, as though better to hear.

"Ye be certain of this, Prince? *Hengist?* Somewhere in these parts?"

"Nay, somewhere to the south," Howel said, rather hurriedly. "He came down the Narrow Sea from Kent with three galleys, and each sail bore the White Horse. My scouts and coast-watchers saw them pass these shores." He frowned his displeasure. "I put forth in pursuit. Shameful that one should be using home waters with not a by-your-leave! Too, he'd have fetched a mighty ransom, could I have taken him alive—the which I will admit is doubtful. In any case his ships proved too swift for me to catch."

"Hengist turned hare?"

"Surprise is on me," Cormac said thoughtfully, "that he did not turn back and fight for the mere pleasure of it."

Prince Howel agreed. "So thought I, knowing his reputation! Surely he had some urgent business to hand. Now word has come back to me that he is *guesting*, among the Saxons of western Gaul. It's friends and kin he has among them."

"Aye, true, he has," Wulfhere said. "By Wotan! This is good hearing!"

"Ye've but now come to these coasts," Morfydd said. "Strange that ye heard naught of it on the way."

"Not so strange. It was by night we traveled, and careful we were by day, to lie well hidden in lonely places. It's hardly our best fighting condition we're in at present."

Wulfhere glowered at the Gael, and spoke from indignance. "But yet ten times better than most! Ah! Hengist and Sigebert both within our reach! That caps it, Cormac! We'll not be leaving here until we've finished with those whoresons!"

"Both of them? God's light!" Howel laughed merrily. "Your hate for Sigebert I know. What have ye against Hengist, Captain?"

Cormac's eyes rolled upward. "Och, ye know not what ye ask. I trust ye've ample time and to spare for listening."

"WHAT?" Wulfhere thundered, drowning out Cormac's voice ere the Gael had finished speaking. "What have I against the swine? Know ye naught of his history, Prince? Hengist is a Jute, for one thing, as I am a Dane. There be more death-feuds between our peoples than—than betwixt the Saxons and your own! We Danes moved into Jutland and drove out the Jutes with weapon-steel, generations agone. Some remained . . . as thralls, or carles or warriors in service to Danish chiefs, and sure it is we found many of their women worth the keeping! Many others fled in ships to the coast of Frisia, a sodden land and no good home. The sea's an invader that steals the fields little by little. They can either humble themselves to a mean life fishing and fowling, or take to the pirate trade. I've no time for Jutes, but I grant ye this: they be not so lacking in manhood that they will choose the former!"

Wulfhere wet his throat and continued.

"Hengist was one of those stayed in Jutland. He served my grandsire, Hnaef. Now, Hnaef's sister Hildeburg was wed to a Jutish chieftain in Frisia, and there Hnaef went with his hearth-companions—Hengist among them, may monsters eat his corpse!—to visit his brother-in-law. All went well at the beginning. Then, because of bad blood and old feuds, trouble arose. The damned swinish Jutes . . ."

Wulfhere paused, swallowing, his face having gone dark with fury. "—the pig-sired Jutes did treachery on their guests and attacked them in whelming force in the night. Though they had been surprised, the Danes of course got themselves into battle-order and made ready to sell their lives at high price. They fought. Grandsire Hnaef was cut down and slain, early in that fight. His companions were grief-stricken—and enraged! They fought like blood-hungry demons, they did, slaying and hacking and slaying until the Jutes gave back before them. Then came Finn, the Jutish chieftain, he who had done death on his wife's own brother. That leering traitor offered them their lives an they'd swear peace and friendship! Aye! Now I put it to ye, Prince. What is a man to reply to such an insult as that?" Wulfhere shook his head. "Yet, the alternative was death. Too, Hengist was now become leader of the Danish company Ye see? That damned Jute. Belike he felt his Jutish blood speak to him, though blood-ties should never count above loyalty to a chieftain."

Howel made a faint grimace at that. Cormac was Cormac; set of face and slitted of eye, he showed nothing. Still, he felt as Howel did. They were Celts. Ties of blood and kinship to them were supreme.

"The snorting pig prevailed upon the Danes to accept Finn's terms! A shameful, disgraceful thing it was, but never has *Hengist* known what scruples are save for tripping better men with. He's a *Jute*. They suck treachery with their mothers' milk. Worse than Franks, the Jutes." Wulfhere paused then, seeing that Howel, who knew more of the ax-throwing Franks than he did of Jutes, was openly incredulous. "Aye," Wulfhere repeated. "Worse than Franks, Prince! Anyhows—Hnaef's band was not altogether lost to shame. They gave no thought to returning to their own country with such a tale. Among the isles and lagoons of Frisia they remained, living as neighbours to Finn's Jutes."

Wulfhere paced a step, swung back to fix fjord-blue eyes on Howel. "That did not last long. Word of what had befallen wended back to Hnaef's kinsmen in the north of Jutland. Naturally they made ready to pay Finn and his fellows a visit, and in numbers, all armed and war-shirted."

"Well, naturally," Howel said nodding. "How old were you?"

"I was not! Hengist is *old*, Prince, old—he'd lived too damned long twenty years agone! He gave aid to those Danes of Jutland's north! Aye! He who had broke his oath to Hnaef once Hnaef was dead, now broke his oath to Finn the Jute whilst Finn yet lived, and helped the Danes to slay him! Victorious, the Danes returned home, and their kinswoman Hildeburg with them. *Hengist* was left in Frisia—in power!"

Wulfhere paused and stared at Howel until the prince shook his head in disgust, and the giant went on.

"Thought ye the Franks were treacherous, eh? Now Hengist became a pirate chieftain—and one for the reckoning with. Natheless Frisia was and is no good place to live. He looked about with his pig's eyes, bethinking him of a better place to make his home."

"Aye, and I know what happened after," Howel said.

Wulfhere went on as if he'd not heard. "Was the worst thing that halfwit king of the Britons, Vortigern, ever did! To hire *Hengist* and seven shiploads of his wolves to fight the Picts, once the Romans were well gone and Britain unprotected by the legion and beset from many sides. Thor's thunder, any man who knew Hengist could have predicted the outcome. He commenced calling in other sea-rovers who wanted homes in a land that squelched not under their feet. In great numbers they came, like called pigs to the trough."

Cormac, from in-sloping Eirrin that squelched under foot as often as not, and well familiar with Britain's fogs and fens, was almost smiling. Almost.

"When Vortigern saw what was happening,"
Wulfhere said, when a movement of facial muscles indicated Howel might essay to speak, "he
sought to stop it. Too late, too late. He dealt with
Hengist, prince among princes of treachery.
Naturally, Hengist turned against *him*. And now
. . . now old Vortigern's dead and Hengist's a
king himself. In *Britain*, as well ye displaced Britons know . . . calling himself not Jute but *En-
glisc*, along with the Saxons who have also moved
in, jowl to cheek with Angles."

"King," Cormac said, and again in the tongue of
Eirrin: *"Righ!* King of a tiny patch like Kent! King
over as much of Britain as his hand and hams will
barely cover!" Wulfhere was his old friend, a
friendship conceived in prison and born in escape
and grown asea to be ripened by the saving each of
the other's life, more than once. One sneered at
one's friends' enemies.

"All this I know," Howel said, indicating the
wine. "Still, Kent is a *wealthy* little patch of Britain."

Wulfhere jerked, sloshed the wine he was pouring and glowered. "Hengist swore loyalty to my
own grandsire and then proved false! He is Loki's
left hand and my own blood-enemy. Aye, blood-
enemy. I snatched some loot out of his hands,
years agone. He revenged himself by taking captive eight of my men. At my offer to ransom them,
he laughed. The leprous pig-snouted dog
hanged them with his own hands, then sent me
their corpses with the message that he wished me
joy of them!"

"Peace, Wulf," Cormac said quietly. "Ye cannot

have thought on you that other folk know the story of all the blood-feuds ye have with all the rovers afloat! Blood of the gods, it were simpler to tally those ye have *not* enmity with. They cannot number above a dozen."

"Listen to him!" the huge redbeard snorted. "Ye have made foes of your own in plenty, battle-brother. Hengist for one! Ill-will hung betwixt yourself and him ere ever I met ye. Who was it took that grey madman's battle-standard of white horsetails from the middle of his camp, and has crested his helmet with 'em every since?" And he indicated mac Art's helm, which was unusually ornate for his sombre, unbejeweled attire, with its flowing crest.

"Policy," Cormac said, straight-faced. "An angry foe cannot think."

He thought on it, whiles Wulfhere made churlish complaint about how wine left one with a drawn mouth and thirst curable only by tankards of ale. Hengist was not to be taken lightly. The grizzled devil had achieved what no Caesar ever had; a lasting foothold in Britain. His name thundered over the North and Narrow Seas like a storm. Wulfhere had told naught but truth of the man's early deeds; all those things Hengist had indeed done. Aye, and he'd grown more terrible in his grizzled eld, not less.

"Hengist," Cormac said with a grim matter-of-factness, "likes to kill."

"And he'd rather betray than drink!" Wulfhere snarled.

"Has age brought him no infirmity?" Morfydd asked.

"Only in the head," Wulfhere said.

But even that was not true. Hengist was crafty and clever as ever. A giant he was, huge and powerful as Wulfhere, despite his grey mane and beard like brine or hoarfrost. None knew the number of his years, because nigh all of his generation were dead. Threescore years and more, surely. Hengist remained—and flourished. Year after year he raided, plundered, slew in ever wilder excess. He showed no sign of weakness or mercy. It was as if by behaving as a wildling yunker he could cheat death itself. Some thought he had; some thought him supernatural.

Hengist had no need of plunder. Piracy was his pleasure these days, not his livelihood, for no livelihood was necessary to him. King! Had he wished, he might have sat at ease in his dun on the Isle of Thanet, which commanded the trade of the north, and grown yearly richer without lifting a hand.

He did not. He feared that. Aye, he feared precisely that, did Hengist, who feared neither god nor man nor demon. Others might believe him immune to age. He knew better.

Women no longer interested him. Each winter the fear gnawed in his brain that his lungs or thinning blood would betray him in the cold, so that he, Hengist the terror of the wide seas, would die unworldly in straw. Each summer he fared and bullied forth in greater fury, hoping for a warrior's end. Each summer it eluded him. He sought the occasion of death, but slew and slew and showed his wiles and thus avoided the fact of death. As sometimes haps when a man actively seeks Hel's embrace, she passed him by as though he bore a charmed life. And she filled her chill hall with those he made enemies, and then corpses.

In a few summers more, surely, he must find himself too ill for voyaging. No choice would be his then but to decline and rot like a sessile tree.

That fate Wulfhere Skull-splitter had every intention of sparing him.

"So," the Dane said, softly now, "Hengist is nearby, eh?"

"It's . . . other business we have in hand, Wulfhere."

"Surt's burning breath!" The voice lifted to a roar again, as Wulfhere proved how man could be mule. "Other business? Other business! YOU go and farm pigs, Cormac! This is *my* business! This is a debt owed to my slain crewmen, to my betrayed grandsire, and I'll not let it slip unregarded into time for Ver—"

For Veremund or all the silver ever mined from this earth, he was about to say, Cormac knew, and Cormac forestalled him. He raised his voice against the Dane's in a bellow that rendered Wulfhere's words incomprehensible.

"Blood of the gods! Now ye'd shift to Latin and spout *veritas odium parit*, would ye?" he cried, striving to warn. "Must we squander the men we have left on every grudge ye've ever harboured? What of Sigebert One-ear, yonder in Nantes, opening his windows to the stench of Thorfinn's green rot? Let us be dealing with him, at least, ere we concern ourselves with three shiploads of Jutes and an unknown horde of Saxons!"

He and Wulfhere stared at each other while their hosts remained very still, nervously swallowing.

"Besides," Cormac said on in a more moderate tone, having quelled Wulfhere's giving away of secrets, "we cannot go hunting Jutes over the water, Wulf. It's overhauling *Raven* wants; have ye forgot?"

Wulfhere drew and gusted forth a sigh to fill a galley's sail, and his belt buckle flashed aureate. "Aye, that's true," he said, grudgingly. Having given some vent to his wrath, he began to use his wits—he who'd once said in a time of quiet that Cormac was his wits. "Hmmm, hmmm. Look ye, Wolf, we must draw *Raven* up the shore and dry her out, or her timbers will soon be waterlogged, and she too heavy for rowing. Well it is that your Armorican summers be bright and warm, Prince! Then the battle-bird must have her careening and re-caulking, for if such work be done not this summer, will mean greater delay next year."

"True."

Another sigh; grudging and mournful. "That we cannot afford."

"Aye. True also," Cormac said relentlessly.

"Well, then . . . it needn't disadvantage us, surely? It were maybe foolish to use *Raven* in any case. Our battle-bird of the seas is too well known on these coasts. Surprise be the way to deal with Sigebert."

"Right," Cormac said, recognizing the nigh wheedling tone of his comrade and playing him as only he could. "Right as the words of a spaewoman."

"Ah . . . well then . . ." Wulfhere's voice trailed off. "What think ye that we should do?"

Cormac gave him a gift: "Going to be keeping your own plan back to test mine, is it? Why, that must depend on our host. What say ye, Howel? Will ye be lending us a ship, that we might be making a little run to Nantes?"

Howel was sure not to glance at Morfydd, who was frowning. "And gladly!" His smile was genuine. He knew that Wulfhere had been angling for this favour, but knew not how to ask it for himself. The Dane was after all a stranger, while Cormac was the corsair prince's friend, known to him of old. "It's the right man ye ask for the loan of a ship, Cormac Art's son! Ha! When that first Caesar came to these shores, he was amazed to find my ancestors building better ships than any in use on the Mediterranean! He defeated them only because the wind failed them at a crucial time. Even then many escaped to the west of Britain. Great seafarers we have been, in all the generations since! We builded seaworthy ships of oak when the men of the northern lands hadn't yet heard of sail! No force in that. I'll be providing you both the means for faring to Nantes—and ye will bring me that verminous Frank's other ear, won't ye?"

Wulfhere blew flutteringly through his lips in the manner of a restive horse. He'd his own ideas about the respective merits of southern and northern ships. He was also the prince's guest. Heroically, he refrained from speaking.

8

Demon On A Black Horse

"It took two or three centuries—from the fourth to the seventh—for the decline of the Roman Empire to pass into the creation of medieval Europe. . . . Little by little the Roman roads disappeared beneath the weeds. . . ."
—Larousse Encyclopedia of Ancient
and Medieval History

The big black horse crested the rise above a forest glade. It stood for a moment, silhouetted all sleek and shining against the summer sky, while its rider looked this way and that and cocked ear for the sound of the hounds. His finely shaped mouth twisted unhandsomely into a snarl of displeasure. Rotten was the hunting, this day!

A lithe, athletic figure and richly clad, he none the less presented a bizarre appearance, atop his black horse. A stiff mask of black leather covered the man's brow and cheeks. Indeed, it concealed all his face down to the jawline save for the nose, mouth and chin. The mouth, at least, had healed.

Another man rode up beside him, not so well mounted or clad; his huntsman.

"By death!" the masked man snarled. "As well might the weather be howling storm as this bright summer that is a lie, for all the game we've roused! I ought to have you flogged, Vafres!"

104

Vafres's craggy face lost colour. When his master spoke of flogging he was seldom merely giving vent to idle talk. Nor was it any small punishment for a man to receive.

"I ha' aroused yourself game when no other man could, sir," he protested, with respect. "And will again, if 'm spared. This today 'uz the luck o' the chase. 'Tis God's will, belike."

"God's will!" Sigebert One-ear said contemptuously. "Be silent!"

They had fared far afield in their quest for game. Sigebert decided they were out of the Roman kingdom altogether, and into the forests of Lesser Britain. He knew not for certain, and cared not. He was who he was. He hunted where he would. Armorican peasants and villagers could be no different from other such vermin. Let them beware and be wary.

Behind the leathern mask, hazel eyes narrowed. An arm sleeved in beautiful russet leather soft as cotton lifted, and he pointed to westward.

"Your sight is sharp. There! A village among fields, is it not?"

"Aye sir."

"We will gather the dogs and make for it. Who knows? There may be some amusement to be had."

Sigebert's hand had tightened unconsciously as he turned toward Vafres, and his horse made slight objection to the pressure at its mouth. Sigebert jerked viciously, with both hands. The animal grunted and backed in its attempt to escape the hurtful pull. Vafres shivered, and this time not on his own account. The long ride and lack of game had put his foul-mooded master in a still fouler disposition. Seeking amusement in a little peasantish village, and him in such a mood, could mean that not only the horse would feel his ire. Yet Vafres ventured no comment, but made efficient shift to collect the deerhounds.

They set out through the winding forest ways toward the village, with Sigebert cursing low branches as though they reached out for him apurpose.

Normally he was more urbane than at present, not that he was then more reassuring to be with. He merely inflicted terror in a soft voice. Now, however, his raw facial scars were sending him mad. Pain sent the arrogant young man's reason aflying. The mask protected his cheek and ear from wind, as it would for some time yet ere they became insensitive enough to tolerate weather. Was his sweat that caused the agony now; it soaked into the mask's padded lining and irritated the scars so that they itched fiercely. Naturally they could not be scratched and a perverse pride forbade the Frank's taking the thing off to wipe his face.

The pain of his missing ear was worse. Hot skewers seemed to jab into his head through the hole and burn his brain.

"May those pirate scum be accursed and accursed," Vafres heard his master mutter, as he savagely broke away a leafy branch.

Sunlight slanted down through dense leaves to scatter coins of brightness on the forest floor. They shifted liquidly across Sigebert's cloak and the watered-silk hide of his magnificent horse as he rode. After him came Vafres on his grey nag, and the trotting hounds with their tongues out.

All trod silently on the soft game trail flanked by haw and willow-herbs.

The grey-skirted woman gathering firewood was taken by surprise. Tall she was, big boned and gaunt, aged beyond her years. Hers were the eyes and lined face and gnarled hands of a work animal. She had added more sticks to her sizable bundle and was lifting it to her shoulders when Sigebert came upon her.

She looked around, up, and stared. Her dull eyes widened at sight of the tall black horse bestridden by the finely-clad man in the macabre mask. Black-masked, black-cloaked, black-vested man on a black horse. Black gloves holding the reins. She stared.

Sigebert looked at her contemplatively. She had no beauty and thus did not interest him. His first impulse was to ride her down. Then another thought struck him and, throwing back his head, he laughed wildly.

At that laugh without mirth the woman dropped her bundle and fled.

"Vafres!" Through the neatly-pared holes in his mask, Sigebert's eyes now showed sparkling and merry. "I've raised quarry at last! The master teaches his servant how to ply his trade! Now I shall have sport!"

He laughed again and tugged off one glove to thrust two fingers into his mouth. Whistling up the hounds who came happily and hopefully, he bayed them on the peasant woman's track.

Already she had run far down the winding forest path, racing desperately with her skirt about her hips. Blue-veined legs churned, grey-brown with dirt. Doubtless she thought she'd set eyes on that monster Satan, spoke of by the priests.

By the time Sigebert's pack was well started, she had emerged from the wood and fled across the cleared ground bordering her village. No need had she of a backward glance; her ears told her what pursued. The hounds of Hell!

Without hesitation she legged it across the fields, a pathetically ludicrous figure that took a wide ditch in a leap to land running on harshly knotted calves. Yonder lay the houses and the small stone church. All were stoutly built, as they had to be for fear of beasts and robbers. Her own house stood nearest. Her heart pounded and her feet pattered and she thought that surely she could reach it. She'd no time to cosset such weaknessess as the pounding of her heart, the rawness of her throat and the beginning burn in her calves. She shrieked her man's name as she ran.

Behind her streamed dogs and riders, black mask on tall black horse. The man shouted and laughed maniacally; the dogs bayed and slavered, loping.

Outside the quarry's hut, in the shade of its projecting thatch weighted at the corners of cord-wrapped stones, her man sat fitting a new handle to a reaping hook. He heard her scream, call his name. At first the dull fellow had not recognized the mortal fear in her voice, but took it for shrewishness. When she screamed to him again, and then again, and he heard those other sounds, he lifted his head, much irked. Then he simply gaped.

His wife, whom he oft berated for her slow movements, was running like the wind toward him. Behind her flowed a river of black and brindle hounds, amid a hellish clamour. And behind them galloped a horseman on a tall jet steed, riding as if he owned the world. His rich black cloak flapped about him and streamed like a hellish banner. This man the peasant had never seen afore. He did not have to know him or of him. He knew the kind.

His wife drew close enough for her man to see her bulging eyes, the gape of her mouth and straining cords of her throat as she sucked for air. He stood frozen, staring. She staggered and her arms windmilled and she recovered and came on. The hounds were thirty paces behind her and loping, running faster than she and closing the distance.

They came like the wind itself, and the wind came from Hell. Now the peasant could hear the ragged whistle of his wife's breath. He calculated distance . . .

He moved at last.

Handle and reaping hook dropped, apart. He darted into the hut and slammed the door with all his strength, literally in her face. Her nails clawed splinters from the rough wood she'd helped him hew from a great tree. She was hurled back by the impact and her nose and mouth were bloody. Even her shriek emerged as a bubbling moaning cry.

Sigebert's baying hounds loped and leaped and covered her from sight and the noise was hideous.

Cathula had been working in the fields when terror came riding across them. Like her father, the girl of not-quite fifteen stood frozen and appalled for a long time, staring at her fleeing mother and the chasers. When Cathula acted, it was in a very different fashion from her father. He had seen the choice: aid his wife and die with her; hold open the door for her and slam it—and be dragged out to die with her, or try to save himself. He had opted for pragmatism. The peasant was beyond emotion.

Scrambling out of the ditch whose sides she had been trimming with a hoe, Cathula ran fleetly toward the awful scene by the hut. The hoe came with her, clamped in a grimy hand become a vise.

"Mother! Mother, NO!"

Sigebert saw her coming. Under the mask, his brows rose. With a smile on his mouth, he urged his mount between Cathula and the snarling yapping raging pack.

The girl did not hesitate. Squinting up at him where he towered over her, she planted her feet and snapped her other hand onto the hoe's handle. She swung it thus, like an ax, with the determined purpose of imbedding the blade in his head.

The leather mask moved urgently aside. Sigebert felt and heard the hoe's edge hiss past the one ear that remained to him. The handle struck his shoulder so hard that the wooden stave broke, and the iron blade fell harmlessly away on a short stick. Before the astonished Frank had recovered himself, Cathula was spitting fury and thrusting at his belly with the splintered end of her hoe handle.

The thing gashed his forearm ere Sigebert gained a grip on the crude spear.

He pressed his knees hard to the black horse's flanks, and Sigebert's thighs and calves bunched

with the musculature of any accustomed rider
who had many times remained mounted only
through the use of those sinews. Dragging
Cathula close, he caught her by the arms. He managed to haul her across the saddle before him
without toppling from it himself. Was no easy
task, with the girl fighting him frenziedly and
squealing the while. The horse whickered nervously. The broken hoe handle fell to the ground.
Still smiling, Sigebert seized his captive's brown
hair, which hung in oily sheaves through being
dirty. He struck her in the throat in such a way that
she had to end resistance and fight for breath. Her
eyes bulged and she made gasping choking
sounds; airless sounds.

Sigebert dragged her up to set astride his horse,
dragging her hands behind her back and high
between her shoulder blades in a relentless double lock. She was strong and coming on fifteen;
Sigebert was at prime male strength.

"Now—bitch—do you but—*watch!*"

Little there was to watch, now. His savage dogs
had made short work of their ghastly task. Vafres
beat them away from their shredded, disjointed
kill. Their jowls ran scarlet. At sight of what remained of her mother, Cathula made a sick mewl-
ing sound and shut her eyes. Her tiny belly
lurched.

"Vomit over my leggings and I'll impale you on
that hoe handle," Sigebert told her. He bent this
way and that to run his gaze appraisingly over his
catch.

The brown hair might have been a lot cleaner.
So might her tight young skin, and mud from the
ditch blackened her feet. Still, the pressure of her

taut backside was most pleasant and her rucked-up skirt displayed enticing legs, and her body was better.

"Not bad," Sigebert muttered, to none but himself. "She may even prove pretty, once she has been cleansed." And he added in a mutter, "—and de-loused. Vafres!" He tossed a purse to the huntsman. "Coax that quivering coward out of its hovel and give it a gold piece for its offspring, here. Nay, stay!" He laughed in a burst, as at a fine jest. "Nay, give him thirty silver ones instead! That is more appropriate for a betrayer! Then follow me on the road. I return to Nantes forthwith."

No longer did the Frank sound petulantly harsh. High good humour fair shone from him. As for the possibility that Vafres might take the purse and flee in another direction, Sigebert never considered it. How would such as Vafres explain his possessing so much money? Besides, even with such resources he lacked the personal resource to try.

Cathula had ceased her struggles. She stared at the blank, unrevealing wood of her home's door—her father's door, barred from within—and her eyes were blue ice. Slowly she turned her head toward the village church. There stood a spare figure in black, silent and unmoving. The black horse passed him by at a walk, and the priest of the cross said naught.

Sigebert turned his masked face to look directly on the man. He shuddered and sank to his knees, soiling his soutane as he drew the sign of the cross in the air. Perhaps he superstitiously believed that Satan had come to his village. Perhaps he was not far from wrong. It scarcely mattered. Once a man and then a priest and now neither, he uttered no denunciation and called down no curse in the name of his hanged and risen god.

Having done naught, he now said naught.

Sigebert went on, at the walk. Even the trees of the forest seemed to draw away. Cathula sat still, arms twisted and held high behind her back. She did not test her captor's grip. The big horse came to the long, dusty road leading east.

"There is no place you can flee where this horse cannot follow and trample," Sigebert said, and released her arms.

Knowing they were too stiffened to be of use for a few moments, he thrust both his hands in under her upper arms, grasped her firmly, shook her. Her teeth clacked before she clamped them together. When he let go, she made no attempt to twist free. He had clutched her where none other had touched her, high on her chest. She swallowed, compressed her lips, and made no attempt to twist free of the one hand he kept on her. With the other he took up the reins.

She could not escape him; there was naught in the village to which she could return or cared to, and nowhere else to go. Sitting quietly before the Frank who had so casually destroyed her mother's life and seemed bent on hers in a way she well knew, she gazed blindly ahead. Her mouth was a line that might have been sliced across her face with a dagger.

"What a fortunate wench you are," Sigebert told her, speaking in her ear. His fingers moved and she sat stiff, not letting him feel her flinch. "I've a house in Nantes such as you have never seen, with linens and silks you may wear when you are somewhat cleaner—and doff by lamplight when I so bid. By Death, but you will live a life such as you'd never have known else! You should thank me!"

Silence.

"Mute, Ha?" His fingertips ground in. "No bad thing either, an it be true. Many men wish their women were voiceless—nay, I remember you cried out, yonder. Well then, Empress Theodosia, you merely need encouraging to speak!"

Sigebert kicked the black horse into a wild gallop—and let go any hold on his captive.

He rode superbly, a flowing part of his mount. Cathula jolted and bounced. Her head rocked and flew wildly back and forth and her hair stung the lower part of Sigebert's face. Desperately and yet surreptitiously, she let one hand slip forth to grasp the horse's mane. He had seemed so tall; now lethal hooves flashed in the dust of the road close, so close beneath her. To fall would mean broken bones at the least.

Even so she uttered not a word, whether to curse or to beg, nor did she gasp save when it was slammed from her lungs by sheer impact of flying horse on hard turf.

9

The Ravens Are Flying!

Hooves rang on the pave as the big black horse entered the walled yard. Arbors and flowerbeds breathed scent to one side, while trellises entwined with vines formed a partial roof above. The stable was beyond. Although cleaner than most, it smelled as stables smelled; yet Sigebert never noticed. Many a street of this city of Nantes reeked worse.

With an athlete's grace Sigebert One-ear alighted from his saddle. Not a trace of burlesque or mockery informed his manner as he helped the girl Cathula to dismount. She accomplished it far less stylishly than he; her limbs were stiff, she who had never ridden before in her life.

She shuddered uncontrollably when he took her hand. Rather would she have been touched by a coiling adder. Her eyes were those of a trapped doe. After what he had done this day, this black-masked rider on a black demon masquerading as a horse . . . his studied courtesy unnerved her more than open brutality. At least she could have comprehended that.

"You shiver," Sigebert said, "and of a warm summer's night! And you never cried out whiles we galloped! Indeed my dear, you must suffer in winter! Well, well, never dread that. Who knows?

You may not have to endure another winter." He let his captive peasant feel a threatening tightening of his strong hand on hers. "*Austrechilda!*"

That bellow brought a creak from the massive main door of Sigebert's mansion. It opened to spill forth the yellow light of candles. A woman of formidable proportions emerged. Her features were like iron and her arms big as Sigebert's. Household keys chimed at her belt. She gazed upon Cathula without astonishment.

"Take this wench and make her presentable. Burn the clothes she wears."

"Aye sir," Austrechilda said, with no more concern than had she been told to sweep the yard. Less, in truth; that she would have considered beneath her position, although she'd have obeyed none the less. Would be madness for a servant of Sigebert One-ear to do aught else when he spoke.

The big woman took Cathula by the wrist. Her thumb and fingers overlapped, though the stout farmgirl was not tiny. She was drawn within the house while the master watched the girl's backside. She made one small effort to hang back and desisted swiftly when she felt the strength of Austrechilda's grip.

Glancing at the big woman's face, Cathula despaired of finding sympathy. Not that Austrechilda looked cruel. No, it was worse. The peasants of Cathula's own village wore Austrechilda's expression, year in and year out. Stolid, it accepted all, questioned nothing aloud and little in silence. It said, "The great ones of the world do as they please, and however bad they may be, we must bend our necks and like it, or they will do worse."

Cathula felt a sudden scalding upsurge of hate. No! She was here, with no way to go back. So be it. She would watch and listen, however filled with danger that might be, and perhaps . . . perhaps she'd learn of a way to do her captor some great harm.

She had not yet even had time to mourn her mother.

Tucking her head down to hide the wild gleam in her eyes, she went meekly with Austrechilda. Her bare feet made no sound; Austrechilda was silent; her keys jingled, reminding all that the master's mistress of household passed.

In the stableyard, Sigebert tossed his horse's reins to a groom. Though he gave over his latest concubine to another to burnish without supervision, he would not deal so with his mount. Unusually for a Frank, the One-ear was a superb rider.

Sweat prickled on the groom's unwashed hide at the prospect of seeing to the beast under those masked eyes. The rubdown had better be satisfactory. Sigebert had an affection for his horse that he showed no other living creature.

"My lord Sigebert!"

Sigebert turned at the hail, ripping forth his sword. The figure emerged from the shadows stopped dead while he repeated his greeting to a naked blade. Sigebert recognized him, and put up his sword.

"Faraulf! You are alone?"

"I am, sir."

"You have word for me? Come within."

The portal banged shut behind them and Sigebert drew its bolts. Hearing them snib, the groom expelled a breath of relief. Not even to himself did he wonder as to the stranger's identity or purpose. Was no affair of his. In this household a lack of curiosity helped one live longer. He led the raven-hued horse to its stall.

Sigebert One-ear preceded the messenger through the richly furnished halls of his mansion. Lighted candles vaunted wealth.

The house went with his position. The city's previous chief customs assessor had acquired all this by turning a blind eye to the dealings of a certain merchant with pirates; shares in the plunder came to the official. This had proven his mistake, and at last it had caught up with him. Sigebert was appointed to replace him. The treacherous Frank had done so right briskly. Both merchant and former official were dead now, executed in grisly fashion at Sigebert's orders. Nothing to do with manse and furnishing save give them use . . .

In an arrased chamber on the upper floor, Sigebert lit more tapers. The wavery light imparted a sinister, even an inhuman look to the black leather mask he had not yet troubled to remove. The man Faraulf stood uneasily in his linsey-woolsy and leathers. He knew Sigebert of old, and had heard of his recent disfigurement.

Sigebert folded himself lithely into a chair. "Well?"

"I bring word from our lord Clovis, sir. 'Tis this: *The ravens are flying!*"

Sigebert hissed softly between his teeth. The pre-arranged code he had waited to hear!

"So soon, then!"

"Aye, sir. Our lord Clovis moved swiftly after he heard of your . . . misfortune."

"Faraulf," Sigebert said very quietly, "you court . . . misfortune, yourself, by speaking of that."

Faraulf paled. " 'The ravens are flying!' " he repeated, for a change of subject—any change of subject. "Now, sir. This moment as we talk!"

"The black birds of war," Sigebert muttered, and laughed aloud. "The death-birds! That is good to hear!"

Beside his chair squatted a small table on dog-curved legs. It supported a flagon of wine and five goblets. Sigebert swept the mask from his head with an exultant motion as he turned to pour. The taper-light fell on the unscarred side of his face, smoothly shaven, fair of skin, handsome beyond the ordinary.

"And do you know what means this word you have carried me?"

"I do, sir. The Frankish kings march against Syagrius. My lord Clovis added a word from himself to yourself; that when he has taken the kingdom, you shall be Count of Nantes."

"Splendid." The word was a soft purr of satisfaction. "Well, my friend, you have come far. I'll hazard you are both weary and thirsty."

Sigebert turned with deliberate suddenness to hand the messenger a brimming goblet—and to display the gashed corner of his mouth, the savagely scarred cheek on the earless side of his head. He saw the effect with twisted amusement: Hard as he was, Faraulf came nigh to dropping the wine-cup. He did splash golden liquid over the brim. And he drank deeply, swiftly.

"Thirsty indeed," Sigebert One-ear murmured. "You may find yourself a bed, Faraulf. In a day or two I will send you back to our lord Clovis with my thanks."

It was dismissal. Dismissal from him who'd be Frankish lord of Nantes, once Clovis and his Frankish army had crushed the last holding of Rome in Gaul. Glad to receive it, Faraulf drained the wine to the lees. He set down the goblet, bowed to his lord Clovis's one-time master agent at the court of Soissons, and departed.

Sigebert lounged back in his chair, smiling, stretching forth long, good legs.

Good tidings to receive! Aye, splendid, as he had said. He had been greatly chagrined to be sent from the court of Soissons, to take this insignificant if lucrative post. Plainly Syagrius had begun to distrust him. Well, that distrust would not matter long, now! He'd be swept into the rubble of the past where resided all broken kings and "kings" and shattered kingdoms—and the empire of Rome. In place of the Roman realm would stand a Frankish one. This boring time of obscurity would be over; Sigebert would stand powerful and highly placed in the world again. He chuckled softly, savouring his reward in advance. Exultantly he emptied his cup and filled it anew with topaz-hued wine.

As he sat drinking, he bethought him of the girl he had carried off. He'd not intended to enjoy her this night. Anticipation was also a pleasure, and she'd be filled with wonderment and apprehension; and too he had ridden far this day. Now . . .

he smiled. He changed his mind. The word brought by Faraulf fired him with exhilaration. The girl should be bathed and prepared by now. His smile was gloating. Just a bit more wine. Then he would show her the pleasures of the body, along with the pleasures of pain.

The tapers throbbed and faltered as if nearly bereft of air.

Darkness seemed to intensify in the chamber, to press palpably down on the feeble sources of light. Sigebert froze in mid-movement, and he frowned though his eyes had widened.

An odour filled the Frank's nostrils . . . a smell as of musty feathers. His throat seemed to close. He had difficulty breathing. The chamber seemed smaller, as though giving way before another Presence.

Wildly Sigebert thought, *I have felt this afore! When?!*

Huge, round yellow eyes gleamed at him from the shadows like pools of the very wine he drank.

No! Madness! Begone! He held the cup of wine from him, regarded it as a traitorous friend become enemy. He looked back to the eyes. They remained, and now there was other movement . . .

A shape stirred there, a blocky black shape with a sinisterly tufted head. Immense wings ruffled and Sigebert *heard* them. Visions from a half-remembered—nightmare?—returned to him. Words had been spoken to him then, words that had since slipped his mind. It had been impossible anyhow. He looked upon that nightmare, now, materialized here within his privy chamber in his own home, in his waking hours. Eyes of topaz, wings of onyx.

Sheer freezing panic rooted him to his chair.

I have returned as I promised Sigebert of Metz. Dost thou know me?

Sigebert choked on words. "Not I, by the gods!"

I am the soul of Lucanor the mage. Luke-anner, magus. Indeed, your memory fails you. Once before, when thou wert wounded and ill, I came thus to thee. Neither wounded nor ill art thou now. Behold me, and believe.

"Believe?" Sigebert gabbled. "Yes, yes, I must! The soul of a wizard? Are you then a ghost?"

Nay. I enjoy bodily life yet. Mine is the power to leave my body and travel the night in this form, Sigebert of Metz, and my body is even now in Nantes-city. Far and far have I come on many a weary road, seeking thee.

"Seeking me?" Although chilled by this malevolent Presence, Sigebert One-ear maintained control over his nerves. Despite that it was uttered by such—such unnatural horror, this had the sound of the language of bargaining.

Siegbert said, "Why?"

We have mutual enemies, thou and I.

Sigebert was regaining confidence and aplomb. If what the apparition said—said? Sent, into his mind?—were true concerning its origin, the sorcerer had a fine sense of drama. Now Sigebert was supposed to ask "Who?" He would not. It was natural to him to seek to gain ascendancy; to hold it; having lost it or seeing it threatened, to regain and reaffirm. He sat silent, and forced the . . . owl, to tell him what it had to tell, unaided.

Their names be Wulfhere the Skull-splitter and Cormac mac Art of Eirrin.

"Ahhhh." Sigebert gusted a slow, vengeful breath as those names unlocked the gates of memory.

Aye, this monster had appeared to him afore now. It had spoken then of those piratical thieves, reivers; had given him news whereby they might have been destroyed—and aye, he remembered: it had also predicted then that he would give no heed. As he had not. The black owl! Again! He remembered it. It had predicted too that when it came to him again, he'd give listen.

He would indeed.

"Aye," Sigebert said grimly. "Now I call it to mind. A king over in Hispania cast you forth because of them, and would do death upon you, could he capture you. Was that not the way of it?"

It was.

The brief acknowledgment made the room suddenly heavy with a miasma of hate. Sigebert grinned, feeling himself on surer ground. He shared the hatred—and he knew it weakened a person, even though he did not seek to put it from him. His awe of the ghostly presence in his chamber diminished a good deal. Human, this Lucanor who sent giant owls in his stead, and driven by hate. Ah yes.

"And now here in Nantes, in your corporeal body?"

I have said so.

"Your human body."

So I have stated.

The haughtiness covered unease and Sigebert

knew it. He did not know that Lucanor's fleshly body was ragged, filthy, almost starving, and slept now in a stinking alley by the river front. The black owl was impressive and horripilating. It could feign to be free of these considerations and inspire terror in ways that a man, a most mortal man indeed, could not. The black owl could even kill. It was not merely a ghostly apparition; it was real.

Yet the black owl was Lucanor, and bound to his body. It dared not allow that body to be harmed.

A man had come to tell Sigebert that *the ravens were flying:* the black birds of war and death; Clovis's war on Syagrius of the Roman kingdom. Now another bird came to tell him other news . . . and once again a bird was involved, and once again it was the black bird of battlefields. *Raven,* for such Sigebert remembered was the name of the ship of Wulfhere and Cormac.

"It is a season of birds," Sigebert muttered, and aloud, smoothly, "Well then, come to me in your own form on the morrow, and we will join forces."

What said thee? It had the sound of an order. Bare, helpless to my talons and beak, you dare speak of joining forces? Foolish man! I am not here to accept thee as my equal, but because I can use thee. Beware! I can rend thee apart and find another tool!

Horripilation crawled over Sigebert's skin like a migration of ants and a little frisson went through him. The creature could do as it threatened; he doubted that not. Yet . . . would it? Did it dare? Had it come for a tool or for an ally?

Was he not strong, Sigebert of Metz soon to be Sigebert of Nantes, and coming on for being stronger? He thought to recognize the bluster of desperation in its seeming strength and big words. Was it not there?

Two things Sigebert the Frank was not: true coward, or poor judge of men. Indeed, his was judgment that kings might envy and seek. If only one knew . . . if only Clovis would hasten to take more power, and more; soaring power! Then, Sigebert thought, then will Sigebert come into his own. Valued, valuable, powerful . . . rich! As, of course, he deserved: surely advisor to Clovis, truly King.

Having thus bolstered and gathered his courage, Sigebert spoke in response to the threat of this fell creature.

"Then do so. Waste no more time on threats. I say that you bluff—and lie! None but I, Sigebert, will or would shelter you. None but I will give you your chance of vengeance and house you after. You know this, creature! An you can deny it—strike!"

The silence that followed his challenge was terrible.

In all the world Sigebert was aware of nothing but the lambent topaz eyes of the thing he faced, and of his own maddened heartbeat. He'd gone sodden from armpits to belt, and running sweat tickled. He bore it, unmoving, wishing that he had contented himself with the word "bluff" and not added the directly angering and challenging "lie."

The huge black owl screamed. Never had Sigebert heard a more frustrated cry. In raging anguish it acknowledged that whether he walked in his own unimpressive body or winged abroad in baleful spirit-form as greatly enlarged bird of prey, Lucanor the mage of Antioch was a meager being who had need of a powerful ally . . . a powerful master.

The Frank suppressed his smile of relief. He sat impassive—seemingly—and he stared with flat, hooded eyes.

The vast wings beat wildly—and the black owl was not there. It vanished.

Sigebert sat for a time ere he reached for the flagon. Even after that pause it slid in sweat when he lifted it, and he must set it down again until his hands had ceased their shaking. He wiped them on his clothing and felt their chill. He lifted and looked at them with a sort of remote curiosity while they trembled. And then, cynically, he laughed. It was release.

"By the gods! Had I been wrong—!" More release, that; the sound of his own voice helped. Now more wine was required, and more.

The girl Cathula was not troubled by his attentions that night, after all.

10

When Villains Plot Murder

The sun shone bright and warm next day on Sigebert the Frank. He was at practice with swords in his courtyard. A rack of long Frankish blades stood to hand. Five of Sigebert's barbarian soldiers were present, in their close-fitting trews and hard leather vests. Three watched whilst two engaged their master simultaneously, at his bidding.

Sigebert was unmasked. Clad as plainly as his guards, he put from him consciousness of the thickness, the pounding of his head. This was both necessity and recreation, and Sigebert loved it.

He shifted position, caught a stroke on his shield and drove his point at the man's side above the hip. At the last instant he pulled the thrust so that it did not pierce the leather. Even so, the man knew he had been touched. He made a soft gagging noise and reeled.

Now the other was prevented from coming at his master. Stranded on the far side of his stricken partner, he had to move smartly to rightward, and by then Sigebert was prepared for him. The long double-edged swords glittered in the sun.

The soldier cut at his master's head, feinted a blow with his leather-covered shield, and swept his swordtip quickly down in an attempt to skewer Sigebert's foot. The foot was not there to be transpierced. It flashed aside, moving with a dancer's ease. Had been a foolish ploy anyhow, as the foot was too small a target, and forever amove.

The soldier paid for it. Sigebert brought his shield's rim jarringly down on the man's arm. His sword clattered on the courtyard stones. Sigebert feigned killing him.

There arose some sycophantic applause and comment. Sigebert One-ear ignored it, scowling and preoccupied. He raised his eyes as the messenger Faraulf arrived.

"Good morrow, my friend. Saw you that?"

"The end of it, sir, aye. Was ye fighting *the pair together?*"

"And won! Do not make it sound so awesome, for we both know better. I've discovered that two men are weaker than one alone, when the one knows what he's about. They lack his coordination . . . tend to stumble in each other's way." He squinted along his nicked sword-edge. "Also, these be my men. I suspect they are not fighting so well as they might. The trick that last dog tried, stabbing at my foot as if he held a spear, was a little too clumsy. He verily *gave* me the bout."

"Mayhap he requires training," Faraulf suggested.

"I'll see that he has it! Aye, till his body cries for respite and his lungs ache for breath, day after day! When he faces me again, he'll not incline to treat me gently in hopes of preference! I, too, require hard training. Do these fools think I am playing idle games, they must learn otherwise!" Sigebert's voice rose in passion, and Faraulf blinked.

"Was clever use of the point, on that other man," Faraulf said. Shoulder length, the messenger's hair looked as if he'd fallen into a tun of hot blubber.

"Ah, you arrived in time to see? Aye, Faraulf. The point is much ignored. D'ye know that when first the Romans came here they hardly used the edge? Over these centuries swords have lengthened and now the use of the point—so!" he cried, skewering the air—"is nearly forgot. I'm told that Cormac mac Art uses it well. Therefore I try its employment. I find that it works quite nicely. The shortest way to a man's throat or vitals is best." And Sigebert repeated softly, "*Cormac mac Art.*"

"The pirate?"

"The same. One of those black-haired Celts. Came from their stopping off in Spain on their way to tearing Hivernia away from its previous people, I reckon. I've cause to think on him from time to time. It's in my mind that we may meet again, that Hivernian dog and I. Should it befall, I'd not be unprepared." Sigebert's gashed face twisted appallingly. "One of his men gave me these scars."

Faraulf was wisely mute, and the customs assessor turned to one of his soldiers.

"Have the highwayman fetched hither." For a moment Sigebert watched the fellow make obeisance and leave, louting. Then he said, to Faraulf, "Fear not to question me! By death, man, you bore me welcome news! You may speak if you wish!"

"What highwayman be this, sir?"

Sigebert shrugged. "Some fellow who was taken drunk at an inn, with his band of throat-

cutting robbers far distant. Betrayed by his trol-
lop, I believe. I cannot recall his name. However,
he is well-born, and by reputation he handles a
sword well, which is all that matters.''

Faraulf did not ask how a captured highwayman came to be a captive of the customs assessor, and in his own manse. An Sigebert had a
use for him, he'd have found it simple to contrive
the robber's ''escape.''

Two Frankish soldiers returned with a tall,
yellow-haired man in a doeskin tunic and short
leather boots. Filthy from travel and prison grime,
he yet stood insolently straight and stared from
eyes the colour of granite. Faraulf had thought to
see remnants of breeding in that lean face, and
sought them. The signs of reckless violence and
wasted power were far plainer. The miscreant's
arms were bound to a wooden pole laid across his
shoulders.

''Well,'' he said coarsely, staring. ''Seek you
dogs to affright me with this scarface? Who be ye,
the local frightener of children?''

Sigebert smiled with unfeigned pleasure. He'd
been told this animal had spirit. A movement of
his hand stayed the soldier who had been about to
strike his prisoner with a spear-butt.

''My name has no importance,'' he said, ''to
you. I am the man who will do death on you, here
and now—unless you can slay me!''

The highwayman received the news stoically,
and did not lose his sarcasm. ''Then I reckon I'll be
the loser,'' he grunted, ''since my hands be bound
up. There's been no blood going through these
arms in hours.''

''It shall return. Your wrists shall be freed,''

Sigebert promised, and watched the fellow blink. "I would have your name."

"You know my name. And jape me not about untying me."

"No japery, fellow. And no, all I know of a name for you is what they call you in that area where you plied your trade. I'd have your name—ere one of us stretch the other cold and bloody."

"What they call me's good enough, and I don't give a tinker's pot about your name."

"Very well then, Lynx. Time shall be yours to exercise, to work out the stiffness in those bound limbs, and you may choose a sword from yonder rack. You yourself may say when you wish to begin. Then—we fight to the death, you and I!"

Lynx's bloodshot eyes widened. "Ye say? Supposing I have your life, man?"

"Then you may have a fast horse and an escort from the city as well. Freedom! These men have been given their orders, and bound by oaths. They will not harm you an it prove that I cannot."

"Such as you harm me? O-ho-ho! Plainly ye be mad, and certainty's with me that ye lie—but Satan's eyes, what odds? Unbind my arms and place a pretty blade in m'grasp, and I'll accept my chances!"

"Sir, this is folly!" Faraulf protested. "Single combat with a felon who's naught to lose? As well face a wolf!"

Sigebert looked at him. "I intend to, a wolf named Cormac. For now—only a lynx, methinks. It is my whim. I require a man who will fight. I trust you have no thought of interfering? Nay? Then stand you back."

A dagger's blade caught the sun, sawed briefly.

The highwayman stood unfettered. He rubbed his big-boned wrists with white hands. The hands darkened as blood returned. He flexed his shoulder muscles and flung his arms about to set the blood moving. Ignoring the ready soldiers, he went to the rack and handled each sword there, trying them for balance and weight in the manner of an experienced fighter. His eyes narrowed, then widened to stare and narrowed again, as he studied the blades for flaws. At last he chose one. He made it keen through the air. He surprised them all, then, by chopping into the rack.

"Easy lads," he said with a flash of smile. "I'd not meet your master with a weakened blade, now would I? I like this one well enough, Scarface."

The anxious gaze of every eye went to Sigebert, but he only smiled his thin smile. Incredible. The mere mention of his face would gain another a flogging, or worse.

"Give me a shield."

A soldier tossed a shield to the man called Lynx. He caught sixteen or more pounds of iron-bossed, iron-banded wood handily, with his left. He slipped it up that arm, flexing his forearm against the strap. His knees bent and he practiced a few simple strokes and guards. There was no showing off. Faraulf took this to mean that the thief had skill and did not wish to betray it in advance. Lynx, eh? Were he unsure of himself, he'd have attempted to look better than he was. A lynx. Rufous-furred, sharp-eyed little bastards, eating anything they could overpower. Ferocious when threatened or cornered. A lynx. The big wheaten-haired man might be well named at that. Faraulf pondered Sigebert's sanity.

"I'm ready," the rogue said, with an oath—and rushed upon the word.

Faraulf caught his breath at the savagery of that onslaught. He'd said it himself: this man had naught to lose. He charged to slay on the instant.

He did not; swords rang so that pain to Faraulf's ears made his face writhe. Shields clashed together like slammed doors. The two men moved under the vine-trellises, knees bent, eyes fixed, then darting, to return and stare fixedly again; circling each other, the unkempt wheaten head and the exquisitely barbered brown with its sides and Romish bangs arranged to hide the ugliness where an ear had been. Their feet whispered, shifting, shifting.

Sigebert smote at his adversary's leg. Lynx's shield flashed down in time to save it. Even while sword was banging off round buckler the highwayman was hewing murderously at the Frank's neck. He failed to reach it (shriek of blade parrying blade in a blaze of metal in dappled daylight) and slammed his shield-rim into the Frank's side. Sigebert made a croaking sound of pain. For a few moments he fought a desperate running defense while he regained his breath—and while the thief attacked and attacked, using every trick he knew to slip past Sigebert's guard. He made attempt to trap Sigebert in a corner darkened by hanging vines. The Frank slipped away, backing from beneath the trellises into the open courtyard. His breathing sounded more natural again.

His brain was working, working, too; the highwayman was meant to rush after him with his face to the sun and receive that white dazzle in his pale eyes. He did not. He laughed shortly even while he moved sideward more swiftly than a scuttling crab—forcing Sigebert to do the same—and maintained a more equal sharing of the light. His eyes stared, and they had become pale blue gemstones in the bright sunlight.

"Frankish pig! I'll not be caught by a trick as old as that!"

"Manners," Sigebert said, neither moved nor seemingly disappointed.

While Faraulf and Lynx noted how this excellent Frankish fighter showed nothing, he attacked.

Light on his feet, supple and nimble as a dancer, he made but small use of his buckler. He was content to employ it only to catch the other's strokes. Yet his sword flickered like a thing alive, a rigid serpent of blue-flashing silver.

It occurred to Faraulf that for all his praise of the point, Sigebert had not used it once in this death-duel. Nor had his chosen opponent. Although an able fighter, the man called Lynx seemed limited to the edge.

Even as this occurred to him, Faraulf saw Sigebert catch a lethal cut on his shield's edge. Sparks leaped amid the scraping sound as a shrieking swarm of enraged bees. Then Sigebert's own long sword and arm extended in one driving line, over the rim of the highwayman's shield. The point slid through the blond man's throat to grate on spinal bone. That swiftly, that simply. Blood burst forth. In the cloudless daylight it sprayed intolerably red.

Lynx's eyes bulged. His mouth gaped in an effort to speak, mayhap to pray. No sound emerged save a rattling croak. His knees bent the more. His arm commenced to twitch. His entire long body lost proper articulation and he fell, a graceless crimsoned sprawl in the courtyard.

Blood continued to spurt. It would soon slow. Sigebert stood panting.

Faraulf shook his head. He'd known Sigebert since they were boys. Both had been trained in weapons-play, as befitted Franks of good birth. Yet Sigebert had never cared for it, maintaining that a surer road to power lay in letters and politics. Faraulf and others had made fun of him for sharpening his speech and his grammar rather than swords and axen. Although a fine athlete and graceful, Sigebert had not seemed to have the makings of a *fighter*. When news reached Faraulf that the other had become a polished courtier of the Roman king's court at Soissons, Faraulf had felt more certain than ever. His boyhood acquaintance must be swiftly forgetting all such fighting skill as he possessed!

Not so. Plainly something happened to make him remember. What Faraulf had seen this day seemed implacable obsession—or outright madness. The man of letters and politics and guile was determined to be a weapon-man—and was.

"Take this rubbish and sink it in the river," Sigebert said, cleaning his blade on the robber's soiled doeskin tunic. "Let none observe you."

"Yessir!" one of the soldiers said, as though respectfully replying to a general. He and three others carried away the corpse of Lynx the highwayman. Another fetched a bucket of water to sluice the shed blood from the stones. They'd be darker, now.

Hardly had the four left when a guard entered

from the direction of the great house's gates. Faraulf, about to speak, closed his mouth.

"Sir: there is a fellow at the gates says he must see you. He *demands*, lord! I'd ha' sent him off with busted bones, save that you ordered us to watch for such a one—but I swear sir, he's a base and beggarly scut, for all his fine language."

"Ah," Sigebert said, thinking of last night. "Has he given a name?"

"Lucanor Antiochus sir—spoke as he mighta said Emperor!"

"Fetch him hither, and do so gently. I myself, be there need, will convince him that he is not a wearer of purple."

The soldier departed smiling grimly; Sigebert almost laughed when he returned escorting the stranger. Base and beggarly, by God and the gods, was an understatement! This Lucanor owl-Sender might have been the half-starved shadow of an unsuccessful midden scavenger. His odour wafted ahead of him.

"You?" the Frank said in open unbelief.

Lucanor knew what the question implied. His back straightened.

"It was I and no other," he replied, making his voice ring.

Sigebert looked into the robed man's strange black eyes, and believed.

"Then wash," he said. "You are the second guest in as many days has arrived here requiring a bathe and new garments. I'll not speak with you in a closed room as you are!"

Lucanor pressed his lips tightly together, locking in words. That he resented such high-handed treatment was most obvious. He had not long to wait ere he'd be convinced that, from Sigebert, this was naught to complain of. Less than an hour, in truth.

Shorn and cleanly, he was escorted into the Frank's presence. Sigebert dismissed the guards with a curt "Let none disturb us" and closed the door. He turned a deadly stare upon the mage.

"And such a thing as you dared address me as 'foolish man'!" he said. "You could use me, could you? A tool, is it? I am not acceptable as your equal? You'd rend me apart and find another tool if it suited you, would you? You!"

His black fury was not assumed. With a snarl, he gripped the smaller man in a way that made Lucanor cry out in pain. Almost he had raised an ancient god, and subverted a kingdom as he had its queen, and now he was come to th—

Sigebert jarred all such thoughts from his mind by slamming him violently against the wall four times. He hurled him then to his hands and knees and kicked him around the room until the Antichite grovelled for mercy. It became worse for him then, with the Frank's rage cooled a bit, for now Sigebert placed his kicks more carefully.

At last he desisted and, nostrils flaring, seated himself.

Chillingly self-controlled on the instant, he spoke. "You have escaped lightly, though I daresay you do not appreciate it. I'd have the life, and slowly, of any other who offended as you have done. I may have yours yet. It will depend on how well you serve me . . . Lucanor."

Lucanor dragged himself painfully from the floor, glanced at Sigebert low, and collapsed into a chair.

Though he'd been glanced at, Sigebert asked in the mildest tone, "Have I said that you might sit?"

Lucanor would have taken sincere oath that he was physically unable to stand again, and he was a physician, among other things. Yet at Sigebert's softspoken question he found himself on his feet, trembling.

"Better," Sigebert said.

"Sir—my lord . . . I—am not well! My travels and travails . . . privation and hunger . . . your . . . punishment . . . I beg to sit. I may faint else."

Sigebert could have instructed a king in the way he waved a hand, and to the monarch's benefit. "Very well. Now attend me. From this moment, you are no more and no less than my man. I am no other than your master. Should you forget that, I doubt that any demon you control could prove more cruel than I shall be."

Lucanor sat still, hearing those words spoken quietly, as plain statement of fact. He could not disbelieve.

"You came here for vengeance on a pair of pirates," Sigebert said. He caressed the place where his ear had been, softly, meditatively, while a strange look kindled in his eyes. "You shall have it. Rather we sh—I shall have it, and you may savour it with me. Be certain of that, man from Antioch. However, Wulfhere Skull-splitter and Cormac mac Art must wait. Greater things are toward.

"North of here, war is abrewing. King Syagrius the Roman prepares to resist invasion by the Frankish cousin-kings, Clovis and Ragnachar. The fate of Roman Gaul hinges on the battle between these two forces, and well they know it, both. *I* wish to know early, and with sure truth, how it has gone. You learned of me through your sorcery; you set your *fylgja* to find me across leagues of distance. It must be possible for you to . . . *see* this battle."

"Possible? A simple matter," the mage said, and saw Sigebert lift an eyebrow, and added with some haste, "sir. Although . . . to fly forth in my spirit form and view the battle thus . . . that cannot be done. Full sunlight will destroy me when I am out of my corporeal house." He touched his chest, and went on before Sigebert could demand of what use he was. "Happily, it is not needful that I do so. Power is mine to scry and prognosticate events. The closer they may be in time, the easier the mists to dispel and the more clearly I can discern what lies beyond—what lies ahead, in time. In this case . . . meseems it is your wish to be informed of these bloody events *whiles they are happening*? Not, that is, to predict them?"

"Just so. I fancy your predictions can have but little value. Were you able to read the future with any true skill, your own fortunes had never come to this sorry state."

"One's own fortune, sir, is ever nigh-impossible to read," Lucanor said stiffly. "I had in my power a queen, and a land to come—and a single *pirate* disrupted that and thus reduced me! Two pirates. I made the error of trusting other forces, those I had set in motion," he assured the Frank, not wishing to say that he had planned poorly and prodigiously underestimated a certain man of Eirrin, and him far younger. "I have a small mirror of opaque black glass I use for divinations. The mirror itself has no magical powers, of course; those reside in me. I might scry in a simple bowl of water, as others do. It merely haps that I am accustomed to the mirror—"

"By death! This does not fascinate. What care I of the *how* of it? You may take your head between your legs and look into your own backside, for aught it matters to me! I slew yesterday and fetched home a comely doxy; today I had passage at arms with a strong man of weapons and slew him with a sword in this hand. It is action fascinates me—and information. Give you me false information, and I will give you molten lead to quench your thirst."

Again, a plain statement of fact, almost dispassionate, after Sigebert's first passionate outburst. Lucanor nodded. "That is understood," he said, with no sign of fear.

"Ah. Confidence upon this matter? Good, then!" Again Sigebert waved a hand, for he had slain one man this day, and bested two others, and reduced this one. He sat his chair as though enthroned. "Mayhap now you should rest, and later eat your fill and wash it down with good wine without water. You will have need of restoring your strength."

The utterance gave warning to Cathula, who was listening at the door.

Swiftly, silently and with her heart apound, she fled away with hardly a rustle of her new clothing. Was the second time she had eavesdropped on the demonic master of this nightmare house to which he'd brought her. She had been listening the night before when the monstrous black owl appeared in his privy chamber, and she had managed to gain a glimpse of it as it flew away. Cathula neither knew what it was nor had aught of deep thoughts on the subject, having understood little of what she had heard. She was a peasant, and not of this land, and not yet fifteen. She assumed merely that the creature was Sigebert's familiar demon, and that they challenged each other. She had heard of such; that preternatural forces were hard to control, and endangered the person who sought that control.

What mattered to her was that she now knew names that belonged to deadly enemies of the scarfaced Frank, her mother's murderer; the names of two pirates.

Wulfhere the Skull-splitter and Cormac mac Art.

11

When Vengeance Reigns

"She will do, Wolf!"

The ship was a ponto, flat-bottomed and therefore shallow of draught. This gave advantage in some ways, although a strong wind might blow her sideways across the waves like a scudding wooden tray. None the less, she was sturdy and well rigged, with the same effective iron anchors *Raven* was equipped with. Indeed, Cormac had discovered the value of iron anchors on these same coasts in his days with the reivers of Eirrin, and shared the knowledge with Wulfhere later.

The latter appeared well satisfied. "Aye," he went on. "There be ample room in her belly to hide us all, and harmless she looks, a mere trader. Were we to fare in one of the prince's corsair galleys we'd have closer inspection to face!"

"So thought I," Cormac said, "and despite our friendship, one of Howel's galleys had been much to ask. He loves them as his children."

"They be sweet vessels," Wulfhere agreed, and added in duty-bound chauvinism, "for southern ships."

Turning, he tramped down the timber jetty where the ponto was moored, her wooden fenders squealing with friction as she rocked forward and back. Huge, immense of height and thew, with his fiery mane and beard, his mail shirt and weapons and his golden jewelery, he resembled some great autumnal tree that, hung with sacrifices of battle-gear, had heaved up its roots and taken to walking about.

Beside him, Cormac walked with tigerish litheness. Wulfhere's Gaelic battle-brother was one of the few men who did not show meanly by comparison with the hulking Dane. Part of the reason lay in the extreme contrast they made.

Where Wulfhere was massive, Cormac's form was lean and rangy, yet instinct with savage vitality—like the wolf he was called. On him were no glittering, flashing ornaments of gold. His black mesh-mail shirt, and the helmet unadorned save for its crest of horsehair, sorted well with the grimness of his dark face. Thin-lipped it was, shaven and marked by a number of scars. Set in that somber mask, his cold, narrow grey eyes had a peculiarly sinister look.

Prince Howel awaited them on the beach. Morfydd stood beside him, her long black hair blowing wild in the sea-wind. Nine Bretons were there as well, the air of seamen bred about them.

"What think you?" Howel asked.

"She's a good choice for the work," Wulfhere said. "I'm indebted to ye, prince."

"It's little enow."

Howel indicated the foremost of the Armorican seamen, a smallish, hard-bitten man with a seamed face mostly nose. Was a nose that seemed to have been violently struck once at least from every direction. Shrewd eyes nestled close to it, seemingly for shelter, looking with tough-minded appraisal from beneath sandy brows.

"This is Odathi," the prince told them. "He and

his men are to take the ship into Nantes for you—
and bring you safely out again when you have
your vengeance."

Cormac remembered Odathi of old. He couldn't
have asked a better man for his purpose. The Armorican was a skilled mariner, and able to hold
his tongue. He merely nodded by way of greeting.

"We will come out again," Wulfhere said con-
fidently. He turned to his Danes. "Look ye,
blood-spillers, there is our ship! And since it's
ours she is for this little time and this one purpose,
I'll be naming her anew. This voyage, her name is
Norn!"

He named the three women of Northlands belief; harsh goddesses who wove on the loom of
Fate, and whose decrees not even Odin could
reverse.

"I call her that," Wulfhere said loudly, in a
moment of fancy unusual for him, "because she's
to be the instrument that brings Sigebert One-
ear's weird upon him!"

The Danes roared with laughter, shaking their
spears and clashing swords or ax-heads on their
shields of linden-wood. Was the sort of fierce joke
they appreciated.

Cormac said quietly to Morfydd, "No Sight to
offer us? No prophecy as to the outcome?"

Morfydd smiled with a kind of tranquil com-
passion. "Suppose I had, Wolf of the blue sea?
Suppose my prophecy were evil? Would you or
your friend or any of your men abandon your
vengeance because of it?"

Cormac shook his black head.

"What if I prophesied success? Could that add
the faintest aught to your determination?"

Again the reiver shook his head.

"Then I should not speak but to wish you good fortune—as I do, Cormac Art's son, from my heart."

Cormac looked at her for a moment, and for no reason he could name he thought of Samaire of Leinster in Eirrin. Then he must clasp Morfydd's hand and Prince Howel's, and lead the tramping Danes aboard Norn, for it was time to go.

The weather was clouded this day, and turbulently windy. Standing on Norn's high stern, Cormac and Wulfhere watched the waves lashed to a running waste of foam, while the sails of thin dressed leather were strained taut as drumheads. The masts creaked. Wulfhere's great beard streamed before him like a flame.

"Two days," he said softly, fondling the haft of his beloved ax. "Two days at most will bring us there, Cormac."

"Aye," the Gael agreed absently. He'd been gazing at the sky, thinking how dark it had suddenly turned. A strange note rode the wind . . . a storm brewing? Or a squall about to strike! He turned his gaze upward again, and felt his body shudder.

"Wulfhere!" he said hoarsely.

The Dane followed his line of sight. For a moment, he saw only dark clouds tumbling before the strong wind. Then they parted, and terrible shapes swept out of the murk to fill the great empty spaces of the sky.

Women rode naked on wild-maned horses. Their arms, holding the reins, were red to the elbows with blood. Their eyes looked eastward, alight with exultation at some greater slaughter that only they could see. Dreadful laughter twisted their mouths. Black flocks of carrion birds kept pace with them, hungry and expectant.

Such were the precursors. Behind them, huger even than they, rode a lone horseman. Although a wide-brimmed hat obscured his face, one icy eye glittered from its shadow, merciless and forbidding as the spear he carried. Loping like hounds by the feet of his eight-legged steed were two wolves. Even as he watched, Wulfhere saw the nearer throw high its head to howl. The second shivered between the ragged clouds.

Then they were gone, rushing eastward.

"Hel's teeth!" Wulfhere croaked. "Battle-brother, tell me, even if ye lie, that I've not been stricken with madness! Tell me that ye also saw!"

"I saw," Cormac muttered, shaken as few had seen him. He breathed hard, and swallowed with effort. "I saw right enow, and I'm thinking that this be no wise time to mention the name of your Hel of the death-demesne."

"A true word. Yon bloody-handed hags might be her very daughters." Wulfhere laughed harshly, and stopped the noise short when he heard how it sounded. "To think the foolish poets make them honest, virtuous war-maidens, those Valkyrior! I'll break the back of the next who chants such stuff in my presence."

Cormac stared. "Wulfhere—"

"What is it?"

"What is it? A pertinent question! *Of what be ye talking?*"

"Eh? Cormac, was yourself showed them to me. Ye saw them first! Valkyrs, their arms dripping gore, riding the sky along with the birds of battle-death, and their father Odin behind them attended by his wolves. It's a portent. Some great battle is brewing over eastward. The Father of Victories doesn't ride abroad for little things."

Cormac mac Art continued staring.

At last he said, "Suppose I tell ye what it is I am after seeing. A hunting pack of pure white hounds, Wulfhere. The dazzle of them like new snow in the sun or bright foam on the sea. And their ears a burning scarlet, and their jaws as red, open and baying. They ran as if they'd run down the world and make it their prey! I saw not your Father of Victories looming behind them. Was a figure of Vastness all cloaked in grey shadow, riding a grey horse. Upon the rider's head were twelve-tined royal antlers, and the pale death-fire played over them like slow lightning. His face I could not see, and by the gods, it's glad of it I am!"

Wulfhere was staring at his blood-brother as if the Gael had come up daft.

"Wulfhere, it was him we call the Grey Man, the lord of death and rebirth. Among the Britons it's as Arawn the Hunter he's known, and it's *Cernunnos* also he has been named: the Antlered God. Nigh as many names and titles he has with him as your Odin! Yet it's him I saw, not the Father of Victories."

Baffled and angry, Wulfhere struggled not to say aught he'd regret, such as giving Cormac the lie to his face. The dark Gael was not lying. Even Wulfhere, whose perceptions were far from subtle, could see that Cormac was in earnest. He'd seen what he claimed to have seen. Yet— Wulfhere knew what *he* had witnessed.

"Ye must have been mistaken, Wolf," he said at last. "This death-lord of yours . . . ye took the

One-eyed All-father for him, that's all.''

"Since when," Cormac snapped, "does the One-eyed have an antlered head and bear a hunting horn jewelled with black stars?''

"Oh, he bore a hunting horn gemmed with stars now, did he? That's a thing ye forgot to mention the first time around!''

Cormac opened his mouth, was struck by the argument's absurdity, and shut it with an audible click of teeth. Glancing into Norn's midship deck, he saw that which turned his mind swiftly to practical matters.

"Wulfhere," he said, "let us agree that each of us saw something, and it was a dark omen, whate'er the details. But by all the gods, it's down there we'd best go and take control at once, or the Armoricans and our Danes will be panicked together. Look at them!''

The Skull-splitter did. Three of Odathi's mariners were yammering in his face whilst the rest were attending but poorly to ship's duties, and the reivers' two-and-thirty Danes were muttering among themselves with every sign of unease.

"Right you are," Wulfhere growled, clambering down from the high sterncastle. "Do you handle the Bretons, Wolf. You are closer to them by language and race.''

He himself confronted his own men, glaring. "What be this havering?''

"We've seen the valkyrs riding," muttered Einar. "This venture's accursed. Best we turn back and try another time!''

"Not for all the valkyrie that ever stirred up war!'' thundered his leader. "Why do ye suppose

they ride for us? I say they ride to fetch Sigebert
One-ear, and I'll show ye how right I am when we
reach Nantes! Turn back? Now there's a thought,
Einar. And we could do so; beg these Britons to
take us the way we've come, and us barely a few
hours out of the Mor-bihan, because we saw
spectres in the clouds! Aye. That'd be a fine ex-
planation to make the man who loaned us this
ship. No dishonour therein at all. We could still
hold up our heads."

Wulfhere's heavy sarcasm had the desired effect. Men glanced sheepishly at each other. Some
looked to the now empty sky. None spoke further
of turning back.

When Wulfhere turned around, he saw the Armorican seamen back at work. He didn't ask how
Cormac and Odathi had managed it. Mayhap they
had simply convinced the crew that the Danes
would slaughter them all, did they falter.

What they had seen, they did not dwell on. The
vengeful hunger was in them to rend the guts of
Sigebert One-ear, and each sea-mile brought them
nearer to Nantes. The wind held. By nightfall they
had reached the mouth of the Loire. Another day's
sailing up the wide estuary would bring them to
the port.

"We'll go on by night an ye wish," Odathi said.
"Will be slower, more careful going, but what of
it? Thirty-odd Danish seamen there be, to work
the ship while mine sleep, and none will spy them
from the river-bank in the dark."

"It's well!" Wulfhere said eagerly. "That will
see us at the city's docks i' the forenoon."

"Let's be having the smallest noise we may,
then," Cormac advised. "It's far voices carry

across water at night and there just may be someone listening somewhere who knows Danish when he hears it."

Thus Norn moved up-river through the short summer night, a shadow of vengeance ghosting over the waters.

At last, false dawn lightened the sky.

"Time ye were all getting below," Odathi said. "I'll awaken the lads, and we will bring the ship to the docks."

"Aye," Cormac said curtly. He disliked this part of the scheme. It had on it too much the smell of placing his fate in another's hands. "Leave yon hatch open, Odathi. We'd suffocate were it closed and battened."

Wulfhere descended into Norn's capacious hold, grumbling. "It likes me not, to skulk down here!"

"Nor I," Cormac said. "Knud, and yourself, Half-a-man—do off your armour and look as much like common seamen as ye can."

"What?" Halfdan Half-a-man, so-called by reason of his shortness, did not see the necessity. "To what purpose?"

"So that ye both may keep watch above decks when Odathi goes ashore. Odathi I'm inclined to trust, but he has eight seamen by my count, and . . . it requires only one traitor savouring reward for our heads to ruin all. Ye're to take a fighting knife each, and if any Briton save the sailing master and whoe'er chooses to go with him should try to leave the ship—prevent it! No wish is on me to be trapped in this hold by Sigebert's soldiers."

"Sound sense," Wulfhere nodded. "How certain be ye that ye may trust Odathi?"

"I'm not. Naught in this world is certain, but that we must chance. Someone has to go ashore, and it's too conspicuous we both be. And the rest of us here be too clearly warrior Danes."

Tensely they waited, in the creaking gloom of the hold.

Not long after dawn, someone called that Norn was approaching the docks of Nantes. Wulfhere sent Halfdan and Knud on deck, and sweated. The business of mooring followed, and after that, more of waiting. And sweating.

At last, Odathi came down the ladder.

"Chieftain," he said, as one who knows what the answer will be but asks for form's sake, "this enemy of yours; be he brown of hair, with Romish dress and manners? One who erst was handsome but is no longer?"

"Ye have seen him?" Wulfhere demanded, thrusting his face forward.

"He's in the custom-house yonder. He is there now. I spoke to him and answered his questions. There be sword-scars upon his face that he hasn't had for long; not so long as a year, surely."

"Sigebert!" Cormac breathed. "Why should it astonish us, after all? Chief customs assessor is the office he holds. Why should he not be there?"

"Within our reach!" Wulfhere shouted joyously. The hold reverberated to his voice. "Here on the waterfront! Cormac, we can slay him now! 'Tis needless to wait for night and attack his manse!"

"The place is aswarm with Frankish soldiers," Odathi warned.

"The worse for them. It needn't deter us. So would his mansion be!"

Cormac was thinking quickly. Wulfhere's impetuosity oft had much to commend it. Their original plan had been to wait, and seek the Frank's house after dark, although that left the entire day for some unforeseen little thing to betray them. Now they could strike quickly from Norn, retreat to her as quickly after slaying Sigebert, and make escape.

Against that was to be weighed the seeming madness of an attack in full daylight. Cormac considered it, briefly. He decided it was no real objection. The very audacity of the notion gave it promise. Besides—holding back Wulfhere now were bull-wrestling.

"True for you, Bush-face," he said with a savage grin. "It's better Black Thorfinn's ghost will rest this night. Let's be at them!"

That morning was spoken of on the Nantes waterfront for years thereafter. Nigh three dozen fighting men appeared as from nowhere, to spill over the decks of an ordinary trader and charge down the gangplank, yelling. Many did not wait, but sprang to the rail off the ship and thence to the dockside, drawing swords as they landed. Steel blades and helms flashed in the sunlight like silver and flame. Their beards and bright helms announced them. Folk scattered before them on the crowded waterfront.

"Saxons! The Saxons are here!"

"Follow me to Sigebert's heart!" Wulfhere roared, striding through the panicked rout. He did not trouble to smite such unarmed folk as inadvertently got in his way. He simply shoved or shouldered them aside or dealt the merest love-taps with the flat of his ax. Cormac, beside him, acted similarly. Behind and about them their men widened the path their leaders had opened, with battering shields and jabbing spears.

"There's the custom-house!" Cormac snarled, pointing with his sword to a powerful stone building. "Behl and Crom! It might be a little fortress!"

"We will take it!" Wulfhere said.

Even as he spoke, Sigebert's bodyguard of Franks came arunning from an alley beside the custom-house. Their long oval shields rattled together and they howled like demons. Cormac had time to judge their numbers at thirty, before the two parties met.

They clashed like colliding waves of bone and metal. No civilized fighters these! The Franks in their leather vests, with their deadly long swords and hand-axes, were as ruthlessly fierce as the Danes. If the tough oxhide protecting their torsos was somewhat less strong than the Danish scale-mail shirt, it was also less weighty and allowed greater freedom of movement.

Blood spurted; deep fierce war-shouts drowned the first death-yells.

Cormac glared into a snarling face under a fringe of mouse-coloured hair. The Frank warded a cut with his long shield, then chopped at Cormac's shoulder. The Gael's point flickered like lightning to drive into the fellow's mouth and through the back of his neck. His spine severed, the Frank toppled, emitting a death-gurgle. Cormac trod ruthlessly over the corpse, his blade taking further toll as he went.

Wulfhere was howling like a berserker. His terrible ax made nothing of the Franks' oxhide vests, splitting leather and ribs alike, while the iron boss and rim of his skillfully handled shield broke limbs as they had been twigs. Aye, for this day he wielded his ax one-handed.

"Sigebert One-ear!" he thundered. "Dog! Cur and torturer of wounded men! *Where be ye?*"

"Here, you blundering oaf!" Sigebert's voice answered, mocking and amused. He leaned in the custom-house doorway, sword in hand but as yet unblooded. "Come if you can reach me. You shall be welcome."

Wulfhere snarled his frustration and his blue eyes blazed. A knot of Frankish soldiery stood betwixt him and Sigebert; he could only fight his way past them. His ax thundered, rose and fell with a racket of breaking shields. Three Danes broke from the melée to aid him. The Franks went down in their welling blood.

"Come!" Wulfhere panted, and charged.

The custom-house door slammed in his face.

No matter that it was made of iron-bound oak. Wulfhere attacked it with an ax he wielded like a madman. The door began to splinter.

Cormac, cool and deadly in battle, had seen and heard what befell. Guessing that Sigebert had gulled Wulfhere into charging the front and would now vanish out the back, he sent five Danes to prevent it. His powers of command were tested greatly to separate them from the murder boiling in the alley and make them go. Just as he made to accompany them, several Franks came running. Mac Art found himself in a desperate rearguard fight.

The Franks spread out to flank him. Cormac got an alley wall at his back and glowered at them.

One lean wight moved in too recklessly; his foot slipped on the blood-greasy stones.

Instinctively, Cormac leaped forward, a man who was ever happier taking the initiative. His shield-rim broke the man's exposed neck almost in passing. Then immediately, it was interposed between himself and a Frankish sword swung two-handed. Cormac's own point vanished into that man's belly, and his knees buckled.

In the mean time, Sigebert One-ear departed the customs-house by its rear. With him were three stout soldiers. They emerged just in time to meet the five Danes dispatched there by mac Art, and Sigebert ceased to laugh and mock. He tasted cold fear. The red-bearded giant would be upon him at any moment.

Snarling in desperation, Sigebert fought like a demon.

This was his first experience of real battle, and he went well at it, goaded by fear and necessity. Hungry Danish swords sought a way past his shield and blade. Dropping almost to one knee, Sigebert rammed his point into a bearded pirate's crotch. Though that harsh thrust failed to pierce the skirt of the man's shirt, it dropped him writhing in agony for all that. His face a snarl, Sigebert straightened and all in that motion his point ran into a Danish throat. Beside him an ax cut through the cheekpiece of a Danish helm and into that pirate's brain through the temple.

Sigebert took that opportunity to run. His horse was tied in the customs yard and he knew he had acquitted himself well. With a sweep of his blade he cut the black animal free, and sheathing his sword he leaped to the saddle. Behind him, ignored and unsung, his Frankish guards were dying.

Wulfhere burst into the yard in time to see the horse's tail vanish.

He wasted no time in outbursts of rage or disappointment. Striding like a colossus, he crossed the yard and gained the street on its far side. Sigebert had kicked the horse into a gallop, to trample pedestrians as if they were so much rubbish. His short cape flapped from his shoulders.

Wulfhere raised his huge ax, and hurled it.

The terrible weapon flashed through the air, turning almost gently, flying for Sigebert's backbone. Wulfhere began to run, even while the missile was in the air. It needn't slay Sigebert. Gods! An it merely knocked the cur-begot bastard from his horse's back, or struck the horse itself and caused it to throw Sigebert, that would be enow. Wulfhere yearned only for the chance to get his hands on the swine. Of that there could be but one end.

Ever after, Wulfhere cursed the fools who made that street too short. Sigebert had reached its end and was turning the corner to safety by the time the Danish ax caught up to him—and hissed by. The head caught his flapping cape, tangled therein and ripped it from his shoulders. Though rocked in his saddle, Sigebert was untouched. His horse galloped.

Swearing mightily, Wulfhere continued his ponderous, armoured run and swore the more. The iron scales of his byrnie jolted and rang with each step. A woman, helping her young brother from the street after Sigebert had ridden him down, shrank fearfully aside from the big redbeard. He never noticed her, nor gave thought to the possibility of being mobbed by the people.

They showed no sign of wishing to meddle with this enraged giant loose on their city. The contagion of mass fear had convinced them all in moments that they had a Saxon invasion to dread.

Wulfhere grunted with satisfaction to see his cherished ax lying in the street, enwrapped by the Frank's rich cape. Seizing the weapon, he left the garment in the muck and returned to the custom-house, bawling for Cormac.

"Wolf!" he roared, absently knocking a wounded Frank aside with his shield when the fool—still on his feet—seemed to want to attack him. "The slimy dock-rat's escaped us! He's run, the mangy scum, and left his men! There's no more to be done here!"

"Bad," Cormac said, betraying little emotion. "We must leave. It's defeat we've put on these Franks, but if we tarry, the Count of Nantes will be sending a little war-host against us. This time, let us be very sure we leave no wounded, for that polished filth to play with."

Wulfhere, fully agreeing, began to shout orders.

Cormac ran to inspect the three Danes by the custom-house's back door. Poor old Horsejaw had his helmet off and his brains showing. Unquestionably he was dead. Another lay in his blood with a sword-thrust through the throat. Anlaf's gullet, windpipe and arteries were severed, all. Cormac took in the nature of that particular wound, and did not miss its significance. His icy eyes slitted briefly in thought.

The third Dane was Einar, still suffering greatly from that blow in the stones. He'd lurched to his knees, sweating, grey-faced and bent over, but he needed Cormac's aid to rise and walk. On the way to Norn he vomited; once he'd gained her deck he sank down groaning. He'd lack interest in women for at least a month, mayhap for life.

"Out of here, swiftly," Cormac bade Odathi, and added with harsh humour, "Best ye be not come trading again in this port!"

Odathi chuckled. "I'd not ha' lent myself to your scheme if I'd any pressing need to return! Your enemy, chieftain—did he die hard?"

"He died not," Cormac said bitterly. "It all went for naught. It is the rest of the day ye mean to stand there babbling?"

Grimly, they counted their dead. Those numbered not so many as Cormac had feared; indeed fewer than he'd dared to hope: three only. Some others were sore wounded, and most, including Cormac and Wulfhere, had at least minor hurts.

"The first good thing in this business," Wulfhere growled as they cleared Loire-mouth, "is that no trap was set for us this time."

He was thinking of their first meeting with Sigebert, when they had almost been captured. That had been a most carefully planned trap. Few could have scaped it. Even Cormac and Wulfhere had found it needful to abandon their hard-won loot in order to keep their lives, and cross the tempestuous waters of the Cantanabrian Sea to evade the Romish warships that pursued them.

"Sigebert cannot have dreamed we'd dare set foot in Nantes again," Cormac said. "He knows better now, curse him—and it's even greater care he'll be taking to safeguard his putrid life!"

Morbid silence descended on them both. Three

men slain, others hurt, and naught gained. Further, Einar was victim of Sigebert himself and so, Cormac thought, was Anlaf.

They knew not of the lost and hating young girl Sigebert kept in his house. They cared not that their bold attempt on the Frank's life was the talk of Nantes by midday. Sigebert's guards were those who spoke of it loudest and most vehemently, for they had greatest cause. The names of Wulfhere Skull-splitter and Cormac mac Art were freely bandied about. Cathula recognized them with great joy when the story came to her ears.

12

Omens

Bright was the weather as Norn eased through the straits of Mor-bihan, bright the weather and gloomy the mood of the reivers. As the vessel moored, a horse came plunging along the beach. Its rider unhesitatingly urged it up the timber ramp and galloped recklessly along the jetty. He drew rein at the very end and leapt down from the saddle.

He was Prince Howel of Bro Erech. The reverberations of hoofbeats on timber yet echoed while he greeted them.

"Cormac! And Wulfhere, I see! No wounds that show?" Then he looked again, seeing Cormac's moodiness and the thundercloud darkness on Wulfhere's brow. "It went not well, did it?"

Cormac shrugged, then vaulted the ship's rail. He performed the feat with ease and landed well balanced, despite the weight of his mail shirt. The links of it chimed together on his body. Howel's horse shied a bit. The prince patted its shoulder, soothing it with an absent, "Sa, sa, my beauty."

"It went not well," Cormac admitted. "Almost we had success—bah! *Almost!* The beggar who squats naked on the midden can say that he's *almost* a king! All he requires is different parents."

Wulfhere trod down the gangplank. It bent like

a drawn bow under his weight.

"Three men slain! With those who had their death in a sea-fight with the Basques, far south, there be nine-and-twenty living of the two score sailed from Galicia with us. And neither vengeance nor plunder to show for any of it! Sigebert yet breathing! I think that bastard of Loki's get must bear a charmed life!"

Howel swore in genuine disappointment. "That be worse than a sorry business. What will you do now?"

"Return to Nantes and make a new attempt!"

"Nay, Wulf," Cormac said. "That we'll not be doing. Sigebert now knows we be about, and hungry for his blood. He'll not be exposing himself to weapon-steel of ours again. Nor will he omit to have every ship to dock in Nantes searched most carefully from now on, the moment it touches the quayside! And it's thrice as many guards Sigebert will surround himself with, now."

"Franks of the likes of those others?" Wulfhere snorted. "How will he get them? Conjure them out of the air? And if he makes do with Gallo-Romans, I fear them not."

"Something in that, mayhap," Cormac conceded, "although it's many Frankish warriors there may be serving as mercenaries or levy troops in the Roman kingdom." He sighed. "Yet my main argument holds, even should Sigebert be unable to get any such. He *will* be expecting us again, and take all the precautions he can. It's too long the odds are, Wulfhere."

Wulfhere spoke angrily, knowing it was not feasible but hating to give up—and hoping Cor-

mac would devise a scheme to make it succeed.
"We might try an attack from the landward side."

Cormac considered the notion. At last he shook
his head. "Not with such few men as we have left.
We'd never get through the city gates. It's unlikely
that we could sneak over the walls at night; but
supposing we did, Wulfhere. We'd just about be
after reaching Sigebert's mansion—and die there,
not even slaying him, but once again failing to
slay him. Bear the truth, Wulfhere. We have
failed." Cormac added grimly, "For this time."

Gnawing his beard, Wulfhere snarled, "So! So!
When we have been to Jutland and gathered a full
crew, though—"

"Oh, aye!" Cormac said. He gave Howel the
thin-lipped ghost of a smile. "Your gallop along
the jetty was fine to see. Although some might say
it wasn't befitting your princely dignity, quite."

"My princely dignity is my concern!" Howel
answered. "And strong enow to survive, I'm
thinking. I'd been exercising this horse along the
beach when I saw Norn's sail. The day I return
sedately to my hall and sit my throne looking
splendid while a friend's fate is in doubt will—
will—"

He sputtered briefly, searching for words to de-
scribe what sort of improbable day that would be.
Cormac's heart lightened. He clapped Howel
lightly on the shoulder and proceeded along the
jetty with him. Their destination was the great
hall, Cormac dreaming of shedding his war-gear,
of bathing luxuriously and donning fresh clothes.
He did bend an appraising gaze on Raven.

The war-bird's lean dark length had been
drawn far up the shore, beyond reach of the high-

est tide or any likely excess of storm-lashed sea. Rough triangular cradles had been made for her from timber baulks, and tenting of sail-leather was folded nearby to prevent rain from delaying her drying out. Some few of Howel's seamen had begun scraping weed and barnacles from her hull.

Wulfhere, ambling beside his Gaelic blood-brother and the prince, cast a middling jealous eye at this activity.

"Those planks near the prow that were sprung in Galicia—they want renewing, Cormac," he said. "Remember ye when we rammed yon deathly barge and sent it splintered into the arms of Ran?"

"Who could be forgetting? Was made of monstrous bones," Cormac explained to the prince, "and it burned with fire that did not consume. The crew were sea-women of spectral beauty, or seemed so, though in truth it's monsters they were, in a disguise of illusion. We smashed their craft and slew them all . . . and the look in your eyes warns me ye have doubt on you that it's the unadorned truth ye're hearing."

"Never!" Howel said valiantly, and they entered his hall.

Evening fell, warm and dark blue. In a chamber panelled with beechwood and lit by oil lamps, the two reivers sat clean and freshly clad. Morfydd was present, in a gown blue as the gloaming. Gold-worked at the border it was, and gold cinctured her tiny waist. For once, her hair was decorously coiled atop her head. Prince Howel stood with feet planted wide, his strong features heavy with concern. His tunic was almost ridiculous on him; plunder it was, off a ship out of

Greece. The tunic was silk, and deep blue and silver bordered.

"I've held converse with Odathi," he said. "By the Great Abyss! I like not the omens that haunted your voyage, Cormac!"

He used the word carelessly. Two days' run to Nantes was scarce what Cormac would have called a 'voyage,' or Howel either, had he been thinking about it.

"They were summat . . . disconcerting." Cormac agreed. "It's with Odathi ye've spoken, ye say. With his crew as well?"

"With some of them. All spoke of Arawn leading the Wild Hunt through the sky—"

Wulfhere sighed deeply. "By your leave, prince, not one o' them knows whereof he speaks —and Cormac here is in error for once! Was Odin the Spear-Brandisher, on his way to some great battle in the east, with his valkyrior! Ask any of my Danes. They, too, were there."

Cormac shrugged, and spoke to Morfydd. "There it is, lady. The Skull-splitter knows what he saw, and so do I. What make you of this?"

"Peradventure it is not the mystery it seems, Cormac. Captain Wulfhere . . . your Spear-Brandisher, Odin the One-eyed . . . he is a god of death, is he not?"

"Of death in combat, aye," Wulfhere answered, looking askance at the wise-woman, wondering what she was about. "Slain warriors revel and fight in his halls until the day of the last battle for gods and men."

"My people have known Arawn the Hunter for very long. He too is a god of death, and all that live is his warranted prey—but equally he is the god of rebirth. The one-eyed wanderer or the antlered huntsman; what matters it." She gestured. "These are the guises of poetry and common memory. It's in my mind that neither of you saw what was truly there. No matter; surely was a presage of great death coming. A war perhaps—and there is usually a war. I'm satisfied it does not hang over this realm of Bro Erech. I would know."

"It may be that I will add to that, very soon," Prince Howel said. There was a note in his voice that none could have taken lightly. "We're hard upon Midsummer, and I am priest as well as prince. The rites may tell us more than we'd comfortably wish to know."

"Why, here's a thing, prince!" Wulfhere chuckled. "Ye follow the old ways still, and intercede before the gods for your people? What does this Christer bishop over in Vannes think of such?"

Morfydd's eyes flashed. Although the query was addressed to her lord, she bit back an angry outburst of her own. Cormac observed it, and sympathized with her. The subject was a sore one with him also.

Howel grimaced as if he had swigged ale from a barrel with bad wood in it. "Paternus? He says little to my face! To be sure, he knows the people still keep the rites of Beltaine and Samhain, Midwinter and Midsummer as the year turns, and he likes it not. He's too wise to provoke trouble to no gain. I suppose he fancies that Bro Erech will come within his Church's net gradually."

"It's no fancy, that," Cormac said, and his bearing was grim. "Given time, this Church will destroy the worship of all other gods. Hang your Bishop Paternus, Howel; see him swing and make it known ye'll be having none to replace him. An rulers enow act so, the Cross-worshipers may yet be stopped."

"Not by the hanging of bishops!" Howel said. "Were it so simple, Cormac, the spread of this faith had been stopped long agone, by the rulers of Rome's Empire. The gods know their power was greater than mine, and yet they failed."

Morfydd gripped his hand and shoulder. "Listen to Cormac mac Art, my dear lord! You can do something, if you cannot do everything! Well may you save yourself from seeing the ruling power slip into the Church's hands within your lifetime, our people tortured and slain for worshiping the old gods!"

"True is that," Cormac agreed. "Is knowing on ye what the Christians dare claim? Ye must have heard it time and again from the Bishop of Vannes! They say their god is the only god, all others being false demons who deceive men. They say that Arawn—Cernunnos, the Horned God, as the Romans called him when they found him worshiped in Gaul—is the greatest and worst, and make him one with their own arch-demon. I forget me what name they give him."

"Satan," Morfydd supplied.

"It's only fools they are," Howel said impatiently. "The Antlered God was worshiped in Gaul and Britain ere Christianity was ever heard of, or Rome either."

"As we well know! The Christians do not, or care what is true—the ignorant, rigid-minded clods! They're after believing whatever their bishops tell them!"

"Enough!" Howel was beginning to grow angry. "I know my own demesne, Cormac, and by the gods I still rule it! You will see. Come to the ring of standing stones in the Forest of Broceliande upon the Night. It is very near now. See what multitudes of folk attend the old rites, long though the journey is. Then tell me the Church and its bishops are a threat!"

Well, Cormac thought wearily, I tried. Mayhap Morfydd can make him see sense, when they are abed together. He loves her. Knows he not the Church calls her a witch, and would joyfully burn her alive?

"We spoke of the Horned One," Howel said. "You will be knowing I personify him in the rites, and take his spirit upon me. Mayhap then I will know what these skyward portents mean. I cannot promise to recall it fully when I am a mortal prince again, but an I do I'll share the knowledge with you, Cormac."

"Cormac . . . why should you not take part in the rites yourself?" Morfydd suggested. "You too are a descendant of kings."

"I?" Cormac was half startled, half drawn to the notion. "What should I do?"

"Be Winter, in the combat of Winter and Summer." Morfydd looked at him, appraising his height; his hard, rangy form leanly muscular as a wolf's; the black hair and dark, sinister face. "You more than look the part!"

"I should," Cormac said broodingly. "It's at Midwinter I was born . . . all save the most hardy babes entering the world on that night are keened for ere spring."

"Who could be better?"

"Hmm. Who's to personate Summer?"

"Garin the shore-watcher. He's known to you."

Cormac nodded, thinking of the golden-haired, outgoing warrior. Aye, Garin was well chosen for his part in the ritual conflict. Twice yearly it was fought, at Midsummer and Midwinter, and held strong meaning for folk whose lives were regulated by the changing seasons. In the depths of the bleak season, the symbolic defeat of Winter by Summer gave hope for the future, when it seemed the dark and cold might swallow all the world forever. At the height of Summer, the outcome was reversed, as a boding reminder that time was burning and that after this night, the Sun's power must commence to wane. It lent a certain spur to industry at the harvest.

"A good man," Cormac said, speaking of Garin. "Well then, I'll be matching meself with him at the standing stones."

"An it's Winter you're to be," Morfydd said smiling, "it were best you not wear that talisman you have about your neck! Surely it partakes of the power of Behl, the Blessed Sun."

"I've been told so," Cormac answered, noncommittally. He balanced the Egyptian sigil on his hand, frowning at it. The mage Zarabdas's words rang in his ears.

. . . and sorcerers stand across your path, and wraiths of darkness fly from the shadows. Whether you or they will triumph, I cannot know. In this only can I advise you helpfully; keep ever on your person the golden sigil you once showed me. It will aid you.

Words!

Had the serpent of gold aided him to see the Basque ships as they really were, in that southern sea-fight? Cormac doubted it. He put small faith in sigils and talismans. Besides, he was among friends here, and surely it was true that would not be fitting for him to wear a symbol of Behl the life-giving Sun for his chosen part in the Midsummer ceremony. He'd give it to Garin then, just afore they entered the ring of standing stones in the forest north of Vannes. Any dark power would be hard tested to touch him at a place of such holiness!

"Garin may wear it, during our 'battle'," he said.

13

Shadow from Hell

Expectancy wafted sweet over Howel's land.
Every farmstead and tiny village felt it. From the
town of Vannes it was shut out in a measure, held
at bay by the stone walls, the stone streets, and the
stone houses, and by the disapproval of the
Church. Yet as Midsummer Eve approached,
many folk went out through the gates even of
Vannes, to travel north. They went alone, and in
pairs and in family groups. The roads Rome had
built were yet in sufficiently good repair to make
the going easy. Two such intersected in the ancient, sacred forest of Broceliande, where a
number of Druid groves had survived the axes of
Caesar's men because secrecy and magic had kept
them hidden.

Then came Prince Howel himself, from his island estate in the Little Sea. His indigo-sailed
galley rowed into the harbour of Vannes with
the prince, his lady and a bright entourage
aboard—conspicuous among which were a massive redbeard from the northern lands and a grim,
dark warrior in dark mail.

"I mislike cities," Howel said, sniffing the air.
Rank it was with the taint of rubbish and sewage
in too-great amounts. "They stink, and hem a man
in. We'll be parting for Broceliande on the morrow, but this night I must pay a courtesy call on

Bishop Paternus." He smiled with heretical sarcasm. "Would you and Wulfhere like to bear us company, Cormac?"

The Gael's thin lips curled in answering mockery. "Not I, thank ye. I'll not be speaking for Wulfhere. He might enjoy it. What say ye, old sea-dragon? Here's a golden chance to have mended those mildewed places in your soul."

Wulfhere snorted. "Thanks for naught, hatchet face! The last time I spoke with one o' these cross-worshiping bishops was in Britain. Some swindling smith had taken me for a gull, so I showed him his mistake by hauling him into church by the scruff of his dirty neck, and a haltered heifer with my other hand. I cannot say which bawled louder! I forced the local bishop to marry them there before the altar. It might have been a good joke, but the Christian marriage ceremony proved so tame it fell flat, and I burned the church to ease my disappointment." Wulfhere shrugged. "I cannot say if this Paternus has heard of it, although he may have done. 'Tis sure that if he's heard any sort of description, he'll know me by it . . . there be not two men like me anywhere . . ."

"Agreed, and the gods be thanked!"

"Thus I'll bide here."

Morfydd smiled. "You are splendidly tactful, Captain. I'd as soon do likewise, but among other things, I'll not have this robe-wearing fellow think I fear to confront him."

So Howel and Morfydd, with a few trusty personal servants, spent the night in the house of Bishop Paternus. The rest of their entourage readied horses and provisions under the orders of

Garin. All preparations were well made by the time the rulers of Bro Erech returned the next morning.

Their party was strongly armed against robbers or possible raiding bands of Franks; they met with none. Wulfhere showed some disappointment. His muscles would grow flabby, he complained, from lack of exercise. Yet a certain awe was apparent even in him, as they followed the Roman road deeper and ever deeper into the Forest of Broceliande and he began to have some notion of its vast extent. Nor was the giant easily awed. Hailing from the land of the Danes as he did, Wulfhere Skull-splitter was familiar with country covered by great tracts of impenetrable forest. But Broceliande had a timeless, brooding presence like unto naught Wulfhere had come upon elsewhere.

They left the road, leading the horses in file by winding paths. Men swore while they lugged chests and bundles in the tail of the party. A rearguard, burdened by weapons and mail only, followed them. Cormac and Wulfhere marched with those men, through a world composed entirely of trees. The sky hung low.

The paths led gradually upward. At last they came to a low hill with shelters and cooking places newly refurnished around its foot—and atop it, like a crown, reared a circle of regularly spaced standing stones.

Prince Howel had disappeared. None made comment, or asked questions. They knew that his part in the Midsummer rites was to personate the Antlered God, and no mortalman could take so

mighty a spirit upon himself without going apart
from other men to prepare. Was one of the mys-
teries, and it was not for the speaking of.

The pilgrims of ancient Celtia ate their last meal
before the rites were to be held. Then, with great
thoroughness, they covered the cookfires with
earth and stamped the embers to extinction. The
like was being done with all fires, throughout the
land. Not a coal or rush-light was left burning, nor
would any be kindled anew until the prince's fire
was seen to blaze on this one hill. They were
similar, the ceremonies of Midsummer here in
Armorica, to the rites of Beltaine as they were held
in Eirrin . . .

Cormac drew his thoughts sharply away from
that. He had promised himself he would cease to
think of Eirrin.

Night came down. The dark was warm, breathing and heavy, like some great live creature
embracing the world in arms of black velvet. The
stars hung all fuzzy and dim, aureoled in fog.
Tendrils of sluggish mist coiled among the stones
of the sarsen circle. Somewhere in the wood an
owl hooted. No Celt he, some wag said.

In the very center of the ring, a conical stack of
logs and brushwood had been heaped. Now three
men in their youth came in from the dark, and
Morfydd blessed each one as he knelt, tracing a
sign before his face. They set to work to make fire.
Their labour was hard and long. Soon they were
sweating in the warm night, while their hands
ached from constantly spinning the large bow and
drill.

Gathered outside the stone circle, the people

were no less tense. Would this be the year it failed? No fire, however skillfully the chosen ones worked? No renewal of life?

The drill sang its persistent song. The fire-makers felt pain become part of the bones of their hands. Sweat ran into their eyes and dropped from their lashes, and they strove while the waiting mass held its collective breath.

Then, at last, came the grey twists of smoke . . . the glitter of sparks—and the first bright tiny flame! It leaped white in the punk and straw, then grew to feed on wood. The needfire at the center of the stone circle began to crackle.

A wild, joyful cry arose from the crowd, cut short abruptly by awe. Enthroned before the fire, indifferent to its growing heat, was a tall figure, naked, oiled and shining, with the head and antlers of a royal stag. The antlers that won the doe in battle, that grew, and fell, and were yearly renewed in the way of all life. The antlers of Arawn, lord of death and desire and rebirth.

They hailed him in ecstasy, whiles the needfire grew.

Two by two, they slipped between the grey stones and began the Long Dance of Midsummer. It threaded in and out of the circle, moving ever in a sunwise direction. Out there in the dark, on the hillside below the stones, vats of liquor were ready, and the dancers scooped wooden cups full as they went. Moving in the interlocking spirals, they lit torches from the central fire and carried them outward again, until they resembled a swarm of bobbing fireflies.

The dancing grew wilder. It wasn't on account of the liquor, which in truth was scarcely needed.

Fires began to shine fuzzily on other hills,
through the light fog, signalled by the beacon of
the prince's blaze.

Seemingly of its own accord, the Long Dance
fulfilled its pattern, and ended.

Two powerful figures rushed from opposite
sides of the circle. With the high-burning needfire
between them and the immobile, antlered form,
they met to clash like fighting bucks. Rebound-
ing, they began to circle each other.

One wore leggings of grey wadmal, a black
leather tunic and helmet. Pinned cape-fashion across his shoulders was a grey wolfskin. Its fierce
jaws snarled beneath his own chean-shaven jaw.
He'd a dark face, and grim. His slitted eyes shone
in the firelight, cold as winter ice.

The other was gold, as his antagonist was onyx.
Yellow-haired and yellow-moustached, he was
fair of skin deeply bronzed by the summer sun.
Save for golden ornaments and sandals, his tough
limbs were bare. He wore a warrior's tunic of
brown leather over a madder-dyed orange shirt.
Upon his breast jolted the Egyptian sun-symbol of
the golden winged serpent.

Of course, he'd never have dreamed of wearing
such a thing into a real fight, to irritate and distract him. Not bouncing free in this wise. He'd
have worn it under his tunic, if at all.

Each symbolic combatant carried a shield with
a bull's-hide cover, the dark man's black, the
other's pied brown and white. Only their actual
weapons differed in kind as well as hue.

Cormac's was a mace. Its handle was made from
the heart of a century-old oak, seasoned well and
hardened in fire. The grip had been wrapped in

black leather and bound tightly with iron wire. The striking head was scarred, battered lead. Although a ceremonial weapon rather than a warfaring one, it could brain a man at a stroke, given a strong man to wield it. Cormac sensed its sorcerous power as he hefted the thing. It suited him. He liked the way it felt in his hand.

Garin's spear was ancient and ceremonial as the mace. Yet it too was a functional, well-made weapon. Too short for throwing, it had been fashioned for stabbing and thrusting solely. To balance the broad-headed blade of gilded bronze, a solar orb of the same metal had been affixed to the butt. Thus could a man reverse it quickly in his hand to strike with either end.

Garin was playing at that now, a series of showy juggler's tricks and feints with spearhead and weighted butt alternately.

Cormac mused grimly, *It's little this would gain him in real combat. Unless—*

It happened even as he thought of it, a sudden crosswise blow with Garin's brindled shield. Swift as light—or, more aptly, as a fissure in winter's ice—Cormac's shield was interposed. The two rang like muffled drums.

There followed harsh, bruising struggle, spear against mace, shield against shield, shield against spear, shield against mace. The leaping fire threw gold over them, and deep shadows. The warriors lost the sense of being themselves.

In small remote crannies of their minds they remained men, fighting as men—but the major part of their souls was possessed by contending Powers, even as Howel's. They were ancient as Celts, ancient as Cimmeria and Atlantis, as the world. Garin, the brightness of summer, knew he must drop and lose at last; not because it was arranged and so rehearsed, not even because Cormac mac Art was the better warrior, though he was. No. The thing was inevitable as Fate, as the turning seasons.

Mace slammed on Garin's shield with an impact that shook all his bones. He thrust with his spear. The point struck through black bullhide and slewed awry, scoring splinters from the wood beneath. Garin reversed the spear sharply and upon the instant, so that the bronze ball on the butt swung over to strike Cormac's shoulder. Garin pulled the blow at the last instant, not to snap the bone. Cormac's shield sagged low as it would not have done had they truly been seeking each the other's life. Garin, excited, thrust into the gap so left in Cormac's guard.

His spear-point never reached its mark.

Cormac unprecedently *lunged* with the mace. His arm and the handle formed one straight line, as if he held a sword. The steely strength of his wrist and fingers was taxed to the point of anguish to keep that leaden head from wavering. Yet he did.

He too pulled his blow at the last instant. Instead of crushing Garin's throat, the blow sent him to the ground choking helplessly for breath. The bronze spear dropped from his twitching fingers. On Garin's breast, the golden sigil from Egypt jumped flashing with his attempts to breathe. He clenched his left hand spasmodically on the grips of his forgotten shield.

From the people of Bro Erech rose the sound of a faint, drawn-out sigh. Winter stood grimly triumphant above the champion of warm summer, a promise and a warning that winter would return. Yet it was bearable now, at this time of year. Were it to happen at the Midwinter feast it would be unbearable, a sign that the world would die into bleak darkness forever.

Cormac sighed deeply with them, descending centuries to become himself again. The fire crackled and bellowed at his back.

A wild yell burst from hundreds of throats.

Something terrible came.

Out of the sky it slid on black wings five men's height in span. They beat fiercely, braking it above the stone circle. The monster dropped sharply. All saw huge flexing talons and fiery yellow eyes like embers from hell.

The demon came down on Cormac as an eagle drops on a hare.

Instinctively Cormac flung himself flat and rolled aside. Mace and shield he retained; they hampered him briefly, in getting to his feet, but he did so with creditable swiftness despite that. His sharp wits had already told him what he had glimpsed, and he wasted no time in inner complaint that it was impossible. It was there, and to be dealt with.

The black wings thrashed like gale-blown sails; black sail.

The naked man in the stag's head mask had risen from his seat, quite humanly amazed. He crouched a little, his empty hands spread as if to grasp something. Garin, still choking for breath, had also gained his feet, somehow. He was a warrior. He had weapons in his hands. Here was a threat.

Bro Erech's people remembered the sight for decades, and talked of it to their children. The circle of ancient, firelit stones; the roaring central blaze, gold and vermilion and pure white, gouting sparks to the sky; the Antlered God, arms outspread, seen through the flames; the demoniacal black predator, flapping like a spurred fighting cock ready to leap and strike and rend; and the armed personifications of dark Winter and golden Summer, rushing upon it from different sides.

Garin thrust with the consecrated spear. It glittered hotly as the sun-symbol on his breast, given him by Cormac.

The black owl flapped madly away from him, whirling upward. Its pinions sent gusts of wind through the stone circle, and the fire danced wildly. Despite the warmth of the night and the fire's parching heat, that wind was numbingly cold.

Garin reeled. Cormac set his teeth and stood fast, waiting. He expected the black owl to descend on him again.

It did not. Wulfhere Skull-splitter had shouldered his way forward, colossal in the leaping firelight. He lacked both armour and weapons—he'd been occupied with a pretty Armorican wench he'd caught to himself for the Long Dance and its aftermath—yet little seemed he to care. He came striding on and him no Celt, his bearded mouth stretched wide and venting a Danish battle-cry.

The black owl swooped upon him, eerie horror itself.

Full on his mighty breast it struck, sinking hellish talons into chest muscles like slabs of weathered topaz; glared at him from a range of inches. The cruel beak snapped, eager to strip his face from the front of his head.

Wulfhere caught the awful thing by the neck. Snarling, he sank his fingers deep. Clearly he meant to wring its head off. Maddened by pain, he might have done it, had he grappled a thing of flesh and blood. But there was no solid resistance to his grip. His iron hands encountered what seemed layer on layer of shadow-dark feathers, numbingly cold. The strength went out of his arms.

For one of the few times in his life, Wulfhere Skull-splitter knew fear.

Cormac reached him. Swinging the mace with all the power of his deadly war-arm, he struck the black owl a blow that might have shattered the skull of a bullock. An ordinary weapon had achieved naught; the leaden mace, like Garin's spear, had been sacred in Midsummer's rites time out of mind. It had gathered to itself power of a sort the new Church rejected with horror. So much the worse for the Church! To this place the power of cross and book did not extend.

The battered, stone-dull lead sank deeply through the black owl's body. It shrieked once, hideously, an unbearable screech that tore men's ears. There ensued a moment of preternatural cold, a sickening fetor, and the being was gone . . . was gone, as a bursting bubble is gone, without a sign.

Wulfhere staggered against one of the stones. He steadied himself with a spadelike hand. With the other, he clutched at his breast in the way of a

man with a dagger in his heart. The black owl's
talons had sunk tearing into his flesh. Cormac had
seen it himself. Yet Wulfhere's tunic did not hang
in shreds as it rightly should. Nor was there aught
of blood.

The big Dane realized it himself, through his
bewilderment of pain.

"Surt and all the giants!" he snarled. One-
handed, he tore his tunic in half from neck to
waist. It hung agape, exposing a curling mat of
copper-red hair, over chest and belly muscles like
one of the moulded cuirasses worn, long ago, by
high-ranking Roman officers. Still cursing vehemently, Wulfhere ran his fingers through the
shaggy mat, testing the hide beneath.

There was no blood. Incredibly, the skin remained unpierced. Yet . . . not unmarked.

Morfydd had drawn nigh, holding a fiery brand
above her head. In a voice unlike her own, she
said, "I beg you, stand still . . . so. Now let me
see, Captain . . ."

She reached up, her diminutive stature making
it a stretch for her. Cool fingers parted the Danish
giant's chest-hair. For once, Morfydd the wise-
woman turned pale.

Black as pitch, two groups of stigmata showed
on Wulfhere's fair northern skin, centered upon
the nipples. They were the marks of predatory
talons. In each group, one pair of claw-marks
stood above the nipple and another pair below, as
they would be made by two claws facing forward
and two back, in the fashion of owls.

"Hell!" Wulfhere said harshly. "I've never had
pain like this from such tiny pinpricks erenow!
'Tis cold, too, like the stab of daggers frozen in ice

for ten thousand years! Think ye that shadow-thing had venom on its claws?"

"Not of any material kind, perhaps," Morfydd answered. "'Tis outside my experience—and against most of it! Cormac? Have you seen such a thing as this?"

Cormac was watching the sky, alert lest the black-winged monster return. He did not trust its obliging disappearance. Yet he saw no sign of it, either then or again that night.

To Morfydd's question, he was forced to answer nay.

14

Broken Owl

In the richly arrased chamber wherein he
transacted his most important business, Sigebert
One-ear stood fingering his facial scars with a
slender hand. He did so without being aware of it,
just as he stood tensely when he might have sat.
His gaze was fixed upon Lucanor the mage.

The Antiochite lay on a couch draped in
aquamarine. He had eaten well and regained
some flesh since entering the Frank's house. Just
now, however, he looked desperately unwell. He
lay in trancelike sleep and moved in faint spasms.
His fleshy, blade-nosed face was the colour of ash.
From his appearance, Lucanor might well have
been dying.

Sigebert hoped not. He wanted the mage to
live—so long as he remained useful. Greater yet
was Sigebert's desire to know what befell in
Armorica. He gloated at a vision of Cormac and
Wulfhere dying in agony under the beak and talons of the black owl. *Could I have but seen so fine
a sight!* Yet that was impossible. He could not. He
must see it through Lucanor's eyes—in Lucanor's
words. How much longer would the eastern lap-
dog lie senseless?

Lucanor commenced to shudder violently. His
leg slipped from the couch so that his heel banged
the floor. His lips moved, though no sound

emerged, and sweat gleamed on him. Then his eyes opened. They were full of such fear as even Sigebert had never seen. He gazed on starkest terror, and knew it. The mage croaked wordlessly.

Has the incompetent pig gone mad?

Thus wondering, Sigebert poured a cup of unwatered wine. He handed it impatiently to the other man. Lucanor tried to steady it between his two hands. Both shook. Such was his state that he had to make several attempts ere he could drink, and even then Sigebert heard the chatter of teeth against the cup's rim. Lucanor gulped, gulped.

When he lowered the cup his colour had become less ghastly. Still, only fool or liar could have said he looked fit to stand. His teeth chattered still; his hands shook; his dark eyes stared wildly. He seemed about to collapse.

Tender solicitude was not to be had from Sigebert. "Did you succeed?" His voice was flat and demanding.

"No-no," Lucanor gulped forth, only just loud enough to be heard. He said it again; "No."

"Death and the Devil!" Sigebert strode, ranting. "What use are you? Know you that when first you came to me, mouthing talk of vengeance against these reiver scum, I felt that vengeance could wait—I having taller crops to harvest?"

Lucanor nodded. He had not his wits sufficiently about him to speak.

"I underestimated them," Sigebert said, looking dark. "Never did I dream they would dare seek vengeance on me—and here in mine own city!"

The Count of Nantes would not have been pleased to hear this Frank talk so blandly of the

city as his own. To know why Sigebert did so
would have filled Bicrus with horror and rage,
and ensured his customs assessor's swift arrest.

"They did so dare, as you know," Sigebert
ranted, pacing, wheeling. "I punished you not for
failing me, because it was I had commanded you
not to be concerned with them—then. Yet when
they entered Nantes and almost had my life, and
made escape without harm, I saw they must be
dealt with!" He glared at the shaken sorcerer.
"How confident you were that you could destroy
them! 'They are as good as extinct,' you said! I
bade you choose your own time—so long as it was
nigh. You chose Midsummer's Eve, for all magics
be more potent on this night. And so, trusting in
your vaunted abilities and assurance, I left time
and method altogether to you! Only results concern me."

"Sir—"

Sigebert's malicious glare and pointed finger
silenced the mage. "What did you? Sent your
fylgja forth from that quaking body to rend and
slay . . . and now you sit blubbering before me
and confess that you failed. Failed! *How*? How I
say! Answer me, you clott!"

"It is true," Lucanor said. "All magics are more
powerful on this night. I did not bargain to find
Cormac mac Art"—he enunciated the name with
loathing—"partaking in rituals of magic himself!
All my experience of him has shown that he mis-
trusts such matters. Yet he was there, he and
another. They had ancient, sorcerously potent
weapons in their hands, one of them a spear consecrated to the Sun. They used them against me!"

"Ah—and what would you expect them to do?

No more of your bleating self-pity. *What happened?*" Sigebert added grimly, satirically, "This wonderful spear sacred to the sun does not appear to have harmed you greatly."

Lucanor shuddered. "It never touched me. Was not in the reiver's hands. Nay, the other man held it; a golden-haired warrior. And upon his breast hung an emblem of the sun's accursed power more fearful even than the spear! I fled from him! I *had* to. I fell upon the Dane. Ah, I sank my talons deep in his breast! To that extent I succeeded, for those wounds will not mend! The pain will persist, and ne'er grow less. He is a mighty man . . . it will take long. But he must succumb at last, as to slow poison. As, in a way, it is."

Sigebert thrust forth his head, and his eyes glittered. *"Die?"*

"Indeed, sir." Lucanor nodded. "Wulfhere will die."

Sigebert looked skeptical. The mage might well be exaggerating to please him, or lying outright. "It will take long, ye say. How long?"

The mage considered. "Were this any ordinary man, I would say . . . two or three moons. In the Dane's case, five at most. At very most! As the third moon completes its cycle he will be helpless as a feverish child. After that . . . downward, in pain and weakness . . . unto death."

Sigebert snorted. "A pleasant prospect! I'll believe it when it happens . . . How long can the red-bearded swine remain fit and active? That concerns me more."

"Twoscore days . . . mayhap half a hundred. No more. No more," he repeated, almost smiling. He was guessing, and thought it a fair guess. That mighty northron's powers of resistance were surely great—and so was the power of the sorcerous venom Lucanor had infected him with.

"Twoscore or fifty days," Sigebert said thoughtfully. "Hmm. One can do much in that time. He may find a cure. Or his crafty henchman that Gael may find it for him. Did you set your death-mark on that one, too? The Gael?"

"That, no." Lucanor shuddered. "Ah, black gods of R'lyeh! He smote me sore with a leaden mace of winter darkness. I was all but destroyed. Belike he thinks I was so—nay, nay he cannot . . . he cannot know that what he saw was his enemy Lucanor! I survived, barely. Yet my spirit form was dissolved so that I had neither shape nor senses. It was as groping my way blind and deaf through a strange city, with only the little tie between me and my body for guide!" Again a shudder. "I sensed things groping on my track; things of the sort that prey upon maimed souls and powerless ghosts, the minds of the mad, and . . . flocking to intercept me, too! This night is full of such! Almost I was overcome by them."

"In short, you failed. Tell me not of the dangers you met—or fled. Yours is the knowledge of sorcery. Was for you to foresee what might happen and guard against it. Instead, you bungled. The sorcerer encorcelled!" Sigebert gave his head a jerk. "Ahh," he said, in exasperation. "Have you done aught but bungle in all your life's days, Luke?"

"Wait until Wulfhere Skull-splitter lies dying," Lucanor said, with a kind of evil dignity. "Wait until he lies wasted and dead; then ask me again."

"Five cycles of the moon, eh?" Sigebert shrugged. "Not so very long a time—though hardly immediate! The while, you can be doing that for which I engaged you. Quit your mortal body and watch over the battle betwixt my people and the Romans. I cannot believe the Franks will not triumph. We must! 'Tis certain I worked hard to ensure it, while I was in favour at Syagrius's court! The fool should ha' had me slain at the merest breath of suspicion of me, not sent me here to take this meagre but useful post! No matter. He will pay for his folly."

So did Sigebert sneer at the man who had spared his life from a sense of justice; there had been no direct proof of treason against him, but only vague indications and whispers that might possibly have been malicious. Such uncertainties would not have restrained Sigebert, had he been in the Roman king's place. And so the unprincipled Frank despised the honourbound Roman for it.

"Never!" Lucanor said with a shudder. "You know not, you cannot know! The nearness of those foul creatures of the black world . . . the threat of them—I all unformed and helpless—nay! Never will I venture the more from my fleshly body. I could not, even did I dare. My strength is gone."

"*Gone?*" Sigebert's voice fair dripped scathing contempt. "How much had you ever? Best ye summon strength enow for my purposes, I warn you! I make no demand that you kill. By Death!—were that in my mind I'd send forth a baseborn assassin and think him better fitted to the work than you! You are merely to observe who gains the victory, and inform me what befalls King Syagrius. Even you should not fail at so little an errand." The limpid hazel eyes hardened into glittering garnets. For a moment, Sigebert's face was demoniacal. "An ye do fail, my mage, ye were far better to risk the ugly spirits of the outer dark!"

Lucanor strove for control and self possession, and succeeded only partially. With belated presence of mind, he dared recall to Sigebert his previous words and ability to scry events in his mirror of black; "True Black" he called it. Sigebert gave listen without patience. He remembered.

"Very well. Your methods be your own concern, mage. All that concerns me is to know the outcome of this one imminent battle, the very day it is fought. But mark me!" The finger stabbed again, before eyes gone all round and white-surrounded. "The consequence of failing me in this remains what I promised."

Lucanor bowed deeply, less in submission than to hide the bitter hatred he feared his face was showing.

15

Cathula

Prince Howel kept a manse in the town of Vannes. Romish and all of two centuries old, the house had been well built. It would not tumble in Howel's lifetime. True, it showed its years, as must any oldster. Tapestries concealed the cracked yellow stucco of the *exedra's* walls—without reaching so high as to hide the half-obliterated peacock frieze near the ceiling. Here and there a broken floor tile lay waiting to trip a man and make him curse. Morfydd had furnished the place in the manner of her own people, with heavy chairs and couches strewn with shaggy carpets in several hues.

"Behl protect!" the lady of Bro Erech was saying, seated on a pelt of golden tan. "As he truly did! Were it not for the sigil ye carried from Hispania, Cormac, that had been an ill night for us all. The monster showed itself vulnerable to your mace, as well—yet did not seem to fear it half so much as the power of our lord the Blessed Sun. Were I your menaced self, I'd be keeping the winged serpent upon my body at all times hereafter."

"I shall," the Gael replied grimly. "Another gave me the selfsame advice, in the Suevic Kingdom. It's hardly wise I was to forget it."

Wulfhere slouched against the wall, saying

naught. Wulfhere was hurting and all knew it. The battered planes of his face were harsh with unassuagable endurance of pain. Morfydd had promised to do for him what she could, once they returned to the island where her sorcerous effects were kept. She had admitted to holding little hope. With hope or no, it never became a warrior to whimper. Wulfhere endured in silence.

Cormac likewise said naught. His heart was twisted within him by concern for his battle-brother, yet his way had never been to talk when he could not do. One tiny clue; the faintest trace of the means to effect a cure, and he'd follow it over the sea-rim and into the lairs of demons, if needful. They had no such clue.

"A strange thing, this," Prince Howel said. "Once, not so long agone, concern was on us to know the meaning of those omens ye saw asea, Cormac. Trifling it seems now, when I can give ye the answer."

"Seems? Maybe." Curt and moody the Gael felt, and something of that was manifest in his voice. "And yet—ye've knowledge, Howel?"

"Aye, even though the rites were disturbed." Howel's eyes seemed to look into haunted distance beyond the world. His voice reverberated with a timbre not quite canny. "The god came upon me. I rode through vast spaces on a great, death-grey horse and saw the world spread below me like a tapestry that unfurls. Fields no bigger then squares of quilting. Houses mere chips of wood. Spectres moved in the sky above, and phantom armies, and there was a confusion of many noises. My face turned eastward, and there I saw war abuilding. 'Tis Frankdom that marches!

Frankdom that lifts its axes against the swords of the Roman Kingdom! The cousin-kings Clovis and Ragnachar lead their hosts within the month. I *know* it. Syagrius will meet them in strength. Corpses of men slain redly will cover the ground, and rivers in the Frankish marches will run crimson, even to the sea. Such is the meaning of the omens I saw. I *know* it," he repeated, and all understood that he was not sure *how* he knew.

"Blood of the gods," Cormac said softly, into a shaken quiet. "Said ye this thing seems 'trifling'?"

Howel made no answer. Morfydd spoke in a brittle voice, as if afraid.

"It is not. But it scarcely need trouble yourself, Cormac, save insofar as there be plunder to be had out of it. Me thinks my lord means that Wulfhere's plight is of great moment to him and to you."

"Truth," Cormac acknowledged.

Prince Howel had recovered his normal voice and demeanor. "We may have to look to ourselves here, should the Franks win. They may not rest content with ravaging the Roman Kingdom only."

Gloomy silence rested in the chamber. Wulfhere stirred, scratching the depths of his beard. Even that appeared to have lost its fiery hue, somehow reduced to drabness.

A knock at the door jerked them from their reverie.

"It is Garin, my lord," a voice answered Howel's query, and was bade enter.

The tall golden warrior came in wearing an expression of puzzlement. He gave formal greeting to his lord and lady, and a more casual one to the pair of reivers.

"Lord, this is a strange thing, and one that concerns Cormac if anybody. A wench is here, a young woman—"

Cormac's eyes rolled in Wulfhere's direction, and he frowned. No comment from the Dane. The inveterate womanizer *was* hurting and feeling low, to say naught about who might be concerned with the advent of a young woman!

"Strange? Strange how, Garin?"

"Strange," the shore-watcher said emphatically. "You must see her to know! Yet I'd not trouble ye with her, save that she mentions Sigebert One-ear. Claims she was a prisoner in his house, and escaped."

Wulfhere came alive. "Sigebert?" He glanced at Cormac, whose cold eyes had narrowed while he stared expectantly at Garin.

"Aye," Garin said. "She's a peasant wench— only a girl really, dirty, footsore and ragged from travel. Even so she'd be pretty beyond the common, were it not for . . ." He hesitated, as though he could not find proper words for the framing of his thought. "Have ye interest in what she has to say?"

"It's a trick," Wulfhere growled. "Sigebert has sent her to gull us! What peasant wench could escape his snaky clutches?"

"Not many, in truth," Cormac agreed. "Yet as a trick, it seems too simple-minded for that Frankish cur. It's something subtler he'd be conceiving. But—the more fools we to send her away without so much as hearing her! Howel,

Morfydd—is objection on ye to Garin's bringing her to this chamber?"

"I've none," Howel said readily. "Let it be now. Indeed, it's interested I am myself."

Morfydd chuckled throatily. "After hearing that, I know I must stay! Best to have a woman present anyhow. An she's false, she may need—frightening. But an she's true, it's more likely she will want reassuring."

"Fetch her in then, Garin," the Prince of Bro Erech ordered, and they exchanged glances, and soon they were gazing on her.

Cormac mac Art, hard son of a harsh age, hewed to a trade savage and ruthless even for his time and place. His comrade's sobriquet Skull-splitter was an earned one. Prince Howel, too, was a pirate who had spilled his share of blood. The Lady Morfydd lived in the same world as they, and knew well what it was like. None of them was naive, simple or inexperienced.

Nevertheless something about this girl chilled them all. She entered the chamber hesitantly, with Garin guiding her by a hand on her arm above the elbow; perhaps lest she take fright and flee. An that were his motive, Cormac thought, he had erred. The girl showed no fear of confronting such high-seated folk. Her hesitant steps were surely due to hunger, exhaustion—and something more. She looked as if she no longer belonged in her body or was quite aware of walking on solid ground. The blue eyes had a remote, empty look.

"Who are you, girl?" Morfydd asked gently.

"Lady, my name is Cathula." She spoke softly.

"I lived in a village north of here . . ." She looked at Howel. "Is you—be you Prince Howel, lord?"

"I am."

Cathula turned her eyes to the immense, red-bearded warrior behind her, and then to the dark Gael. For the first time the direct focus of living concern entered her gaze. "And ye twain—"

"I am Cormac mac Art."

Cathula considered that speaker. The height and sinewy, tigerish power of him, the scarred face. Somehow his scars did not repel her as Sigebert's had done. On the Frank's fair skinned, almost girlish visage, sword-scars were a sickening disfigurement. Cormac mac Art had never been pretty. The scars were part of him, and belonged; to the dark, sombre mask of his features, they made little difference. Too, mac Art's facial scars were years older than Sigebert's. Time had faded them somewhat.

Cathula said, "The one-eared Frank is your enemy?"

"Enemy!" Cormac snarled. "When I catch him, I'll tear out his throat—or Wulfhere there will! Now be telling us how it is ye know this, Cathula."

"Sigebert told her, and sent her here," Wulfhere said, doggedly holding to his belief that she was an agent of the Frank's.

Cathula said simply, "No."

"Then how were ye able to escape such as that man?"

"Because he has greater matters to think on than a girl he carried off to spice up a day's bad hunting. I heard him speak of you. Was't truly you what tried to slay him in Nantes, a se'enight since?"

"Aye. Blood of the gods! A pity it is we didn't succeed! The tale of it was all over the city no doubt, and discussed loudest in Sigebert's own house. So. It is reasonable that ye'd have heard our names. But how knew ye where to find us? And how are ye after coming here?"

"Oh," Cathula said with strange indifference, "you and them Danes came to the city in an Armorican ship. I listened to Sigebert hisself, talking on it."

"Spied on him, ye mean?"

"Aye."

"That demanded courage," Cormac observed. "Still, Bro Erech is not the only Armorican princedom."

"The nearest," Cathula said, and Cormac couldn't forbear a bleak grin.

"And then ye made escape. How?"

"Oh, the hardest part was slipping out of the mansion and its grounds. The next hardest was sneaking clear of the city. One dark night I let myself down the wall by a rope. Then I walked. I went hungry, hid in ponds; I stole food . . . twice I cadged rides in farm carts."

Wulfhere demanded "How," and she said in a perfectly equable tone, "By giving them drivers what a girl has to offer."

She said it with the same detached indifference as she'd spoken all else. Although plainly exhausted she had not asked if she might sit; and judging by what was almost the pertness approaching impertinence of some of her utterances, fear did not restrain her. It was as if, since she happened to be standing, she would remain so until she fell. Nor was pertness a true description of her manner. She seemed quietly obsessed with what she had to tell, so that nothing mattered but the telling. Cormac had the eerie feeling that were she taken out and beheaded once they had heard her out, she would not care.

"Can ye be proving all ye've said, Cathula? It's strong proof I'll be requiring. It's a careful man I've been since I was young and people I knew not were trying to kill me for reasons I knew not."

"You talk funny," Cathula murmured, as if to herself. She thought for a time, twisting her hands in agitation. "There be the village I lived in," she said, and named it. "When the Frank came there he . . . he set his hunting hounds on my mother. They rent her in pieces, and et on her."

Morfydd moved rustling to the girl's side. Taking Cathula gently by the shoulders, she caused her to sit. Both women were pale. Cathula spoke without emphasis, in one tone only.

"She was arunning for our hut. She mighta got there, too, but my father barred the door on her. He knowed if he tried to save her he'd get tore and et, too. I know now that Frank woulda made him come out if he'd let mother in and then barred the door—that, or Sigebert woulda burned 'em both in our house. He barred her out and the dogs was all over her like that. I tried to beat them off with a hoe. I didn't even know what I was about. The Frank stopped me and paid my father money and carried me away. Big black horse. The priest seen it all—he watched and did naught." She said priest as mac Art might have done.

Cormac believed that. Morfydd was clutching

the girl, staring at him, and her face was as if she'd looked on maggots and child-corpses.

"I passed through there, on my way here," Cathula went on. She might have been talking of things that had happened to folk dead a thousand years. "It was night. Nobody saw me and I went to my h—my father's hut. It stank of wine and he was laying drunk and senseless by the hearth. I tied 'im fast to the wall whiles he snored. Then I burnt the hut with him in it."

"Enough," Prince Howel said hoarsely. "Oh, enough!"

"Enough," Morfydd said, ashy-faced, "but not all."

"They's more to tell!" Cathula said with vehemence. "Sigebert One-ear's got a wizard in his manse. He obeys Sigebert and commands a demon, too! I have saw it—a thing like a huge black bird—"

Wulfhere's wine-cup crashed on the floor. "Ye say so, girl! Ah! By Loki and all his get! Cormac— that's a likely thing! Had Sigebert a demon in his service, who but you and me would he send it to attack?"

Mayhap several people, the Gael thought; the Frank was richly endowed with enemies. This, though, was surely proof that Sigebert had *something* to do with that fell owl. Now Cormac realized that it had attacked not long after their attempt on Sigebert. Sent!

"So Sigebert has a wizard in his foul employ," Cormac mused, low of voice. "Tell me of him, girl."

"I've not saw him but once or twice. Got a thin

nose, in a fleshy face. Scary dark eyes, and he's real dark. Name is Lucanor of . . . Atyok?"

"Annnn-tiochhh . . ." Cormac breathed.

"Lucanor!" Wulfhere roared, starting from the wall. "Now that's too much! Surely that cur-son abides leagues to the south—or more likely dead at the hands of angered Basques. The wench lies, Cormac!"

The girl turned to stare at him from a face gone all ugly.

"She knows his name," Cormac pointed out. *"How,* an he be not somewhere in these parts? He could be after escaping the Basques and coming north, you know. By his sorcery he could discover that Sigebert is our deadly enemy. Lucanor and Sigebert! By the *gods,* Wulf, *there* is a partnership to make a man dream ill dreams!"

"That black owl that struck at you and smote Wulfhere—it must be a sending of this Lucanor's!" Prince Howel nigh shouted. "Surely, if any man knows the remedy for Wulfhere's hurts, it will be him! He," he corrected, with a glance at Morfydd.

"A good thought," Wulfhere rumbled. "Aye, a very good thought, Prince. We must capture the eastern cur alive and force him to tell us. Since he now dwells in Sigebert's manse, why, we'll have to slay Sigebert in order to get him!" The Danish giant grinned ferociously. "I feel better even now, just thinking on't." A knifing spasm of pain twisted his face to give him the lie. Cormac saw his fingers twitch and start to curl.

"The cure may be such that your Lucanor will be loath to speak of it, even under torture," Morfydd said, and all looked to her. "I have been thinking, Captain. Cathula here calls the black owl a demon." Her hand remained firm and motherly on the girl's far shoulder. "I had supposed as much myself, for lack of knowledge. The creature may still be a demon—or it may be a sending. An emanation of the wizard's owl soul. An that be so, the remedy for your pain is simple. Ye need only to do death on this Lucanor. The effects of his work will vanish with his life."

"Ha!" Wulfhere growled. "Lady Morfydd, it is sentence of death ye have pronounced on that eastern weasel!"

"Be very sure ere you strike," she said, using the personal pronoun. "Should the black owl be some being independent of Lucanor's soul, after all, you will lose your only link with it."

Cormac felt this woman's warmth, and depth. "First we must lay hands on the misbegot dog," he said, moving swiftly to pragmatism.

"Aye!" Wulfhere's unremitting suffering made him even more tactless than usual, and he glowered at Cathula. "Very well, wench. Ye've explained all save why ye be here, telling us these things. Is it reward?"

"Reward?" Cathula seemed to find the word impossible to understand. "Ye twain is Sigebert's blood enemies! Where else should I go? I want him to die . . ."

"Die he shall," Cormac promised all grim-faced, "and life shall be better for yourself henceforward, an it's truth ye've told. An ye lie—"

He did not finish the sentence. The savagery of his dark face said all for him. Yet the peasant, so young and so old, did not quail. Like so many others, she'd been thrust and dragged into womanhood without having had time to enjoy being a girl.

"What should I fear?" she asked. "I saw my mother die awful. Sigebert One-ear's had me for a plaything. I've did death on my own father. For that I am damned. I do not fear weapons or . . . sendings, or life or death, or man or god. Or demon either. It's truth I tell ye."

"We shall discover," Cormac told her. She was at least half mad, he thought. Knowing what he did of Sigebert One-ear, he was not astounded.

"Come away, child," Morfydd said. "You need to wash, and you need fresh garments and a meal, and rest. Anything else you can tell us will wait. D'you love nice fresh pork, hmm? Come along now—you must tell me whether you love chops best, or the sweetmeats . . ."

Left alone, the three men looked at each other. Howel spoke first.

"What think ye, Cormac?"

"That one's not doing deception on us," Cormac said readily. "Blood of the gods! The peasant wench never drew breath who could act a part in such manner!—and it's peasant wench she is, from her speech to the calluses her hands bear from working in the fields. Attend me: her story rings true." He looked from Howel to Wulfhere. "Nonetheless, we'll be testing it."

"How?"

"By going to this village of hers and hearing the gossip there. My father and Sualtim raised no stupid son! This may be a scheme of Sigebert's however strong the reasons for thinking not. It's warily we'll be going, then. Will ye be lending us a few of your best foresters, Howel, to scout for us and be sure no ambush is laid?"

"Och, man! It's scarce need ye have for asking," Howel said, going all old Celtic, "save as a way of stating your wishes. As well ye know, Cormac mac Art. They shall be found this very day."

"Howel: it's the best of friends ye be. Remember; I shall. Lest there should be fighting to do, we'll take most of the Danes with us. Two dozen, eh Wulfhere? All draw lots for five to remain and work on *Raven*?"

Wulfhere agreed, and so it was decided, amid much feeling of close camaraderie. The curses of those five who drew the losing lots nigh sufficed to wither the remaining wet out of *Raven's* timbers with no need of the sun's summery heat.

16

The Reivers Reived

The girl's body shone voluptuously in the moonlight. Thick pale hair hung down a smoothly muscled back, and water splashed about her thighs as she waded toward the bank. Many moon-silvered drops gleamed on her flesh or fell rolling from her arms. She reached up to grip the twisted root of a tree for purchase.

Knud the Swift burst from the water behind her. She squealed at the digging of his fingers into the flesh of her well-curved hips with a celerity that fully justified his name—which the girl did not know. She called him by the name he had given her: Wiliulf.

She gripped the tree's root harder. Knud had lifted her slipping feet clear of the stream's bed. Still, as he was obviously not about to let go of her, she didn't mind. She hooked her feet behind his powerful calves and settled her rump firmly against his belly. He made connexion from behind. She gasped; he grunted. They were both very busy for a while. The heavy tree-root was almost torn out.

Lying on the bank beside her, Knud sighed pleasurably. Was his own long-held belief that peasant women were best. For one thing, they were not expected to be virgins. No dynasties or estates depended on their being kept untouched for marriage. An they bore children, so much the better. A child was another pair of hands to work, and therefore always wanted. Thus peasantish lasses might lie with whomever they pleased with little fear of consequences. And they did. They knew a life of heavy toil lay ahead of them, and that they would be old all too soon. They were eagerly inclined to take their joys whilst they could.

The girl nestled against him. Her wet flesh felt cool. Was a pleasant feeling, the night being hot. Knud fondled her. She purred with enjoyment.

"Stay among us Wiliulf," she cajoled. "It's good fertile land hereabouts. We do not oft go hungry."

"I'm a warrior, dear. There be places for me in the army of the Roman king. What should I fight here? Marauding crows?"

"Better than having the war-birds come for you when the fighting is over! Your limbs would stay whole, at least."

She meant it. Knud found that downright insulting. He slapped her hip with force sufficient to make her yelp. "I can keep my limbs against most men's efforts to maim them—when I have ax or sword! Syagrius be the likeliest man to give me one. I've earned my eating here, and a bundle of food to take me further on my road. I cannot be staying." For courtesy's sake, having been well reared, he added, "Not even for you, love."

The very young woman was disposed to sulk.

She did not continue long when she realized it would gain her naught, and Knud began tickling her again into the mood.

Considerably later she left him, moving soundlessly across the ripe fields toward her family's hut. The door stood wide in the hot night, its opening curtained with sacking. From the forest's edge, Knud watched her go. Then he turned, and made his way by winding forest paths to where his comrades were encamped. Several times as he approached he whistled, soft and low. He'd no wish to come upon Cormac and company carelessly, be like to receive a spear's point ere he could say his name. True, Prince Howel's foresters had scouted the area close, and reported no trace of ambush or any armed force. Knud had spent five days in the village itself without being seized or coming to harm. He grinned reminiscently. No harm had befallen him indeed! Quite the opposite.

Even so a man could never be certain what might be concealed within a forest of these dimensions. Nigh thirty men that Knud could swear to, for instance, and not a peasant in the village yonder had any suspicion. Belike it could hide a thousand with ease. His comrades would be vigilant. Trust the wary man from Eirrin for that.

"Knud?"

"Myself! Aye and ye sound like . . . Atanwald?"

"Aye, Swift one."

An obscure form showed itself, hand outstretched in the sign of peace. A scale byrnie glimmered faintly in the darkness beneath the forest roof. "Be sure of my voice ere ye come closer, lad. We'd not wish to be over-suspicious and kill each other. 'Twere a joke to make the gods laugh."

"I know ye, man. Lead me to the Hausakluifr."

Knud was soon in the encampment. He was

roundly cursed for accidentally kicking a sleeper wrapped in a long cloak. Erelong Cormac and Wulfhere were awake and ready to give listen to his intelligence.

"All be as the little wench made claim, Captain," Knud said. "They talk of little else in that pigsty village. I'll wager it's the mightiest thing to have happed there in a lifetime. Sigebert's hunting, and the dogs, and the way he carried off Cathula. He paid for her, mind. The girl's mother died. Horribly. Not long since, her father burned in his hut. All the village believes it was a drunken mischance—their 'God's' will and justice. I've even talked to the priest."

"Could he understand you?" Cormac asked.

"By the World Tree! My Latin is not that poor!"

"Was the priest's Latin I had ill thoughts about," Cormac said. "An it's like unto most of his kind he is, the garbled mess he calls Latin would be sounding better from a kittiwake. He supports Cathula's tale, does he?"

"Everything does. The village wenches are rolling their eyes and making guesses about her fate . . . they pretend to be appalled, but they giggle even whiles they bite their lips, ye know?" Knud spat on the ground. "Despite what ye said, Cormac, I'd never ha' believed even a sounder of Britonish peasants could accept a Dane as a Frankish vagabond! Certain I was they'd know me for the liar the instant I said aught so ridiculous! Yet they believed me. They could not tell the difference."

He fell silent, brooding on that in disbelief and some outrage.

Cormac grinned. "Forget fretting, Knud. Not

one of them's been more than a league from the village in his life's days, remember. Well then 'tis settled for me; it's honest our Cathula is." He ceased to smile. "By which token, it's a bargain Lucanor of Antioch has made with that bloody-hearted Frank. Now we can be certain—Sigebert *and Lucanor* are yonder in Nantes, and teamed."

Since the black owl's talons had smitten Wulfhere, he had become morose and silently brooding amid his pain. Now he spoke.

"We have another chance to slay Sigebert, and Lucanor with him! This war of Franks on Romans Howel avows is in the making . . . it helps us. Do the Franks march on Soissons *and conquer*, all the land will be in uproar. Nantes will seethe with panic like a broken nest of ants! Fleeing country folk will howl at its gates in multitudes. In such confusion we can enter—and leave again with none remarking us!"

"An these things happen, Wulf." They looked at each other: blood-brothers.

They settled to sleep. Knud wondered, half hopefully, whether he ought not return to the village for another day or two—just to be wholly sure there was naught he'd omitted to learn . . . His comrades brayed him down. Were the women of this village so eager that he could not bear to depart? They were assured the village priest was the man to ask about that; Knud felt sure that despite what the black-robe said in church, he'd likely had every nubile girl for a league around and some of the wives into the bargain.

With the sun's rising they made a fire and roasted venison killed by Howel's foresters. Cormac and Wulfhere allowed a big cheery blaze, as they meant to leave the vicinity anyhow. Nor were they overly strict about smoke.

By this means did the messanger from Vannes find them. Himself a forester and expert tracker, he'd have trailed them to the camp in any event. The odour of woodsmoke merely made it simple for him. He'd traveled most of the way with an armed party, but finished his journey alone. He bore ill news, he said, the Lady Morfydd having despatched him to bring it them.

"The Lady Morfydd?" Cormac repeated. "Not Prince Howel?"

The man shook his head. Short-legged, heavy-bodied and bald he was, clad in deerskin tunic leggings. "The prince is wounded," he said bitterly. "He may die yet." And he glared at Cormac as though blaming him personally.

"How?" Cormac snapped. "By whom?" There was that in his and sudden complete attention to make the man think again about voicing his own feelings on the matter, or doing aught at all save answer the question fully.

"Hengist, lord. He came with three Saxon long-ships, and raided the Mor-bihan in full daylight! The prince was newly returned to his keep on the island. Hengist made no attempt to storm it, for he could never ha' taken it in any case with three ships' companies. He stole your ship—"

"What?" That from Wulfhere, in a bellow. "Raven stolen?" He made three titan's strides and seized the forester. He lifted the man as if he were a doll. "Hengist, ye say? Ye dare tell me he has lifted Raven from out the Little Sea? From your master's own doorstep? What were his coast-watchers doing to prevent it?"

The forester said into Wulfhere's congested face, "The coast-watchers died to a man! My master the prince led a sortie down from the hall to prevent those Kentishmen's launching your ship. 'Tis how he came to be wounded. When he fell, his warriors carried him back from the fray and covered his retreat wi'their lives—"

"*And allowed Hengist to have my ship?*" Wulfhere howled.

He shook the forester like a flapping sail. Even while the man turned grey in that grip, rage got the better of his common sense. With a violent curse, he spat full in Wulfhere's eyes and reached for his hunting knife.

Wulfhere dropped the man in sheer astonishment.

The man crouched, his skinning knife point upward in his fist. "Rot your ship, and your vast self with it!" he snarled. "Would ye'd both been destroyed ere my lord took a wound for you!"

With a strangled bellow, Wulfhere reached for his ax.

An attack of prudence came on the forester. He wheeled, dodged between two Danes, and vanished down a game trail with alacritous churning of short legs. Wulfhere blundered after him, enraged. He found that his quarry had disappeared into the nigh impenetrable brush. Wulfhere hunted about, beating the undergrowth with his ax. It availed naught.

"I lost him," he growled, returning to the campfire. "Brave little rooster!"

"I'd guessed as much," Cormac said drily. "There's only green on your beloved little toy there. Ye needn't be hoping to see him again, either. He'll not show his face whiles we two remain in Armorica."

Wulfhere shrugged massive shoulders. "He'd delivered his message. Hengist! The bastard! He must ha' learned we be guests of Howel's. Word would get about."

"Aye. It's we he wanted. We were not present when he came avisiting, so he took our ship instead." Cormac's hard fingers clenched over his sword-hilt. "Desire is on him that we seek him out to regain *Raven*. Damn!"

"He will get his wish. Ah, wait! The five men left to finish work on *Raven*! Yon fellow said Howel's coast watchers were all slain, but I frighted him off ere he said what became of our own!"

"Right. Thought was on me of that very thing," Cormac said, shooting Wulfhere a look and sounding bitter. "It's in my mind that we have no need of him to tell us. We can both guess."

Wulfhere swore thunderously. Whirling up his mighty ax with both hands, he struck it deep into the mossy log whereon he'd sat a few moments since. All the power of his giant's body went into that strike, and much frustration. The heavy log split from end to end so that it fell in halves. Fat grubs writhed in its partly rotted center and thousand-leggers scuttled.

"Take up your gear, wolves!" the redbeard ordered. "We march for Vannes, and thence we take ship for Howel's island. We march hard!"

There was no protest. They, too, had heard all.

"An other insults be bandied when we reach the Mor-bihan, Wulfhere, do keep your ax still," Cormac counselled. "Doubtless others will be feeling as yon forester does. Morfydd herself well may."

"What? Blaming us for this?" Wulfhere was taken aback. "Why, Howel's a reiver himself! 'Tis the risk of the game. He might ha' met Hengist on the open sea at any time."

Cormac's thin lips parted in a wry half-smile. "Well done. Good hard sense that is, and none can gainsay. And how much difference might it be making to a woman whose man lies at the point of death? Or may have died, for aught we ken."

"Get of Loki," Wulfhere said, scratching pensively within his beard. "I'd not thought. Well— let us hope he lives. He's a good man, that Howel."

"Among the best," Cormac said quietly. Then, abruptly, "Let's march."

March they did. The Roman road through the forest still existed and not even a legion in the days of Julius Ceasar or Trajan could have bettered the time Wulfhere's Danes made in reaching Vannes. Nor did they pause there. Another day saw them landing on Prince Howel's island estate. Lady Morfydd did not rant or shriek at them, but Cormac knew he'd been right about her feelings. He suspected that she had wept violently and raged violently too, since Hengist's raid. They found the slim, broad-hipped woman strongly under control, determined to be just— and seething inside, against them.

Their five Danes had indeed been slaughtered in the fighting on the beach. They had been the next fatalities after Howel's coast-watchers, among whom had been Garin. Prince Howel was laid low with a wound that might yet prove fatal. He could not rise, or even speak. Morfydd's was the voice that commanded in Bro Erech.

"What mean ye to do?" she asked.

"Follow that old bastard and take *Raven* back from him!"

Morfydd stared. "And you with two dozen men left to you? Captain! If ye be fixed on suicide, there are simpler ways! Besides, how can ye follow him? Ye no longer have a ship."

"Howel's captains have several," Cormac said. "Fury's on them for vengeance against the White Horse, and they'll follow us to gain it—even if they do partly blame us for what has happened. I have a plan, Lady."

"Which they may not care for," Morfydd said.

"It's accepting it with joy they'll be, when they hear the greatest risk is to be ours. That ought to blunt the edge of their resentment."

Morfydd hesitated. Was in her mind to forbid the business without hearing Cormac's plan. Wisdom stayed her. In their present mood, her husband's corsair captains might well defy such orders. These were experienced men all. She could count on them to reject a plan that seemed mad. Besides, she too desired vengeance for Howel's wounds. She became practical:

"What of Sigebert?"

"It's truth the girl Cathula's after telling us," Cormac said. "Our mage Lucanor has leagued with the Frank, it seems."

"Then might it not be better to deal with them first? Wulfhere's injury—"

"Will not stop me fighting!" the Dane snarled. "It does but sting me to a fouler temper to cleave

Saxon heads! I've carried all before me in sea-fights when I had worse wounds on me."

He might have thundered on. Instead, becoming aware of Morfydd's proudly lifted head and angry stare, he drew a deep breath. "Nay, Lady, I be your guest; and that was mannerless. Ye spoke with my welfare in mind. See—I know risk of death whether I fare against Sigebert or against Hengist of Kent. One did not drown in a tempest on yester day, so one slips on a balky gangplank and breaks his neck on the morrow. Who knows what's fated? I know only that I'll not leave my ship—my ship!—to a gaggle of Kentish Jutes."

Nor was that all. Were it necessary, Cormac and Wulfhere might have taken another fine ship for their use, anywhere they pleased; even from the Jutes of Kent in Britain, in just retaliation.

What they could not replace was the five yards of chain riveted to *Raven's* forward anchor, tarnished black with great care and thoroughness to make it seem only plain iron. For in truth it was pure silver, and they must have it were they ever to reach the north and hire a master shipwright for King Veremund.

17

Raven uncaged

Cormac had not been mistaken. He had little work in finding men among Howel's corsairs to sail against the Saxons. The problem lay in inducing some few to remain behind!

Soon three Armorican galleys rowed southward over the blue sea, their bright sails furled to the yards. Their prows were more imaginatively figured than those of the dark serpent-ships of the Saxons; one had the shape of a whimsical seahorse, another a swan, and the third a carven sea-woman whose eyes were mother-of-pearl and whose tresses were green.

Aboard the galley with the seahorse prow were Wulfhere and Cormac mac Art. Ship's master was Drocharl, a cousin of slain Garin the coastwatcher. More even than most, this man had been fiercely delighted by Cormac's scheme.

"I've made my oath afore God," he said, "and the old gods as well, to take nine Saxon heads in payment for Garin's."

"I made mine long ago," Wulfhere growled. "To have Hengist's ugly head!"

Cormac spoke to the sword he was whetting. "It's having your chance ye'll both be. Saxons and to spare there are in the Charente and the islands offshore—and since Hengist is plundering in

Gaul this summer, where else would he be making his base? He has kindred there, too."

"Thanks for telling me," Drocharl said with irony.

Not quite smiling, Cormac said mildly, "I was thinking aloud, man." And scree, scree keened his whetstone along his sword's edge.

He gave thought to their destination, and foes. Gaul had her Saxon settlements even as Britain did. Less extensive now than in decades past, they yet remained strong betwixt the great rivers Garonne and Loire, and plied the Saxon trade of piracy with a will. At least fifteen hundred tough-handed weapon men dwelt in the region—and perhaps as many as four thousand. None had counted their number. They had no census as they had no king. Living as they did under the rule of a dozen or so chieftains who cooperated loosely in piratical exploits—as and when it suited them—the Saxons of the Charente needed no king.

Such was the lair of killers three fancifully prowed galleys scudded southward to strike, bearing two hundred fighters only. Even so, the galleys would ordinarily carry about half a hundred men each. On this mission each ship's complement was close to seventy. An all went well, Cormac and Wulfhere expected to need the additional rowers to fetch Raven back.

All went smoothly on that first day. Next day seas were choppy and winds hostile. The third day was better, though not much. Not until its waning did they come in sight of Wecta's Isle, named for a Saxon chieftain of old.

The two bearded Saxon fishermen drawing

their net were amazed and horrified to behold the seahorse prow loom suddenly out of the dusk. They let fall the net and the taller reached for his spear. His companion scrambled after the sail of their little boat, hoping to flee. Seeing the pale line of oars so rhythmically combing the water at the galley's sides, he abandoned that hope. In the present lack of wind, the oncoming vessel could run down any fishing boat. The fishermen could but wait. Two grappling hooks flew and bit. A mighty voice hailed.

"Come aboard and guest with us awhile, Saxons!"

The taller man snarled and flung his spear at the burly shape that had spoken. Up came a shield, blurringly fast. The spear struck it well with a sharp, echoic thud, and stuck fast.

"Very well," the huge form cried down to them in his huge voice, still genial. "Ye've shown ye be no tame dog. An ye be wise now, ye may even live to boast to your children that once ye hove a spear at Wulfhere Skull-splitter. That, however, is as far as my patience goes." The voice roughened. "Step aboard smartly now, or be riddled where ye stand!"

As punctuation, an arrow thunked into the fishing boat's mast. It quivered there, humming nastily to strengthen Wulfhere's point.

The Saxons clambered aboard. At a word from Cormac mac Art, one of his Danes sprang into the fishing-boat and wrenched the Danish arrow out of the mast. Cormac knew brave schemes had oft gone amiss because of little pieces of betraying evidence such as that left carelessly about. The

Dane jumped back. The boat was cast adrift.

"Well, fishermen," Wulfhere boomed, "ye may keep your lives at the price of sharing one choice bit of gossip with us. *Where is Hengist?*"

"Hengist?" the taller man repeated, taken aback.

"Ah, Wolf," the Danish giant said heavily, and turned to Cormac. "These good fellows have never heard o' him! 'Tis natural enow. He hasn't the fame of yourself or me, after all." He looked again to the fishermen. "Hengist," he explained kindly, "be a poor crazy old man not long for this world, who calls himself King of Kent. Some of us be kindly-natured, and humour him . . . it costs naught. Lately he's been doing things a poor crazy old man ought not, and we're bound to teach him the error of his ways. For his own good, ye understand. Where be he hiding?"

"Lord," the fisherman, said, "what know we of Hengist, or such great ones? He may be hereabouts—sith ye say it, so it must be—but he'd not confide in us."

"Play no games!" Wulfhere snarled, suddenly tiring of his own. "I *know* Hengist's hereabouts. I know how quickly word gets around. Tell me, or by Odin, I'll have your lives! I can see ye're brothers!"

At a gesture from their chieftain, two Danes seized the taller fisherman and bent him over a rowing-bench. Wulfhere lifted his outside ax.

"A good thing there be two of ye," he rumbled. "I can spare one, to show the other my mood is no trifling one. Once more only—*where be Hengist?*"

"With Fritigern Redjowl, on Fritigern's Isle!"

the second fisherman howled. "At Fritigern Redjowl's scalli, on the southern point. Although he
may be out harrying—lord."

"Nay, he will be there," Wulfhere said confi-
dently. He grinned. "He expects us. Well now, ye
pair, we'll just be taking ye with us until we know
whether ye lied or not. An ye spoke true, we'll set
ye free with no harm done. Even reward ye,
maybe. An ye're lying—" He made a throat-
cutting gesture, and an ugly noise in his throat.

The two fishermen were bound and stowed
neatly out of the way.

Muffled oars moved the galleys through the
night, standing well out to sea from Fritigern's
Isle. Named for a chieftain now long in his
burial-barrow, it was ruled—or its southern half
was—by a descendant of his bearing the same
name, to which had been added the cognomen
Redjowl. Host to Hengist!

Ere dawn, the Danes and Armoricans found a
tiny islet barely large enow to boast a cove in
which three galleys could lie hidden. Cormac despatched scouting parties to cover its every yard
of ground to ensure that they had the miniature
isle to themselves entire. They would bide here
through the day, and move against Fritigern Redjowl's guest in the evening.

Mac Art spent nearly all the day in weary, stubborn debate with Wulfhere: the Gael insisted and
insisted that their object was to regain Raven, and
but secondly to do death upon Hengist. Meanwhile sentries kept watch from the islet's meagre
heights, to warn should any ship come near. None
did. Nor was the argument conclusive, and with

dusk they put forth.

The Armorican galleys lay to a scant mile offshore from Fritigern's skalli. This was as near as they were to go, and men looked glumly on the ten Danes chosen by lot. These, with Cormac and Wulfhere, stood ready to enter the sea. They wore leggings and bullhide shoon only. Scabbarded swords were slung over their backs so as not to hamper them. Saxes, the wicked one-edged fighting knives of the tribe for which they were named, hung sheathed at their hips. That aside, they went without shield or armour and nigh naked: twelve men, bare to the waist, against an island of foemen not known for gentleness.

On the deck, five big casks were ballasted with stones to float with a particular side up. That had been tested. Lowered over the wales with care, they bobbed and floated as they ought. To the top of each barrel was attached an earthenware fire-pot in which glowing embers were snugly cached. They would last, for the water was slack and calm, between tides. Gazing upon those gently bobbing casks, Cormac mac Art showed teeth in a wolfish grin that was not handsome.

Twelve men slid quietly into the sea. Two or three to a cask, they gripped rope loops attached to them and commenced to swim with a steady leg-beat. The barrels provided support for the men who pushed them.

"Fortune attend you," Drocharl said in low tones.

Cormac had rather the Armorican had not said even that. Sound carried marvelously well across nighted water, which was why he and those with him had care not to break the surface with their frog-moving legs. The shore neared. Fritigern Redjowl's skalli grew and details became more discernible. Somewhere yonder lay *Raven*. She'd be drawn within the stockade sure, and guarded like a chest of gold. It scarcely mattered; they meant not to strike directly for *Raven*.

The little waves of slack tide plashed gently on the beach. Cormac noted the wedge of rock that ran down to the water and out a ways. Peering, squinting, he descried a faint glitter of helm and spearhead. Shortly the scrape of a spear's butt on rock confirmed the presence of a sentry. Cormac's eyes sought more knowledge. Farther along the beach, four Saxon warships lay on the sand ready for instant launching, with yards lowered and sails clewed up. Eyes narrowed and feet constantly working, Cormac smiled thinly in the darkness.

Those ships were essential to his plan. Nor had he merely guessed or hoped they would be there. Cormac mac Art was more thorough than that. He had known it. Fritigern Redjowl's men were professional pirates no less than the Gael and this was midsummer, the height of the plundering season. Those vessels yonder would not be laid up in boat shelters until the onset of winter.

His steadily beating legs sent him that way, silently.

Two bored carles stood guard over the ships. Irksome or no, Cormac stood long minutes braced in shoulder-deep water with rocks under his feet, until his eyes and ears assured him that there were no more. At last he was satisfied of it. It was time to move.

Quietly, he made his way along the edge of the rocks, squirming on his belly in the sand for the last few yards. The gritty stuff clung to his wet body and leggings. For camouflage, all the better. The sentry, standing atop the ridge of rock, did not see him coming.

Two steely hands took him by the ankles and jerked him down so swiftly he had not time to yell. He struck the sand with a muffled thump. A powerful hand seized his throat, choking back any outcry, and the point of Cormac's sax drove ruthlessly through his eye into the brain. The sentry died with hardly a spasm.

Knud was at Cormac's side almost before the Gael had beckoned. He donned the dead man's helmet and hung the shield on his back to hide his bare torso. Taking the spear, he replaced the sentry atop the rocks while Cormac squirmed past him. Wulfhere came following, his brine-soaked beard sweeping the pale sand as he crawled.

Almost, Knud felt sorry for the pair of Saxon carles guarding the ships. Almost.

Cormac cut his man's throat. The sand drank his blood thirstily as Cormac laid him down in the shadow of the ship. Wulfhere strangled the other; although a brawny fellow, the carle had no more chance against the terrible Dane than a kitten. Wulfhere lowered the corpse with a low grunt of disgust. He'd rather have met the wight openly, with weapons. Sneaking through the dark was not the way he preferred to fight, and he knew he and Cormac were one in that. He comforted himself by

thinking of the shock Hengist was going to have,
in just a little while more.

The gates of Fritigern's skalli were a bare fur-
long away. Guards paced the log ramparts. Most
carefully, Wulfhere's men carried ashore their
five casks. They set to work among the ships in the
concealing night. First they saw to the fire-pots.
The embers were blown to redness out of their
beds of ash, then fed with tiny bits of kindling.
This down between the ships' sides, where the
glow was unlikely to be seen from a distance.
With sailcloth to muffle the noise, they knocked
the end out of each cask.

The barrels were half-filled with pitch.

Bundles of pitch-smeared flax, wrapped in
leather for waterproofing, had been lashed to
each. Men unwrapped the flax and spread it
about. They positioned the barrels of pitch directly under the loosely-clewed sails. The long
ash oars, forty to a ship, were stacked together in
close lattices. They would add nicely to the sudden infernoes created by the firing of the pitch: no
wood burned more beautifully than ash, green or
old!

With the makings of a truly splendid bonfire
thus prepared aboard each of the four craft, Cormac saw no more need to wait. He'd availed himself of the scalemail shirt off the larger of the two
carles, and taken his helmet and shield besides.
Wulfhere remained half-naked; none of the three
dead men had even approached him in bulk.

A whistle brought Knud hastening from his
place on the rocks.

The guards at the skalli saw torches flare sud-

denly aboard their master's ships. The red light
gleamed on half-naked weapon-men; one, two; by
the Gods! *Three* in each ship! Voices called
through the night in Danish accents. That huge
redbeard yonder; he could be none other, surely
than—

"HO, LITTLE MEN!" he bellowed. "Go tell your
masterr that Wulfhere Skull-splitterrr is come
a-guesting! Fetch out that maggoty treacher Hengist, as well! Let none approach closely now, lest
these ships make the finest beacons ever to light
your shore! All garnished they are, and prepared
to burn like dry straw! Be sure ye tell Fritigern
that! He will appreciate what it means!"

Fritigern appreciated it all too well. The skalli
gates creaked open within minutes. Fritigern Redjowl strode forth at the head of forty warriors. A
heavy, balding man was this Fritigern, with a
yellow beard.

"What bawling is this?" he demanded harshly.
"Pull them out of yon ships and strike off their
heads!"

"HOLD!" Wulfhere thundered, in a voice
whose sheer volume stayed them all. "Come a
step closer, and these ships burn!"

"Aye!" Cormac seconded grimly. "It's kegs of
pitch we have aboard them, here under the
sails—and the timbers be soaked in lamp-oil from
stem to stern. Smell it?" The lamp-oil was an
embellishment that he thought safe; an he
suggested it was there to be scented, the Saxons
would smell it. "We fire your ships if we must,
Redjowl, and then we die fighting. It's three of us
there be in each vessel; 'tis a fine ship-burial will

be ours, and slain foes to attend us as funeral sacrifices! Four fine ships! Be the price worth it to ye?"

Fritigern's men howled fiercely, and pressed forward. He turned on them with bellowed curses and beat them back with the flat of his sword.

"Ye be talking, not doing!" he snarled to Wulfhere. "There's something ye want, and ye hold my ships to ransom. What?"

"Now there's a foolish question! We want our own ship *Raven*, that Hengist robbed from the Britons of Armorica while our backs were turned! One ship, in exchange for four ye will otherwise lose! Bring her out, Fritigern, and have her launched. Then will we bid ye a peaceful good even."

Fritigern scowled and went silent. He did not try to maintain that he knew not what Wulfhere and Cormac meant, or that *Raven* was not within his skalli. He didn't ask angrily what Hengist's activities had to do with him. Belike he was *afraid* of convincing Wulfhere that he'd come to the wrong place. An he did, his ships were just as apt to go up in a gout of fire. Was as no civilized man Wulfhere was known.

All possible doubt was cleared away in the next moment. A towering mailed figure came astalking through the torchlit gates. The watery light seemed to shudder away from him. The tall horned helmet, the glittering scalemail corselet, the long iron-grey beard, the cruel face, and above all the immense presence of the man—these things announced him more certainly than any spokesman. He was a giant, as big as Wulfhere Skull-splitter, on whom his cold eyes were fixed.

He bore a shield with the device of a white horse, and a naked sword.

"*Hengist,*" Cormac breathed.

The grey giant took in the situation at a glance.

"So, fools," he said in a voice like the crash of surf, "ye came hither to die with but a handful of men for company? I'd prefer taking ye quick, but doubtless I must be content with your corpses. In, and slay them!"

"*Stand!*" Fritigern bellowed. "Those be *my* ships, and *I* rule here! Pursue your own feuds at your own cost, Hengist! They want Raven; give her to them."

Hengist laughed sneeringly. "Not likely! Raven has served her purpose by luring these fools here! They die tonight. Ye rule here? Why, ye seagull, I might have your head at any time I called for it!"

"In Kent ye might," Fritigern answered dourly. "Ye be not in Kent now. Ye came south wi' three ships' companies, from which ye've had losses. On this strand my men outnumber yours."

"Ye'd fight *me?*" Hengist asked incredulously.

"An I'm pushed to it."

Wulfhere forgot the pain of the black owl's talons in his vast, beatific joy at the look on Hengist's face. Saxon or not, he could have hugged Fritigern Redjowl and called him brother in that moment.

"Loki swallow your ships!" Hengist burst out at last. "I'll replace them! Nay, I'll give ye five! Now slaughter yon dogs!"

"Promises!" Fritigern growled. "Nay."

Wulfhere roared with laughter. "Now that be the decision of a wise man! Promises? Jutish promises? The Jutish promises of Hengist especially? All men know what Hengist's promise be worth—even his oath! Who swore an oath to serve the British king Vortigern against Picts and Scots, and later broke it to fight *against* Vortigern? Who lured Vortigern to a council feast to talk peace, where all present were supposed to be unarmed—and whose followers had each a knife in his sleeve?"

Wulfhere ended his spate of rhetorical questions by stabbing a finger at Hengist.

"Danish dog!" Hengist roared, frothing. "Step down here and fight me! Single combat between yourself and me!"

"Ah, nay! I've come for *Raven*, not your poor ancient head." Wulfhere was enjoying himself. "Besides, I'll not be trusting to your oath, ye forsworn treacherous oath-breaking bastard! An ye wish to fight, step onto this ship and battle me here! Wulfhere Skull-splitter's oath has never been broken; all men know that! I say ye shall go untouched by these comrades o' mine, should ye accept!"

Hengist snarled incoherently. He seized a spear and flung it. Wulfhere sprang aside; the spear hissed harmlessly into the dark, to slay sand. The old bastard aimed well, even by night and enraged to the quivers!

"Nay!" Fritigern cried. "Don't burn the ships! Here, ye fellows, *seize Hengist and hold him!*"

The order was obeyed—but it took eight brawny carles to perform it. Hengist raved and struggled like a berserker.

"Ye men of Hengist's!" Fritigern called. Let none be interfering with this, else by Wotan I'll slay him where he lies. Now fetch out *Raven* and launch her!"

"Aye, Hengist!" Wulfhere mocked. "Hear ye that, old niddering? Hengist the niddering! Why, ye crazy long-toothed dotard, it's home in your shut-bed ye should be, hugging the furs about ye, not faring asea in pretense that your aged arms can still swing a weapon! Mumble over your porridge and remember the days of your youth— when ye saw Caesar conquer Britain!"

There followed more of the same. Wulfhere was hardly subtle. Hengist, roaring like a gale, froth spattering his beard, surged up from the sand and for a moment actually looked as if he might break the eightfold grip upon him. One of the carles regretfully struck him hard on the head with a bludgeon—and then had to strike again, harder, ere Hengist would lie still.

Raven was drawn out through the skalli gate on rollers. Cormac and Wulfhere felt their hearts race at the sight of her.

"Let's be sure she has oars in her!" mac Art commanded. " 'Twould be awkward for us, to pile aboard in a rush and find that we couldn't row! Display us all her other furnishings, too; mast, sail, anchors and such.' "

Wulfhere admired the neat way Cormac had contrived to learn whether *Raven's* anchors were still in her—without betraying his powerful interest in them—by merely lumping them with all her other furnishings. The oars and the rest were displayed, after Fritigern had given an abrupt nod of assent.

"Now let her be launched," Wulfhere rumbled,

"and then let your carles return up the beach at a run, not pausing till they reach the skalli gates, that we may go aboard! It must be done quickly, else *Raven* may capsize, to wallow in the surf unmanned—and must I repeat what will happen, an they move not quickly enow?"

"Ye swear my ships will go unharmed, an your demand be met?"

"Your ships will not burn," Cormac answered. "I swear it by my head! What say ye, battle-brother?"

"The ships will not burn," Wulfhere agreed. "I make oath to that upon my beard." He touched that bristling growth even as he swore.

Fritigern gave the required orders, though he scowled.

Raven was duly set out from shore. In truth, she was too seaworthy to stand in much danger of a capsize, and "surf" was an overstatement at this stage of the tide. The carles who had launched her legged it back up the beach, running past the four Saxon vessels in Danish hands.

"*Now!*" Cormac bawled.

As one, each man in his party threw his blazing torch into the tinder they had prepared. The pitch-smeared flax burned brightly; the barrels of pitch burst into vivid orange flame a heartbeat later. Wulfhere, Cormac and their ten Danes were already running hard for *Raven*, sand flying in spurts from their heels. By the time they reached the water's edge, the Saxon sails had begun to flame.

Cormac cast one glance backward, and laughed. He'd sworn that the ships would not burn. Nor would they. The Saxons were already cutting the sails free and dragging them away. Others were heaving the casks of blazing pitch into the sand, reckless of burns. They would prevent the fires from doing any great harm now that each ship no longer held men prepared to fight to the death.

He had sworn only that the ships would not burn. He'd sworn no oath to refrain from setting fires on them, to occupy the Saxons while he and his comrades departed.

Cormac gripped Raven's side and heaved himself up and up by the strength of his arms, streaming water. He rolled over the wale into Raven's familiar oar-benches. Swiftly he scanned them, striding up one side of the ship and down the other again, lest Saxons should be hidden aboard. He was hardly the only man who could play tricks or employ cunning, as he knew well.

No Saxons were there.

His comrades too heaved themselves swiftly aboard. Wulfhere immediately took the sweep. The other ten Danes ran out oars, five a side, and bent to rowing as they had seldom rowed before. Ten oars, to move a ship usually propelled by forty! Was well indeed that Raven had newly been careened, and that her timbers were no longer waterlogged. She answered sweetly. Her prow turned to the open sea and she fled out of spear-throwing range.

Few spears were cast. Fritigern's men were occupied with extinguishing the last flames in their master's four ships. Hengist's men the while ran cursing for their three, drawn up the beach on the other side of Fritigern's skalli. Their vengeful yells made it clear they intended pursuit.

Wulfhere, handling the sweep like some barechested Titan, the night wind ruffling his beard and heavy chest-hair, smiled unpleasantly.

Cormac stood at the other end of the ship, examining the forward anchor. A mighty relief expanded in his heart. The disguised chain of pure silver remained attached. For certainty's sake, he took his sax and scratched one of the links. The pure white shining of silver displayed itself in the starlight, through the black tarnish.

Wulfhere shipped the sweep. After those first awkward moments of getting Raven properly headed, it was no longer needed in such calm water. He and Cormac took an oar each, to add their strength to the others'.

"I hear Saxon war-shouts, Wolf," the Dane grunted. "They have their ships launched, and be bent to run us down like coursing hounds!"

Cormac only nodded.

Raven crawled on across the water. She had a start, but was frightfully undermanned. Each of the three pursuing ships had nearly her full tale of rowers. The twelve strong men in Raven pulled until their hearts threatened to break.

It was not enough. The Saxon ships drew nearer with every stroke.

Sudden as striking birds of prey, Armorican galleys swept out of the dark. They had guessed the portent of Saxon war-shouts and the urgent beat of oars. Drocharl and the other captains had promptly moved to the rescue, in strict silence that they might not lose the advantage of surprise. Now, as they swept past Raven and bore down on the enemy warships, they raised a battle-cry that drowned out that of the Saxons.

These were weapon-men of Bro Erech, hot for battle against their hereditary foes, hot for vengeance because their prince lay low. They howled like devils. Flung a hail of javelins into the Saxon ships. Grappled to them. Meanwhile, *Raven's* dozen occupants worked fiercely to turn her and reach the fighting. They had been left behind while others went before them into the strife, and they were not accustomed to that.

With a rending and crashing of oars and a grinding of timbers, the warships met. A solid wall of shields along the Saxon rail balked the Armorican onslaught for a few moments; then the sixteen Danes aboard Drocharl's ship broke through it. The Armoricans widened the rift with hacking sword and ax. Elsewhere, without heavily armoured Danes to aid them, the more lightly equipped Armoricans made ferocity do. Each Saxon warship became a hell of red chaos, and payment was taken in blood for the Mor-bihan raid.

Then *Raven* arrived.

Wulfhere entered the fray roaring, a swiftly-acquired helmet on his head, a linden shield on his left arm. He swung the great ax he had not abandoned even for the long swim ashore to Fritigern's Isle. His chest was still bare. He hardly noticed. Not often did Wulfhere fight in the fashion of a berserk, unarmoured, but he'd no objection to doing so when he must. Cormac went beside him in plundered scale-mail, his sword striking like an adder's fang. The timbers underfoot swiftly became greasy with blood.

"Away!" Drocharl roared at last. "More ships come to aid these swine! Beseems their chieftain has bestirred himself! Out of here!"

The other captains, with Cormac, took up the cry and the responsibility of enforcing it. Cormac, Wulfhere, and all their Danes withdrew aboard *Raven*, with a score or so Armoricans. They rowed. Behind, of three full ships' companies that had set out from Kent, scarcely enough of Hengist's Saxons remained alive to make up one—and most of those were sore wounded.

"We harmed not your ships, Fritigern!" Cormac bawled, and Wulfhere guffawed.

Fritigern's four ships gave chase until dawn before turning back.

"Hai, Drocharl!" Cormac bellowed to the Armorican captain, in the morning light. "Are ye after fulfilling your oath?"

"I made a beginning!" Drocharl shouted back. "Two! Two that I'm certain of, y'understand— was dark and confused in that brawl! There may ha' been others, but I'll count only those I'm sure on! Well—there be other Saxons in plenty."

"Aye," Cormac agreed, "there are that." For once, the Gael was grinning exuberantly. He turned to Wulfhere and clapped the redbeard on his mighty shoulder. "Blood of the gods, ole splitter of skulls! It went perfectly! Not a thing went amiss! We've not lost another man, even in the fighting. And nigh half of us battling without war-shirts, too! Belief had begun to be on me that we could do naught with success, so bad has our luck been!"

"Aye," Wulfhere agreed, with as much wistfulness as enthusiasm. "Yet I would fain ha' fought Hengist and slain the curson! I looked for him in the fighting—I called him by name! He was not there. Still senseless on the beach from that nice little blow he took, I suppose."

"Ah well," Cormac consoled him. "Ye did call him niddering and coward to his teeth, and a hundred men are after witnessing it."

"Rather would I ha' split him to his teeth," Wulfhere grunted. He scratched his chest, and Cormac saw him wince. "Curse these talon-marks! They burn like fire still."

Aye, Cormac thought, and worry was on him. *That is a matter we must be seein' to, when again we reach Bro Erech.*

18

The Lord of Death

Three days to Fritigern's Isle; two nights and a day to achieve their object; three days more to return. So it fell out, and they entered the Morbihan to learn that Howel was recovering. Although desperately weak and in pain, as he would be for a while yet, he would live and not be crippled.

"His wounds are avenged then," Morfydd said though without smiling. "It is well! And Hengist—he lives yet?"

She sat in her lord's hall, wearing a plain gown of dark red and no jewellery on her save two rings. Present too was a very different Cathula, exquisitely clean and attired in what was surely the finest skirt—red—and embroidered bodice—white on yellow—she'd ever worn . . . and uncertain as to what to do with her hands. Despite that entirely ordinary insecurity, the look of latent madness had not left her.

"Aye, curse him," Wulfhere answered Morfydd, in surly wise. "Hengist lives."

The pleasure of striking back at his enemy and venting his frustrations in battle had left the Dane. His cheeks had gone lank. Sunken in their sockets, his blue eyes were ringed with dark flesh and stared bright as with a fever. The constant daggerish pain of the black owl's stigmata had begun to waste even him.

Morfydd took note of these signs. She recognized their meaning. Concern sat on her brow. She considered, as if weighing words she had rather not utter; words whose very wisdom she gravely doubted. Yet at last she spoke.

"Wulfhere: Sigebert has used magical sendings against you. Is it your wish to do likewise by him? You may find it possible."

"Eh?" Wulfhere started, blinked, became closely attentive. "How?"

Cormac remained silent. He cared little for the sound of this.

"The Antlered God, the Lord of Death, is abroad with his hunting pack," the lady Morfydd said, with utmost seriousness. "So much we know of surety. In earthly phrasing, it is possible to give his pack a scent to follow and cry them on the chase. Great hate, strongly directed, can do this, an it be focused in a place of power such as the stone circle in Broceliande. Now here we have a triad who greatly hate Sigebert One-ear: your own self, Cormac; and Wulfhere, and Cathula. With me to guide and direct, your combined ill-wishing can raise the death-gods of Arawn. And set them abaying on Sigebert's track to harry the soul out of his body and into the realm of Donn."

Cormac's mouth assumed an ugly shape. Cathula said with dreadful eagerness:

"Yes!"

"Suppose it fails?" Cormac demanded with hostility.

"That were hideously dangerous for us all," Morfydd said. "Arawn is a god, not some lackey to be whistled up and despatched on errands! When the doom is loosed, it strikes where it will, and whom. The lord of Death, the Dark Huntsman, and his pack can as easily descend upon the ill-wishers as on those wished ill. Even should that not befall . . . the casting is a fearful strain, and could leave us broken in body and spirit. I tell you this: I would fear to do it. I'd not be so much as speaking of it, were it not that I foresee Sigebert One-ear will do great harm to Bro Erech one day, unless he be destroyed."

"He—will—be—destroyed," Cormac said. He spoke dispassionately, though the look in his grey eyes was far from neutral. "It's Wulfhere and I who'll be seeing to that, and without the use of sorcery. Ye've put belief on me about the danger that's in it, Lady Morfydd. An I have learned aught in this life, it is that gods are not to be used as weapons . . . or meddled with—or trusted! It's my own wits I'll be trusting to bring me to Sigebert's throat, and this sword to open him a second mouth therein."

Though he'd naturally shown interest, Wulfhere growled agreement.

"No!" Cathula fair shouted, forgetting herself in her fervor. "Where be your manhood? Where be your hate? Be ye twain reivers or whimpering babes? An ye dare not do this thing, I will do't—alone!"

"You will not," Morfydd said, in a perfectly equable tone. "You speak with the loud voice of ignorance, and under a prince's roof. I pardon it, and ask Cormac and Wulfhere to do the same despite your insults, for you have suffered much."

Cormac's shrug said plainly that the outburst of

a peasant girl could not hurt him. Was beneath him to inflict punishment for it. Wulfhere said, "Aye—but look ye to your manners, wench. Not all are as forbearing as I and Cormac."

"Now attend me," Morfydd said vehemently. "Put this thing from your mind, Cathula! Even with the stress of the summoning shared among three, and I to direct, the peril were worse than deadly. For one alone, and that of an ignorant village girl—yes, ignorant—no matter how strong your hate, this were madness and utter destruction for you. I'll by no means abet it, and there's an end."

Cathula's stare was sullen and fanatical. She dared attempt one further sharp protest and was as sharply silenced by Morfydd, and dismissed from the hall. Even she was not so driven as to take the matter to the point of further argument. The stubborn look in her eye, however, had not altered.

19

The Battle of Soissons

"The ravens are flying!"

So the word had been uttered, in Midgard and in worlds beyond. Now had the ravens gathered for the feast. Whichever side conquered in this war, the ravens would be victorious as well: servants of the Lord of Death, death-birds of the battlefield; eaters of death-glazed eyes.

Syagrius, Consul of the Empire, better known as King of Soissons, went forth from his city to meet the Frankish threat. He chose not to remain behind walls and subject Soissons to a siege. Informed by spies that Clovis and Ragnachar were raising a war-host, Syagrius had at once sent word to the counts of the appropriatee cities: raise levies and march! Conferring with them, he had flatly refused to subject Soissons to a Frankish siege:

"No, my lords. The barbarians have chosen their time too well. At any other time, we might retreat behind walls and wait while hunger and desertion thinned their ranks. Now, the harvest is everywhere ripe to feed them. I will not permit them to lay it waste, or destroy it myself to forestall them. They have no cavalry, and we have— Gothic mercenaries, no less! We will cut the Frankish host to pieces just as did the Gothic horsemen at Adrianople, a hundred years agone. Ours is the discipline, the heavy armour, the superiority with missile weapons. The Franks can better us in one respect only: Numbers. They will find it insufficient." Thus had spoken Syagrius, and thus was the die cast.

Now he sat his heavy Gothic charger under an overcast sky full of lead and slate, and watched the Frankish host approach. It looked as if the entire nation of the Franci was on the march. They covered the plain as a river in flood-time. The creak and clank, the odours of leather and iron and unwashed bodies flowed ahead of them even to Syagrius's aristocratic nostrils. He wrinkled them in distaste.

A Roman, this Syagrius. A proud one: last heir to the mighty tradition of soldiering and rule. A Consul of the Empire he was, insofar as the Empire meant aught in these times. He bore too the title *magister militum*: commander of Gaul's mobile field forces. His clean-shaven face might have been represented on an antique coin. He wore the panoply of a Roman general from another time; ornate, red-crested helmet with engraved and gilded cheek-pieces, inlaid cuirass and greaves, and a flowing scarlet cloak. His sword, however, was pure business: a plain Gothic cavalry *spatha*. A weapon for use, not show.

He looked with intense bitterness upon the enemy host. The Frankish contingent of his own army had deserted to Clovis and Ragnachar in the night, three thousand strong. (Too late, Syagrius could guess why.) As a result, he now faced twenty thousand foes with a force of nine thousand.

The three thousand Gothic heavy cavalry Syagrius led himself would decide the battle. These were lancers in scale-armour tunics and plain round casques, their iron cheek-pieces covering the temple and reaching down to the chin. Their massive horses wore armour of boiled leather over their chests and heads.

Two thousand archers and slingers waited in ordered ranks on the hillsides above. The Gothic cavalry had been swiftly disposed on a saddle-back ridge between them. To the rear, legions of armoured infantry provided backing, four thousand men all told. The foot soldier had become ever less important in Roman armies since the crushing defeat of the legions at Adrianople, and phalanx formation had returned with all its vulnerability.

Syagrius hoped not to have to commit these legions to a charge. Far rather would he have them stand their ground and let the Franks weary their strength against them. In truth, he had doubts of his foot. They were essentially *limatani*—border soldiers. Their purpose and training was in the main defense. Aye, and surely they must defend this day; defend the last tattered fragment of the Empire in the west!

Syagrius would gladly have exchanged them all for another thousand horsemen.

The Frankish horde now moved to the attack. They came in long, straggling columns. They wore no mail but only close-fitting trousers and leather vests. Few had so much as helmets. Their steady walk became a brisk, jolting trot . . .

which increased to a dead run as a harsh, rolling battle-cry burst from their thousands of throats. The very earth took note—and would for all time.

The Roman archers drew their bows—to the chest merely, as their forebears had always done, an act at which Wulfhere's Danish longbowmen would have laughed. Alongside them, slingers fitted murderously heavy leaden balls into the pouches of their weapons, and whirled them so that they hummed. Roman might, ancient and disciplined.

The Frankish rush came on. The earth quivered beneath the pounding of their feet. A few shaken spirits in the Roman lines let fly their missiles too soon, and were scathingly cursed by their officers. Closer the barbarians came, roaring, their feet drumming the earth. And closer yet. At last the order was given.

A hellish hail of arrows and leaden balls tore into the Franci. The sling-missiles were the more to be dreaded, for their shocking power was awful. Where one of those murderously heavy balls struck a man on the head, it killed him instantly; where one struck an armoured leg, it shattered that limb; where one struck the body, it smashed ribs, driving them into the lungs, or ruptured internal organs and dropped its victim writhing on the grass.

A volley. Two. A third, when the leading Frankish columns seemed almost close enow to breathe in the Romans' faces.

Trumpets sounded the charge for the Roman horse.

The squadrons began to move, surging down over the ridge where they had waited. These big horses under such heavy burdens did not gain full speed quickly; was like an avalanche of bone and iron, slow in its beginnings and inexorably gaining momentum and power. The Roman archers and slingers retreated up the hill-slopes on either side, moving in disciplined order and leaving open lanes. Through these cavalry rushed in a mailed torrent.

The Franks bayed like wolves. A cloud of javelins and missile-axes swept with an awful hum between the horsemen and the sun, to slash down into the Roman ranks. Here a man reeled from his saddle, shrieking while he clawed at the wreckage of his face. The ax fell to cripple a companion's horse. There a nine-barbed javelin tore at an angle into a dun war-horse's side just behind the rib cage, and deeply pierced its guts. It screamed hideously and collapsed, rolling over on the javelin, breaking the shaft. Its rider's leg was crushed and maimed under the animal. The horse struggled to rise, spraying bloody urine. Its terrible screams went on and on, so eerily close to human sounds.

The charge had been shaken somewhat—without being impaired. Its impetus was sufficient to pound a stone wall into rubble. The squadrons thundered onward. Hooves tore up the hillside and snapped javelins as if they'd been twigs. Clods of earth flew high from the chargers' hooves. Black dots against the sky, spinning in air, raining earth and sod and roots. Iron-tipped lances lowered to turn the charge into an awful moving wall of teeth. Bodies braced in the saddles; horsemen's sinewy thighs clamped.

The crash of impact rocked the sky and reverberated for miles.

Men were instantly impaled, spitted through, swept aside like winnowed grain, stamped under the war-horses' feet while their eyes stared huge as fishes'. The cavalry of Syagrius swept on, uncheckable, a flood-tide on the plain. A threshing machine. The Frankish lines had been broken, ripped apart like rotten cloth. Arrows and sling-missiles came howling down to complete the slaughter.

Yet only the van of the Frankish host had been destroyed.

Its power scarcely abated, the charge rushed on against the remaining columns, the greater mass of the foe. Again javelins and throwing-axes shadowed the sky. That Frankish hand-artillery took hideous toll. And horses pounded on.

Fools, Syagrius thought, with part of his mind as he rode. *Had they discipline, or even sense, they would ground their spears and make a solid wall of shields; spear-butts braced, points jutting out and upward that our horses might impale themselves by their own momentum. It is what the Saxons would do . . .*

Many of the Romans had broken or lost their lances. These drew swords or lifted hideous four-bladed maces from beside their saddles. Those who still bore lances leveled them anew. Smeared and dripping. Hooves thundered. The earth shook. Birds had fled for a mile around. Ravens waited.

Again resounded that crashing awful shock that no human flesh could withstand, however massed. Again the ragged barbarian columns crumpled. Bone shattered. Bodies were riven and men vanished under the blurring fury of hooves. Blood splashed and soaked into the thirsty ground and clods pattered down upon it.

This time the charge had spent itself. Its order was broken. As for the Franks, they had possessed little in the way of order to begin with, and scarcely missed it. Their wild ranks eddied. With order failed, those unaccustomed to it grew stronger. The barbarians closed about the horsemen in a storm of angry flesh. The battle became a vast boiling howling melée.

In the cloudy skies vague shapes loomed as if exulting in the slaughter. Hugest of all was a cloaked, implacable figure on a phantom steed. Were those wolves coursing belly-down before him, or a pack of crimson-eared hounds? No man who saw them was able to say. Did wild horns wind?

King Syagrius noticed none of it. Jupiter and Mithras were far from here, and none saw Iesu, and Syagrius was consummately busy. He rode and fought with a kind of inspired madness in knowledge that the Frankish host must be shattered now or not at all. His sword rose and fell, streaming red. Rome was Soissons; Soissons was Rome; and for Rome he fought as his kind had on this soil for nigh onto six hundred years. He hacked and slashed and hacked, grunted without ever shouting or cursing. The business was to slay and Syagrius, Roman, slew. The trained warhorse under him killed as fiercely as he. Its hooves splashed into flesh and broke bones, its iron jaws caught an enemy by the upper arm, lifted him bodily from his feet and shook him, shrieking, until the biceps tore loose and he dropped in a ruined heap. Syagrius slashed and hacked and slashed.

Incredibly, the Franks were not breaking. They fought like the wild men they were. Closing in, they hacked at the hind legs of horses, hamstringing them with great strokes of axes and long, double-edged swords. They seized riders and dragged them down into the dust and blood of the battlefield. There they strove against heavily mailed men; strove with hand-ax or dagger or bared snarling teeth. Bloody madness reined under a crown of sharpened steel and iron. The screaming of maimed horses was even more horrible to hear than that of butchered men. Clanging weapons were as the anvils of a thousand pounding smiths. Men were butchered and died, and horses, and men and men and men.

Syagrius leaped clear as his own horse crashed headlong. Its thrashing hooves brained a Frank who thought to take the Roman commander's head. Syagrius's sword, washed with blood and streaming blood, bit through the temple of a glaring savage and into his brain-pan. The fierce eyes glazed and the long-hafted ax fell.

Dismounted among his foes, his shield somehow lost in the fall, Syagrius accepted that he was a dead man. It did not seem to matter. Naught mattered, save taking as many of these barbarian swine as he could into the next world with him. He struck out ragingly. A sword broke on his blood-smeared cuirass and he opened the belly of the Frank responsible.

"My lord! My lord!"

The deep-throated yell announced the arrival of a score of horsemen. Their leader bashed out Frankish brains with his mace even as he shouted. His other hand gripped the rein of a riderless horse. Blinking, shaking sweat from his eyes, Syagrius recognized his aide, Bessas the Goth. Too, he saw that for this instant he stood alone. The battle had eddied around him, in one of those unpredictable and constant freaks of war. Seizing the saddle, he mounted.

Syagrius well knew that but for Bessas's most timely arrival, he must have died. Yet there was no time to thank the Goth. Syagrius looked about him, and even his strong heart was chilled.

Death!

Nothing but death. Mangled forms and reeking gore.

How many survived, of his splendid cavalry? One man in four? One in five? the foot legions had moved forward in phalanx, and the Franks were breaking those formations, swarming about them, dragging and hacking men down without recking the cost. Even as Syagrius saw them and watched, the *limatani* faltered. In a moment more they were in full flight.

The Franks, Syagrius had said, *can better us in one respect only*: Numbers. He had forgotten their half-insane ferocity, or underestimated it. Who could believe this rage to slaughter, this willingness to die?

A Roman could. "God!" he said hoarsely. Then, to Bessas, "Help me rally the horsemen remaining. The Frankish losses have been terrible too. We can reach the city . . . hold it against them . . ."

Bessas shook his head. "We couldn't hold the city now, sir. Let them have it! We can only go there and die. We can ride to the western districts and raise fresh levies. Sir."

Syagrius blinked. "Aye," he said slowly. "Aye! We'd no time to raise forces from those regions; the Franks moved too quickly—but now we will have. The barbarians will waste much time in . . . looting." He ground his teeth at that thought. He had said it though; it was as good as done. He accepted. "The best man in those parts is that Bicrus, Comes over Nantes. With his backing I can raise all the country from Nantes to Orleans and march north again. Aye, Bessas! Naught will replace what we have lost here . . . but the Franks cannot replace their losses either, and they are frightful. Nor can they raise a new army, for the bloody barbarians are outside their own country!"

He did not add that they must move swiftly, ere the municipal counts in the north made formal submission to Clovis. He did not add that all hope now hinged on the strength and loyalty of Bicrus, whose example would be required to prevent the bickering counts of the west from doing likewise. Hope was slight enow without such words to dampen it the more. The Lord of Death reigned.

"To Nantes then, sir?"

"To Nantes," Syagrius said, with a fire of decision that burned away his weariness even while his sword-arm commenced to tremble. "As swiftly as may be! Aye—and in Nantes there is a small errand to be accomplished apart from our main business, now I think on't. I sent Sigebert of Metz there, to take up the post of chief customs assessor because I had my suspicions of him. Suspicions! Holy Savior! Now I see that *he* suborned the Franks in my army! That snake prepared them to desert to Clovis and Ragnachar! Need I tell you what is to be done with him when we find him, old friend?''

Bessas spat emphatically. ''Nay sir. Ye have no need to tell me, sir.''

''Well horse—it's Rome you carry now. Fly!''

By sunset, Syagrius and Bessas were riding for the Seine at the head of a grim band of three hundred men. Just over half of them led spare mounts. All were bone-weary from battle and carried such provisions as they had managed to snatch.

Miles behind them, swooping strutting ravens were glutted until they could only just hop. Staring eyeballs vanished down avian gullets in their thousands. Clovis and Ragnachar were utterly victorious. Yet of the twenty thousand men they had led south, barely eight thousand survived to march to the gates of Soissons.

20

An Instinct for Survival

The surface of the black glass mirror swirled smokily, then cleared to its normal vitreous sheen. Lucanor laid it flat on the table and sighed deeply. Sigebert, looking over his shoulder, had seen naught in that surface save the vaguest of moving shapes. They might well have been shadows of his own fancy. Yet they had aroused in him a strange unease.

Lucanor sighed again as he emerged from his far-seeing trance, and Sigebert barked *"Well?"* because he could restrain himself no longer.

"Victory," the mage answered. "Utter victory for Frankdom. Syagrius met the host of Clovis and Ragnachar north of the city. His army inflicted fearful losses—and was itself all but annihilated."

"Ahhh," Sigebert breathed. Then, suspiciously, he added, "But is it truly so? How may I know?"

"I have said so," Lucanor was so injudicious as to say. "Believe it or not, as you please. I *saw*. Syagrius has survived the battle and escaped the field. He rides for Nantes at this moment, with some three hundred of his Gothic cavalry. They will camp in the open tonight, I daresay. Having fought a hard battle, so that most of them bear wounds, 'tis unlikely they can continue at their utmost speed. Nor is a Gothic war-horse the swiftest of beasts, especially when it carries a fully armoured man. Yet Syagrius will not waste time. 'Tis a journey of some—what?—two hundred and fifty Romish miles as the raven flies. More, by road. Methinks he cannot arrive in much less than seven days."

"Hmm. Remounts?"

"They lead some two hundred spare horses. That is another thing—sir; they will have to find forage for so many animals."

"Not difficult at this season, and them constantly moving on. Syagrius can requisition what he wants. He may have met utter defeat, but it will take time for the stupid Gallo-Romans to accustom themselves to the idea!"

Frowning, the scarfaced Frank considered. Syagrius and his band must surely rest each night of their journey. Was high summer; there had been little cloud, less rain, and the ground was dry and firm. So, then. Allow them to cover . . . forty miles in a day. As Lucanor said, seven or eight days seemed about right. Sigebert promptly allowed a safe margin, and gave himself but five days to prepare.

Still, first things first. This time Lucanor had impressed him. Not being an utter fool, however, Sigebert knew that the Antiochite hated him. He considered. Suppose Clovis's schemes had somehow gone awry? Was there not a possibility that Lucanor might seek to conceal the news for reasons of his own? Suppose the Romans had gained victory and Lucanor was lying . . . Sigebert's eyes brightened. His merry smile of anticipation imparted a hideous twist to the scars on his cheek.

"Shall we see how your story resists a little pain?" He drew his dagger.

Lucanor shrieked for some moments, begged for mercy, gasped and wept, groaned, cursed, even threatened retribution—which was empty prating. He knew he dared do naught, for Sigebert's protection was become his only hope of survival. Yet he could not be induced to deny that he had spoken truth.

At last, at blessed, merciful last, Sigebert One-ear ceased to torment him. He wiped the dagger clean. Lucanor lay huddled, tears mingling with blood on his face.

"I am convinced," Sigebert said mockingly. "Such a craven as I know you to be had surely confessed to a lie at the first touch of the steel. My lord Clovis is victorious, then. And King-no-longer Syagrius rides hard for this city?" His laugh was short, sharp, ugly. "I can guess what he wishes to do here. There, get up, man," he said, nudging the mage contemptuously with his toe. "You're scarcely hurt. Why, I've merely nicked you here and there. The blood's out of all propor-tion to the cuts. I took a sword-thrust through the side of the mouth and lost an ear without such blubbering." And he left Lucanor, quivering.

Sigebert gathered twenty of his Frankish war-riors. Thus escorted he went to the manse of Bic-rus, Count of Nantes. Directly Syagrius arrived in the city, he would of course seek this man. In Bicrus was vested power to raise an army from among the local populace. The several counts of adjacent districts would follow his lead and that of Syagrius, if only because they had no wish to be dispossessed by Franks Clovis favored and would reward.

Sigebert had himself announced, with the statement that he came upon a matter of the greatest urgency for the kingdom. He added that he must see Count Bicrus at once. In short order, the count received the handsomely attired Frank.

Bicrus was another in the mould of Syagrius, though not so much man; a believer in the ancient values of Rome, and a soldier. He ruled his district with thorough competence. Was ill fortune that he should lack a subtle brain and yet have to deal with Sigebert One-ear.

"Well sir," the jowly, big-nosed man said, unsmiling. "Of great urgency you spoke—for the kingdom, no less. It's best in that case that neither of us stands on ceremony. Sit, and speak your mind."

"I shall indeed, my lord Count," Sigebert said, and mused, *Oh, thou plain honest fool!* And he watched Bicrus as he seated himself. *Plain, indeed!* A leather-skinned craggy face, three warts on his big chin, another on the side of his arching nose, and ears that stuck out. Honest he was equally as the Frank well knew, and of indomitable character—and a fool he was not. Bicrus, for instance, did not trust Sigebert one finger's length.

"It concerns the rebellion of the Frankish *foederati* against the king," Sigebert said. "My lord Count will have heard of it by now?"

"Against the Consul Syagrius," Bicrus corrected, "and thus, against the Empire! I have received news that the Franks march, yes. I'd like to know how the word came to you."

"My lord, I was once a familiar figure at the court of Soissons," Sigebert said in a tone of faint reproach. "I have friends there yet, and a great deal of time for . . . the right sort of gossip. Word came to me, I dare say, but a day to two after it had come to yourself."

"Or even before?" Bicrus suggested grimly. "No matter. I am listening, believe me, with complete attention."

"Possibly it was even before," Sigebert agreed airily, as though it hardly mattered; as though it could be only the rankest lack of courtesy for Bicrus to demand why, in that case, he had not been informed at once. "I believe it was. Further news has reached me since, my lord, and in this case I am absolutely certain it will not yet have come to you. The battle has been fought, and the consul's army destroyed. Utter victory has gone to the Franks, under the cousin-kings Clovis and Ragnachar." He added unctuously, "Alas!"

Count Bicrus whitened. "You lie!"

Sigebert affected to look shocked, and said naught.

"How can you know? Proof, man! I must have proof!"

"It will be yours ere long, my lord! The Consul Syagrius has fled, and now makes for this city with the remnant of his Gothic cavalry . . . a mere three hundred men, and five hundred horses. Doubtless he means to raise a new army here, to fare anew against the Franks."

"I'll give commands for the levies to be raised at once," Bicrus said in instant decision. "The Consul shall find the matter well in hand when he arrives. God help you, Sigebert of Metz, an your warning prove false!"

"Softly, my lord Count," Sigebert purred.
"Softly! There be no cause to recruit the entire
countryside. A mere one thousand men of training and experience ought to suffice. So many
could whelm with ease the three hundred vete-
rans Syagrius brings with him."

"What said you? Nay, I heard. Treason!"

Sigebert shook his head. "Smooth timing is all
in these matters, my lord Count. What was treason
yesterday becomes mere shrewd foresight tomorrow. What appears loyalty now may well be declared treason in as brief a span. Look ye, the
victory he has won will make Clovis's support
among his own people complete." Mention of
Ragnachar, Clovis's ally, co-commander and
cousin, was conveniently dropped. "He can raise
a new host as easily as Syagrius can raise a new
army. With great ease! The Frankish marches
teem with wild warriors, but where can Syagrius
replace the cavalry so thoroughly destroyed in
this sad battle?"

A telling point. Syagrius, riding to Nantes at the
head of three hundred men? Bicrus shuddered to
think of the slaughter that implied. Why, the Consul had commanded thousands!

Always supposing this Frankish rascal spoke
the truth. Bicrus considered it more than doubtful.

"Nay," Sigebert One-ear went on comfortably,
"since Frankish victory is a fact, wise men will
accommodate themselves to it. The Church, I
make no doubt, has already done so. My lord
Clovis has been at some pains to enter the
Church's favour, and methinks the bishops will

accept his rule. No bishop, after all, need fear to be deposed from his office by a barbarian who cannot read or write! For the count of a city, matters be somewhat . . . different.'' Sigebert leaned forward. ''Consider, my lord Count, the worth of earning King Clovis's favour by seizing this fugitive Consul when he shows his face here.''

Bicrus controlled himself, though Sigebert's smirk made it difficult. He spoke practically: ''You have not explained how you come to know so much.''

''Yes. I suppose it is out of place in a humble customs assessor! Well, my lord, while I was highly placed at the court of Soissons, I was an agent for King Clovis. Aye, even in those days. Softly, I say! Hear me out! I myself prevailed upon the commanders of the Frankish soldiery to desert to Clovis when the battle was joined. Misfortunately, Syagrius began to suspect me, and sent me here to take up the minor post I now hold. Since Clovis has conquered, I can look to hold a higher place in the world again—not before time, in my opinion!''

He chuckled, enjoying himself. ''You see that my goodwill as well as my king's will be worth the having. Act wisely, and you can be one of the few Roman counts to retain his position. You will probably better it, an you deliver Syagrius up as a captive.''

Bicrus seethed. Before him sat a fouler traitor then he had dreamed could befoul his city. That he should invite Bicrus into his dirty schemes with the air of one who conferred some immense favour was not to be borne! It should not be borne!

The count's face crimsoned. ''You swine!'' he

roared. "I'll crucify you—no, by Heaven, I'll keep you prisoner for my Lord Syagrius to have the satisfaction of passing that sentence, when he arrives! Guards! Ho, guards—"

"*Idiot!*" Sigebert snapped. With no further talk, in two long lithe movements, he closed with Count Bicrus and drove a dagger into his throat.

So swift, so ruthless and so wholly unexpected was the deed that even the trained soldier of Rome was taken by surprise. He choked horribly, lifting a hand to the dagger-hilt protruding from the side of his neck. He hadn't even known Sigebert carried one.

Sigebert watched him fall across the table, and thence to the floor. Rome kicked and clawed in his death agonies, attempting to drag himself to the door. His struggles seemed to go on forever. Even Sigebert was appalled, though he did find the sight fascinating. He couldn't take his gaze from the stricken man.

"*Guards!*" Bicrus croaked.

Was his last word ere he shuddered and died on the tiled floor. He'd left a trail of dark blood across the room. It continued now to stain his clothes and spread over the tiles.

The guard opened the door. He was one of Sigebert's Franks.

"Gods!" he said in awe, at sight of the corpse. Then he remembered himself. "All's well, sir. The house is in our hands. These town-soldiers couldn't guard a rabbit hutch. Why, we *talked* them down. Didn't even have to kill anybody," he added with some disappointment.

"Excellent," Sigebert said. "Have two reliable men clean the blood and hide this body where

nobody will see it for a while. Once that's done,
I'll convene the municipal *curia*, or as many
members of that august body as I can reach. My
Lord the Bishop of Nantes must be summoned,
too. Without the late Bicrus to stiffen their
backbones, methinks they will see reason."

"Not if they know who daggered him, sir," the
warrior reminded with the freedom of a barbarian.

Sigebert let it pass. "That is why," he said
gently, "I wish his body concealed for the present,
and naught said. I shall inform the bishop and
curiales that, when my poor lord Count heard of
my lord Clovis's victory, he promptly fled the city
and has gone I know not where. You would argue
further?"

"No sir. That's to say—with respect, sir—" The
warrior's words seemed to lodge in his throat
under Sigebert's limpid hazel stare. "Will they
believe that, knowing Count Bicrus?"

"Of course not! However, I can persuade them it
is to their advantage to feign belief. An they as-
sume the Count has indeed turned craven, they
will more readily excuse doing so themselves. I'll
wager that ere they leave this chamber, they will
have convinced themselves it is true." Sigebert
smiled until the warrior did. "Now do as I bade
you concerning our late friend here! He's hardly
ornamental. His presence disturbs me. And return
me my dagger afterward—cleaned."

Later the warrior repeated those words to his
companions, when they had carried out
Sigebert's orders. "Aye! Just that way he said it,
with the Count's body on the floor between us.
And return me my dagger afterward—cleaned. He
might ha' been saying, 'Have food brought me in

an hour!' By the gods! It's in my mind that he's right when he claims the city officials will decide it be safest to believe him!''

The man was not smiling; Sigebert, at that moment, was. Bicrus had proved stubborn; Bicrus had been efficiently removed. Sigebert had not deemed it advisable to tell him of Clovis's promise to make Sigebert One-ear the Count of Nantes. He would, however, tell these others. Should they think to unite against him and his half-hundred men, they could whelm the Franks easily. Still, Sigebert hardly thought they would dare. Not once they knew they would have to answer to Clovis for it afterward!

Aye! By nightfall, I shall in effect be Count of Nantes! Ere the month was out, he would possess that title and authority in law, and be in high favour with the new lord of the kingdom as well. That, or he would be a rotting corpse . . .

It depended on the outcome of the session he had convened. Sigebert believed it would go his way. Even so, there was doubt enow to make his villainous heart beat high with the excitement of the gamble. It daunted him not. Unlike Lucanor, Sigebert One-ear had at least the courage of his own evil.

21

Fleecing Nantes

Five weeks had passed since that fateful Midsummer's Eve. The month of July was ending and sickles flashed bright in the fields as the peasantry, men and women alike, cut the heads of grain. These would be threshed and stored. Later the stalks would be scythed down for straw, and finally the gleaners would pick through the dusty stubble. These harvest weeks were a time of hard, hot work.

A pretty peasant girl in patched, dun-colored skirt drove a flock of geese along the road toward the frowning city gates. Her goal was the market within. Three ox-drawn wains followed her at their usual plodding pace. Indeed, these seemed to move more slowly than most such wagons, the yokel drivers hardly troubling to employ their long ox-goads. Mayhap they were half asleep from the heat. Mayhap they wished to remain behind the girl with her flock, for she was more than pretty enow to distract the attention of the guards at the gate.

They were chaffing her bawdily, one fumbling after her breasts, as the great wooden wheels rumbled by. The wench's geese scattered, gossiping in annoyance. She swore with as much authority as either guard could have done. One of these drew himself up on the rim of each cart in turn and gave the contents a casual glance.

"Wool for market," he told his companion, who did not appear greatly concerned. Neither of them so much as spoke to the ox-drivers. They were too interested in the wench, who was interested in naught save getting her flock of geese under control again, and passing through the city gate unraped. Was fortunate for her the guards happened to have an immediate superior who was strict about such matters—while his men were on duty, anyhow.

The oxen plodded; the carts creaked. Somehow they missed their way in the narrow, winding streets of Nantes. Instead of the market-place, they came to halt in the weed-grown courtyard of a deserted house.

"Nobody about," one of the drivers grunted.

Another rattled on the side of each cart in turn with his ox-goad. The fleeces upsurged and parted. Bearded Danes in tunics burst out of the wool, gulping the sweet light air. The suffocating heat under the fleeces had turned their faces black-purple and they sweated rivers. Aye, and fleeces had been packed under and around them as well, lest the guards should go so far as to open the wagons' tail-boards. This they had endured all down the long straight approach to the city's gate, beneath the sun of high summer in Gaul.

"Cormac," Karlsevni Ratnose gasped, "your clever ideas will slay us all yet."

Cormac clapped him on the shoulder. "Come, man, it's a fine long restful drive ye've had, when ye might have had to walk! Cease leaning upon the wheel and making mouths like a speared fish. We've work to do."

Heavy wicker hampers were unloaded, and carried into the deserted house. Meanwhile the ox-drivers pitched all the camouflaging wool into one cart, making one full load of it. The full cart then rumbled away to market, the two empty ones to an inn-yard. Two dozen northrons licked their lips at the thought of that latter destination.

The wicker chests contained their war-gear and they busked themselves swiftly. Out of the question to wear it while they rode in the ox-carts, hidden under wool! So much metal, leather and padding would have killed them with heatstroke. They had suffered enow in their tunics!

The hampers contained goatskins of water, also. The stuff was warm. The Danes drank it eagerly, none the less. They had a deal of lost sweat to make good.

"Ah, for some ale!" mourned Knud the Swift.

"Be cheerful," Makki Grey-gull consoled him. "Belike ye'll be drinking Valhalla's mead by next sunrise."

Wulfhere looked ghastly, and not because of his suffocating ride in the cart. His broad face had the semblance of a hollow-eyed, red-bearded skull. Was all Cormac could do to hold his own features impassive as he glanced at his friend.

"Word seems out concerning the Frankish conquest, and truly," he remarked, chiefly for something to say. "The countryside is in a ferment! Saw ye the smoke upon the horizon? That cannot be Frankish troops, marauding here so soon. A sign of some peasantish revolt, I'm thinking, in-

spired by panic. It's placid enow they seem, closer
to the city. It wonders me how long that will last."

Wulfhere shrugged. "No knowing."

"An they've sense on them, the country folk on
the great estates will support their masters to the
hilt, for once. A Frankish war-host on the march
be like a plague of locusts for stripping the country. Remember ye that one small war-band we had
to hunt down in Frisia, a couple of years past?
They left a trail like to that of a thousand ber-
serkers!"

"Aye."

Cormac heard himself talking too much, especially by contrast with Wulfhere's taciturn re-
plies. He forced himself to shut up. Morfydd had
said that a possible remedy for his giant friend's
decline lay in the death of Lucanor Antiochus,
had she not? Then death should be Lucanor's
portion, were he guarded by all the legions of
Rome!

Wulfhere spoke, wearily. "It's a fool's errand,
this, Cormac. Ye and the lads ought not be here.
I'm thinking my weird is upon me, and I were best
to meet it without dragging friends into Hel's cold
arms."

Cormac snorted. "Ye may be dying, for all I
know. When ye begin talking thin-blooded cau-
tion and resignation, then it's far wrong something is! Yet as a matter of simple pride, ye ought
to resent dying at the hands of such a verminous
thing as Lucanor!"

"Lucanor will be waiting for us, prepared."

"It's not Lucanor who gives the orders in this
partnership he's after forming, Wulf. To that I'll
take oath. It's Sigebert who's master, and it's

much else Sigebert has to think on. I'll answer for it, yon two-legged serpent be fuller informed of the war than we, or indeed any man on Gaul's western shore. It's little foresight he'll be having to spare for Wulfhere and Art's son Cormac. Nor will Sigebert be foreseein' that we'd dare attack him again, in Nantes itself!"

Wulfhere sighed gustily. "It may be. I know not."

Cormac shook his head. A different Wulfhere, this one, indeed!

Neither of them knew what Lucanor had once said to his Frankish master; that Wulfhere would lie dead of the black owl's talons within five months at the longest. They knew not of his other boast that, for all his great strength, Wulfhere must become incapable of fighting or other great exertion in forty or fifty days. Such had been Lucanor's estimate, and thrice a dozen days had since passed.

Wulfhere's little war-band hid in the empty house while the hours passed. Immediately after sunset they'd set forth, to move by devious ways on Sigebert's mansion. There, if no better opportunity offered, they would scale his walls and make a frontal assault.

Ere resorting to aught so desperate, though, Cormac meant to capture one of Sigebert's guards. He'd force the Frankish hog to say whether Sigebert and Lucanor were actually within the manse.

An they were not, it would become necessary to learn where they were. Cormac thought it bade fair to be a tricky, demanding night, with poor prospect of success and a likely one of death for them all . . . and it never entered his head to complain or reconsider.

Nor anybody else's. This was for Wulfhere; dying Wulfhere.

22

The Soul of Lucanor

The clamor began well before sunset. The sharp ears of Knud caught it first. Cormac confirmed the Swift One.

"By the light of Behl—there's a riot somewhere!" The Gael grinned maliciously. "All the better. This cursed city cannot hold too much confusion for me, this night!"

All gave listen intently to the uproar, which was in a distant quarter of Nantes. Shouting and babble, with noises of breaking, merged into an undifferentiated hubbub. Screams of starkest agony rose briefly above the background. Cormac grimaced.

"A religious rampage," he guessed. "Some poor fools are being ripped apart for not believing as their neighbours do! Such haps all the time among these believers in the gospel of peace and love. Mayhap it will even spread city-wide, ere it ceases or the Count's men put it down. Time to string your bows."

In silence, it was done. Cormac did not consider the bow a true weapon-man's weapon, despite its usefulness. Still a mob of howling religious fanatics ranked in his estimation more as vermin than men. More than once he had seen what they could do to "heathens" and "heretics." He'd no intention of wasting high-minded scruples on such creatures.

"Cormac," Wulfhere said in a voice like a groan, "yon be no mere gutter mob! Hearken— there! Was the clash of weapon-steel, or I've never heard it."

Cormac listened briefly. "Aye . . . Right ye be, old sea-dragon, and there's the neighing of a big horse, too. Meseems it came from the direction of the gate we entered in the forenoon? Those other sounds be more toward the heart of the city. I wonder me, now . . ."

"What do you wonder?"

"Little of use. For the present let us wait, and see what befalls."

The uproar continued. Once it almost died away. Once they heard unmistakably the clop-clop of numerous hooves, the creak and jingle of horse-harness amid the chiming of the war harness of men. This rattle and clop passed along Nantes's broader and better-paved streets. There followed the ragged tramp of inexperienced men trying to march together—many men, although how many was impossible to guess.

Whoever they were, they shortly ran into fierce opposition. The racket of real combat echoed between walls: war-cries, death-yells, striving and slaying. By this time Cormac and two others had climbed to the roof of their hideaway. That vantage showed them a leaping red glow beneath a pall of smoke in the southern part of the city, near the waterfront. Westward, a flaming sunset blinded their eyes. From that quarter came clearly on the wind the sounds of rioting. Ugly it was, and beastlike. The more purposeful violence of fight-

ing men, soldiers, now seemed concentrated toward the center, where the public buildings rose
hard by the market square. Wherever they looked,
the city was in chaos.

" 'Tis a proper night we chose!" Cormac muttered. "We can move openly through the streets,
achieve Sigebert's death and escape with ease in
this madness—if we survive. The gods know our
chances seem better than aforenow."

He descended. In the smaller of the house's two
courtyards, he found Wulfhere frowning at a
Gallo-Roman boy to whose arm clung a girl
perhaps four years younger than his ten or eleven.
Was understandable, with two dozen war-
accoutered Danes hemming her in.

"See what's come avisiting, Cormac!" Wulfhere said. "They fled the rioting . . . sought a
place to hide, this one says." He jerked a thumb at
the boy. "We were just wondering what to do with
them."

Cormac bent a slit-eyed, intimidating stare on
the boy. In Latin, he demanded, "By what is this
upheaval caused?"

The boy stammered. "Mercy, mighty lord! I
. . . I do not understand."

"No? It's mad this city of yours has gone, with
rioting: fighting and arson. Any fool can see that.
It's the why of it I want. Either ye can tell me, or
not—and the more ye can tell me, lad, the less
inclined we are to do harm on ye."

More boldly then, the boy asked, "Will ye let
my sister be?"

Cormac was impressed with the courage of that,
in these circumstances. Even so, he did not allow
his grim features to soften. Barely glancing at the

terrified girl, he said, "She's too young for ravishing. Besides, it's bigger, harder quarry I'm concerned with this night. Now speak while my patience lasts."

"I will, lord! There—there's been war with the Franks. Our king, Syagrius, has been d-defeated. The shouting in the street says he's come home. He's here now, with his army! Some are for him and some think to submit to the Frankish king, Clovis. As ye say sir, the city has gone mad. Be merciful—this is all I know."

"Ye've no knowledge of what Count Bicrus has done about it?"

"Lord, I have heard a dozen things rumored, ere we were separated from our family. Some say he has turned against the king! Others say that he is dead and the other, uh, officials divided—and others that he stands for the king. I cannot say which is true, lord."

"Likely not. Now attend: we will do no harm on ye. By my advice, ye'll be hiding yonder, in what was kitchen and larders. All solid stone, with easy access to the courtyard. An this house takes fire, ye'll not be burned, or trapped to suffocate in the smoke either. There be hidey-holes, too, where no looters ought to find ye, supposing any trouble in this disused shell of a place, as I think they will not. Understand me?"

"Yes, lord!"

"Good. Keep together and quiet, and I hope soon ye are with your family. My friends and I depart now."

And, after Cormac had told his companions of the exchange, they did leave the place, on their dark errand. Boy and girl watched them tramp away through the courtyard. Both were amazed that such terrible men had not slain them out of hand for the mere sport of it. That wore away enough for them to become sensible children. They hid where Cormac had recommended.

Making a path through the congested streets of Nantes was not easy, even for armoured men with shields and swords or axes. Once the company stopped while Cormac gave listen to a fat man haranguing a crowd. He spoke in favour of King Syagrius, and cursed Count Bicrus for fleeing the city in manner cowardly. Mac Art listened but briefly ere he was convinced that this jiggle-belly knew no more than the boy they had queried— and, while unlike the boy, would never be so honest as to admit his ignorance. Cormac gestured and he and his men pressed on. They were peculiarly his, now, with Wulfhere so obviously and pitifully weakened.

Because they knew Nantes well and Sigebert's manse had belonged to the customs inspector they'd formerly dealt with, Cormac and Wulfhere were able to find the place. No happiness was on them to find it locked and barred. The place appeared deserted.

"I'll wager One-ear's not here," Wulfhere growled. "That one will have declared for whichever side he thinks apt to win, and be active somehow."

"True for you, Wulf," Cormac agreed nodding. "Still, there must be servants, a housekeeper; a few guards at least, for us to be questioning."

"That pig Lucanor may be here!" Knud snapped. Hopefully.

None stayed them as they broke in. Sadly,

neither Lucanor nor his master was to be found.
Sigebert had left not so much as a guard or two.
Belike he deemed it too petty a precaution, with a
kingdom's fate in the balance—and his own shining future. Yet it was as Cormac suggested: a few
servants remained, and the formidable housekeeper, Austrechilda. She knew far more.

Austrechilda was stubborn. Two men had to
hold her face in a bowl of water to make her speak.
Even then it appeared that she might rather drown
than divulge what she knew. A tribute to her
character, mayhap—or to Sigebert's ability to inspire fear. Cathula had told mac Art of Austrechilda. Not until she had come up for the sixth
time, snorting and choking and blowing water
through her nose, did she decide that talking was
preferable to dying now, though Sigebert might
have to be faced later.

"He—he—" she gasped. "—he's at the manse of
Count Bicrus. Some days agone . . . he and the
municipal—curia and the . . . bishop, declared
support for the Franks. What's become of the
Count I know not. It's—ulp! ulp! in my mind that
he—he's dead. Now the city is divided . . . and
my lord Sigebert sits in the Count's manse, whilst
the forces he has raised battle Sy-Syagrius and his
men."

Cormac swallowed and digested that while he
demanded, at once: "What of Lucanor Antiochus?
It's a fleshy-faced man I speak of, with a thin blade
of a nose, and airs about him. Where might he be
found?"

"With—the lord Sigebert." Austrechilda
quaked into a long fit of coughing.

"She may sit," Cormac told the Danes who held

her. To Wulfhere: "This makes sense, I'm think-ing."

Wulfhere nodded. "Dark plots and treason, with Sigebert in the midst of it. Aye. An he's against this king, I be *for* Syagrius!"

"Away out of here then, to the Count's rath!"

That manse stood nearby, close to the forum and basilica. Lurid firelight made the great square almost as bright as it had been ere sunset, for several buildings were ablaze. Towering flames created great lamps. The square was choked with men, all revealed in that evil light of orange and yellow. Armoured horsemen rode down foot sol-diers or smote them with sword and mace, while they were being speared or sworded in their turn. In adjacent streets and alleys, other foot soldiers seemed to be fighting on the side of the mounted men: Syagrius's. The city was indeed divided.

"Blood of the gods! It's little difference our two dozen men will make, in that butcher's yard!" Cormac looked around, his eyes invisible within their slits. "Aye . . . best we place ourselves on some rooftop, choose targets for arrows, and shout 'Syagrius!' as our battle-cry. Peradventure in a while we shall be able to essay more without getting ourselves killed for naught."

Men looked at him who'd become General Cormac, and at Wulfhere who coughed in a sud-den eddy of smoke. "Aye," the giant said, and his eyes watered.

The Danes implemented the plan swiftly with-out standing on ceremony. They chose the build-ing whose roof looked best for their purpose, and they forced a way into it. A horseman actually struck at Halfdan, who ducked and gave no return

stroke. The horse bore that surprised Goth on by,
while the scalemailed men vanished into the
building. They gained the roof by the simple
expedient of breaking a large hole in the tiles.
Between fire and Wulfhere's ax, the roofs of
Nantes were suffering much this night. Soon
they'd found a place to stand and aim: a small
terraced roof-garden that they might have reached
less forcefully had there been less haste on them.

Below, Frankdom's supporters had had their
fill. Doggedly they retreated, still fighting and
forming a semblance of ranks before the dead
Count Bicrus's manse. Seeing them drawn up
thus, Cormac blinked incredulously. *Be this all of
them left alive?*

Probably not. Many must have melted into the
maze of streets, deserting. Few of those remaining
still had shields. Those who had were placed in
the forefront. Between them and the mailed
horsemen was a grisly morass of dead or wounded. That and the short distance made a mounted
charge impossible. The horse-soldiers began
dismounting, to finish the night's work afoot.
Cormac noted that orders were given by a man in
red-crested helm and tattered cloak of crimson.

"It's Sygarius hisself that must be."

"And a beautiful target he'd make were we
against him," Wulfhere rumbled, "asitting up
there on his big horse with his fine helmet and
cuirass! Our arrows would nail it to his backbone!
Why stand we gaping? Shout and loose!"

The Danes laughed, and obeyed. Their bellowed "SYAGRIUSSS!" rolled over the square to
bring heads around in bewilderment, just as two
dozen arrows sang over the carpet of dead and

dying. They thudded deep into the ranks of Frankish supporters. Six shafts actually drove through shields, to flesh themselves lightly in the men holding them. Others found throats, and brains and thighs.

Another flight, humming high-voiced, and another. Danish arrows slew Franks to aid Romans and Goths. Each volley was accompanied by a new roar of "SYAGRIUS!" The enemies of the defeated consul-king continued to go down; not spectacularly, collapsing in a mass, but with a nerve-wracking, inexorable steadiness.

Cormac was not comfortable watching easy butchery. "Knowledge is on him whose side we're on, unless he be fool. Let's be going down to announce ourselves."

"What—by our true names?"

Cormac paused at that. "Hm! Best not, perhaps. We come from Bro Erech with a score to settle, with the One-ear. That is all Syagrius need know of his—allies."

Wulfhere agreed and ordered his Danes to hold fast and continue pulling string until he called for them. He followed Cormac from the roof then, into the slaughter-reeking square. Franks were bawling for bows, and finding none, and going down. Two strangers emerged from the building whose roof rained feathered death.

They faced each other in the midst of the shambles, those men of war; the Roman commander with his tired face and battered, gore-crusted cuirass fitted to his torso, astride his wounded horse; the gigantic Dane with his great beard and ever-thirsty ax; the dark, sombre Gael in his shirt of black mail, treading over the slain in the light of a blazing city. Once Cormac slipped, in a puddle of sticky scarlet.

"Meseems it's to the Consul Syagrius I speak."

"I am he. And yourselves?" Tired that voice— and still powerful.

"Our names mean naught," Cormac said, lying mightily. "Mawl of Bro Erech I am, and this be Brogar, a Dane. It's to settle a score with Sigebert One-ear we've come. He is hated by many."

"I believe it," Syagrius said drily. "Look there! They retreat!"

Unable to withstand a merciless arrow-storm that struck them down gradually and horribly efficiently yet could not be fought, the supporters of Frankdom withdrew through the gates into the late Count's manse. The heavy gates slammed with a crash.

"Save your arrows!" Wulfhere roared to his men. "Come down here! This night's work is to be finished hand to hand!"

While mounted men blinked at that Olympian voice, Cormac spoke to Syagrius: "Be Sigebert in there?"

The consul looked into that face with its incongruous grey eyes, and he recognized a man of his own kind; a man other men followed. Besides, Syagrius had reason to be grateful. Of his Goths, some six score survived. Within the manse and its ground waited Sigebert with fifty Franks and something like a hundred Gallo-Roman traitors. Two dozen such fighters as he now saw entering the bloody square might well turn the scale, especially as they seemed fresh. The giant called Brogar and the dark swordsman who gave his name as Mawl looked worth another dozen, by themselves alone.

Therefore Syagrius said, "The swine now calls himself Count of Nantes, from which I infer that Bicrus is dead. A very good man, Bicrus. As for me—I am here now partly because of Sigebert's machinations. Ere he left Soissons he corrupted a part of my army. The result was that those men deserted me when my need was the sorest. That slimy bas— With Count Bicrus murdered," Syagrius went on almost dully, "all hope of rallying now seems lost. I must flee into exile or die here in Gaul. But by the saints, I shall settle accounts with Sigebert of Metz first!"

"This boon I ask," Cormac said. "Let us have him."

"You ask much." Syagrius frowned. "Still . . . were it not for your archers, I might have lost the fight in merely clearing yon gateway . . ."

"A good man," Wulfhere said. "I'd never ha' admitted that!"

With no change of expression or tone, the consul said, "Suppose we go in together, and agree that Sigebert belongs to him who lays hands on him first?"

Cormac mac Art never had to reply to that suggestion he liked not.

The black owl appeared.

Huge, malevolent and horrific, it dropped from the flame-lit sky. At its awful screech Syagrius's war-horse reared. Not even its training could hold the beast steady in the face of such eldritch terror. The horse threw its rider and bolted. The consul fell heavily.

The black owl rushed down on him with another ear-splitting scream. Its wings were black brooms, thirty feet from tip to tip, that drove the summer air in gusts. Its eyes flamed yellow. Its beak was stretched wide for cracking bones while its feet flexed like twin arrays of metal hooks. Other war-horses scattered in blind fear before it.

Cormac's sword was in his hand without his conscious thought. He slashed at the monster—and felt goseflesh when his sword passed through its body to no effect. It glared, gathered sinewy legs beneath it, and made a hopping spring at the Gael. He went down beneath it.

"Ah no," Wulfhere, groaned, "not the claws—not him too!"

For Cormac all was suddenly darkness, fetor and unnatural *cold*. The vast black wings were a buffeting storm about him. Talons fastened in his thighs with eightfold stabs of agony. The beak darted at his face.

Cormac's hands leaped up. He seized death's own throat, as Wulfhere had done on Midsummer's Eve. Like Wulfhere, he found nothing tangible to grasp. Black feathers. Numbing, weakening chill. Neither flesh nor bone resisted his grip to make it effective. The pain of its talons left him not even breath to cry out.

They rolled and thrashed amid the rubble of war, man and monster, and only one was in pain, awful pain. Cormac's free hand stabbed and slashed with his sword—uselessly. That cruel gape of a beak came closer.

Advice flashed into Cormac's mind as he knew he was to die; advice from Zarabdas and later from Morfydd.

Against every instinct of the weapon-man, he let fall his sword.

Fumbling beneath his mail, barking his knuckles, he tore the Egyptian sigil from his neck. In his haste he broke the chain, whose links cut sharply into his skin ere they parted. Cormac never noticed. He thrust the emblem of the winged serpent, of the Sun, into the black owl's face. And the monster fell back. In that heartbeat of time, Cormac attacked.

His hands gripped the broken ends of the chain as it had been a strangler's knotted rope. He twisted the pendant hard about the black owl's neck. It was inspired, that move: for the first time there seemed to be resistance; solid purchase to his grip. Was as if the old amulet had lent substance to the creature. As if? Like it or no, the Gael knew that was precisely what was happening.

The monster thrashed frenziedly in attempt to flee. Its talons came out of Cormac's thighs. The vast wings beat. Cormac squinted in that wind and hung on while he knotted the broken ends of the pendant's chain immovably together. The round, sinister head turned then; the beak attacked. Instinctively mac Art flung up his arms to shield his face, and hurled himself backward.

The black owl whirled up with an awful shriek. When Cormac tried to climb at once to his feet, he discovered that his legs would not lift him. He groaned at the caustic pain in his muscled thighs; he, who had not groaned when years before he'd been tortured by Picts. The best he could do was rise to one knee. *Blood of the gods—it's crippled me!*

Nor had the black owl gone. It fluttered wildly

in air above the corpse-gutted square. Cormac stared, and thought of an immense black moth that blundered back and forth between invisible walls, seeking escape from a confinement it could not understand. Battering its own wings and body with mindless persistence. A monster presence over Nantes.

Then it began to burn.

It burned. Bright golden fire encircled its neck like a blazing torc. The dazzle hurt the eyes of every staring watcher. Metal poured molten from a crucible had been less painfully brilliant. The flame, fell and preternatural as the victim, spread along the black owl's wings to their very tips, streaming behind, shedding sparks. They fell in bright array toward the watchers below, and winked out in air.

Sunfire, Cormac thought, while his back crawled.

The dark soul of Lucanor the mage thrashed in the bright fire it had tempted once too often. The blaze covered its head, took its head. It screamed one final awful cry and lurched aloft. It flew higher, higher, higher, until there was but a brilliant spark in the sky, a phoenix pyre from which there would come no renewal . . . and then naught.

Silence filled the square. Owl and fire had vanished, and amulet.

Wulfhere broke that silence: he destroyed it. He had staggered and clutched at his mighty mailed breast as the black owl was destroyed. Now he cried out in amaze and relief, and it was a bellow.

"The pain is gone! Gone! It—I'll wager the

talon-marks are vanished, too! Cormac; the curse is lifted! I'm whole again! WHOLE!"

Cormac's legs had been freed as suddenly of the crippling pain. He rose. He stood. Crom and Behl! He'd felt that agony for mere moments. It awed him to realize that Wulfhere had endured it for weeks; had given orders, fought battles, slept, led his men while under such a burden.

"I'm freeee!" Wulfhere thundered. "I shall live!" He lifted ax and fist to the sky, a titan on spraddled legs like treetrunks. "HAAAAA!"

In a shaken voice the Consul Syagrius asked, "What was that horror?"

Cormac shook his head. "We know not. It's attacked us afore, a monster seeking destruction. It's gone, whatever it was."

"Gone, aye. It is in my mind that but for you, Mawl, I should have fallen its victim." Syagrius smiled grimly. "I can offer little reward any longer, but for what it is worth, I renounce any claim to Sigebert of Metz! He is yours, Mawl." The Roman threw aside the remnant of his military cloak and raised his sword. "Now let us go in there and take him!"

They gripped hands in a silent sealing of their purpose, and Wulfhere's huge red-furred hand rested atop both of theirs to make a triple clasp. Then they gathered their men and moved to the attack.

23

The Soul of Sigebert

The gates shattered before a makeshift ram.
Cormac, Wulfhere and Syagrius were first
through the opening. Gothic mercenaries and
piratical Danes poured after them, shouting. The
owl was dead. The men of Raven attacked; the
death-bird's crew flew into Sigebert's keep.

Cormac remembered little of that fight. The
black Gaelic battle-frenzy came on him, that madness peculiarly his that would prompt a minstrel
of Britain to say, "At such times he is more terrible
then Wulfhere, and men who would face the Dane
flee before the blood-lust of the Gael."

His red-streaked sword flashed and seemed to
spring lithely before him, opening throats so that
blood came gushing forth; striking into entrails.
No shield a man could bear was adequate to protect him from that inhuman sword-arm, however
skillfully he handled it. Cormac was a henchman
of death who stalked grimly among those Franks
and struck like a fanged snake.

Beside him strode Wulfhere, a two-handed
ax-man exulting in his freedom from the cold
agony that had dwelt near his heart for so long. He
was irresistible and terrible. Shields broke like
crusts of bread under his ax. Men died headless or

half sundered. Swords skidded off the blade that destroyed their wielders.

And there was Syagrius. Defeated, deposed, careless of life, the Roman fought like a demon. His kingdom was lost. All he wanted here was vengeance. He took it and was resistless in his uncaring advance. Sigebert's Franks fell to his whistling steel, and Gallo-Roman traitors. That night any man who tried to stand before one of the three leaders—or could not flee—died.

Aye, and the trio's men followed their example mightily.

There, across a gore-spattered and corpse-strewn courtyard, stood the doors of the mansion, shut and barred. Sweeping away the last opposition, Goths and Danes together brought up the ram. Molten lead came splashing down from above. Men fell back with howls and curses. Leather leggings smoked and were holed by hissing splashes. Up came shields, high. And those men moved to batter down the doors under an armoured roof of wood and metal. The ram thundered; the bars burst. The foreigners swarmed in, attacking foreigners in the manse built so long ago by the foreign conquerors whose last consul now stomped in under a helmet crested with scarlet little different from the one worn by that first Caesar called Caius Julius.

Ten Franks faced them, ranged on a marble staircase. At its head stood the man they sought, and his smile was all mockery. "It is pleasant," Sigebert said, "to see men so eager for my company. My lord Syagrius, I see." One-ear bowed with a flourish. "And speaking of company—you lower yourself, once-king, by consorting with pirates who await the rope. Do you know the men flanking you to be Cormac mac Art and Wulfhere Skull-splitter?''

"Indeed?" Syagrius glanced interestedly at his allies. "Is this true? I see that it is! Last week I might have had to order your deaths; today: well met! I'll not allow you to sow dissension this time, Sigebert, traitor! Thanks to you, I no longer rule Gaul and have no responsibility to enforce the law against these men . . . even had I power and inclination to do, which I have not. I am come here to deal with *you*. So are they. Since they have a prior claim, in a manner of speaking, I have relinquished mine in their favour." With the courtesy of a king, he turned to his piratical allies. "I have done speaking, my friends. Consider the dog and son of a dog yours."

"You Franks," Cormac called. "Will ye be dying needlessly with your unworthy master, or leave him to me?"

One of the Franks spat on the stair without taking his gaze from Cormac's eyes. There was no other answer, and none of Sigebert's men moved.

"Brave men ye be, and loyal," Wulfhere said rumbling, "but foolish. Think again. By my beard, ye shall live to go free." He stared at a Frank. "We come here for justice. You and I have no quarrel. Why die for *him*?"

At that consummately sensible suggestion, Frankish laughter was a baying of trapped wolves. "We'll see who does the dying, an ye've the hardihood to be first up these stairs!" one jeered. "Come and eat steel!"

Wulfhere sighed. In their place, he'd have used the same words.

"Have it your way," he said, and gripped his ax-haft high up and far down.

The notched and dripping weapons of the attackers crashed against the unblooded ones of the defenders. Murder seethed on the stair; blood spilled over the marble. The noise within those walls was as the anvil-pounding of a god. Wulfhere's ax dropped one Frank with a shattered hip and, twisting a bit, brained another on the return stroke. Syagrius, weary from combat and travel and combat again, at last proved a little too slow. A blow from a Frankish shield-rim broke his arm. His sword clattered down the stair. Timely intervention by a Goth and a Dane in combination saved his life. They trod over a glaring Franci corpse and fought on toward the top.

Cormac himself slew the last of the ten Franks and in his impatience he hurled the follow from the topmost stair. At last, Cormac mac Art faced Sigebert One-ear of Metz, of Soissons, of Nantes; of Frankdom.

The Frank wore a light-flashing cuirass of moulded leather. Refulgent steel epaulettes guarded his collar-bones; an oval of convex steel polished to mirror brightness guarded his bowels. Almost as strong as mac Art's mesh-mail, that cuirass, and a deal lighter. For the rest, he wore a leather helmet strengthened with iron placques, carried a buckler rather than the large Frankish shield, and held, with seeming negligence, a long Frankish sword.

"How impetuous we are tonight," he murmured. "What, pirate? No big talk? No blather of how I'm to answer to you now for that moronic crewman of yours? What was his name; the one who slashed my face?"

"Black Thorfinn," Cormac said, slitted sword-grey eyes watchful. "Nay, no talk. Time enow for that when you are dead, Sigebert, dead. Should I fail, there be Wulfhere to come. But should I fall in combat with such as you, I'll have deserved it!"

"No argument." Sigebert smiled. He was facing his end, Cormac thought grudgingly, like a man with more to be proud of. "Oh yes, I see Wulfhere. He's too big to miss. How is your health lately, redbeard? I've heard reports of—"

The sword, no longer negligently held, leaped for Cormac's neck. The Gael's own blade turned it aside with a teeth-torturing scrape of metal. A less experienced man had surely been taken off guard by Sigebert's mocking banter, and died for it. That cut had been startlingly swift. Cormac bashed back, was rebuffed by shield, shoved hard, pounced to the landing—and only just ducked under a slash that hummed like a breeze.

Mac Art fought coolly, making no showy displays of skill. For now, he was content to hold to the defensive and make trial of Sigebert's swordsmanship. Determination was on him to take no chance of underestimating this man. Others had done that; among them, mayhap, was Count Bicrus.

The blades flickered and rang. Cormac's battered shield met Sigebert's unmarked buckler with a great bam and crash. They struck, feinted, circled. A thrust of Cormac's was deflected over

Sigebert's shoulder by the well-handled buckler. In return, the Frank cut slantingly down at the side of Cormac's knee in an effort to cripple. His sword met the edge of Cormac's shield, cut in through the already much abused rim, and stuck there. Mac Art strained to give his buckler a quick turn in hopes of disarming or dragging off-balance. The Frank twisted his hilt the other way so that his blade tugged free and he sprang back-ward. For him, it had been a nasty moment.

Mac Art attacked with a sword seemingly flail-ing, pressing his advantage. Sigebert eddied away from him like mist, knowing the Gael to be stronger and longer of arm. Now he ceased the retreat, for to turn further had exposed his back to the top of the stair and those who watched, and "honourable fight" was a game for boys. Came a brief savage flurry, almost body to body, legs straining and swords a bright flashing cross of steel between the two men. Their grunts and the stamp of their feet mingled with the sound of clashing steel. Then Sigebert had slipped aside and was safely away from the stair. The rushing after him of Cormac's shield was impressive for the strength in the Gael's left arm, but Sigebert avoided it and flashed a smile at Cormac's grunt.

Aye, Sigebert knew something about the work. He'd a natural talent for it, a coordination of hand and eye and brain. This was the encounter for which he had been obsessively training, half hop-ing for it. In addition, that early training he had indolently allowed to lie fallow for years had come back to him. He remembered it all, and knew much, and was strong and uncommon fast.

Nerve he had too, combined with a devious imagination—and naught in the least resembling a scruple.

Even so, Cormac mac Art could match him on all those grounds save the last—though in combat he also paid no mind to scruples. His advantages of reach and strength were offset by the hard fighting he'd already done this night. There remained his endurance and long experience. These had been hammered into the scarred Gael bone-deep, through years of feud, war, exile, seafaring in all weathers and all seasons; through bitter imprisonment that few others could have survived. These were in his muscle and his heart; in his very marrow by now. They were qualities that Sigebert One-ear, whose life on the whole had been pampered, could never match.

Slowly, the Frank was forced to realize it. In him grew the chilling knowledge that he neared the end of his powers, while this grim dark wolf he faced had yet to extend himself fully.

A try for the neck was caught on buckler. That shield leaped at him, so that he was only just able to get his own shield up to catch the sword-edge that followed Cormac's offensive use of seventeen pounds of iron-banded wood.

Sigebert had one trick left him. So far, he had used only the edge of his blade. Sure that the Gael was deceived and that withheld knowledge would work, Sigebert feinted once, twice, bringing Cormac's shield low—and thrust straight for the throat in a bright, flashing line.

A similar tactic had slain the highwayman in awful surprise. Now, mac Art's swordblade was *there*. It caught the Frank's and swept it out of line with a flash and hideous grate of metal, burrs grating along notches and burns. The Gael laughed savagely. Below, so did Wulfhere.

"Now for that I've been waiting since we began the dance, Frank! Ye fool! Ye did death on one of our men in such wise when we paid our visit to the custom house, remember? I saw his body, thrust through the hollow of the throat. Were ye after thinking I had not eyes to notice it or wits to know what it betided? Blood of the gods! Aye, and when ye warded my own thrust so neatly this night, ye did sureness on me. Now try your last and be accursed, *One-ear!*"

With a howl of pure frustration, Sigebert flung himself on Cormac mac Art, stabbing, slashing. Again and again his blade banged and skirled off Cormac's shield, and then his time came and the blades glittered and flamed together one last time and Sigebert's sword, quite unstained by blood, rattled on the marble. His own sword-arm poured red, laid open from elbow to wrist.

Sigebert's eyes glared wildly. He was helpless.

"Wulfhere," Cormac said, low and deadly, and the Morrigan had never been grimmer.

Wulfhere knew what was meant, and came— without his ax.

"Romans crucify a man," he rumbled. "We northrons have another way."

They stripped a snarling Sigebert of his leather cuirass and threw it aside. He growled like a mad dog, spitting in their faces, snarling, cursing them vilely. Then, while four Danes held him down, Wulfhere drew dagger. He thrust, sliced; again; he cut the blood-eagle on the Frank's body, the dreadful northlands death Wulfhere had never inflicted on an enemy and never would again.

Sigebert screamed like a soul in hell when he saw what would be done. His bulging eyes stared at the ceil, but he saw it not. Horribly rearranged, his body, too, bulged unnaturally.

Many were the things he might have seen: Black Thorfinn, writhing in agony, screaming likewise while infection bloated his belly and death's clean mercy was withheld from him; or Cathula's mother torn apart by hounds while her daughter watched, or that daughter's later cruel reduction and use; or Count Bicrus of Nantes struggling across a tiled floor in his blood . . . or a score of other victims of whose fates the pirates knew naught. Uncounted treacheries lengthened the list of Sigebert's crimes.

He might have beheld any or all of his victims, come from the grey lands of death to witness their murderer's end. He did not.

He beheld great, misty spaces. An emptiness beyond his little comprehension. Bounding out of the mist came a hunting pack fit for nightmares; pure white hounds, save for the ears of them that were red as their gaping fanged mouths and glowing eyes. Coursing down through the night to harry the soul out of his body; to hunt it fugitive through nine eternities. Behind those beasts, towering on a great horse with flaring nostrils, came a shadow-cloaked Huntsman whose head was crowned with royal antlers. Sigebert saw what few saw; the terrible Lord of Death, god of the Celts of Britain and Armorica and Gaul and other lands as well.

And Sigebert knew, and his final screams

formed coherent words while the bones burst from his blood-eagled body.

"The hounds!—aahhhh, mercy, no, no, the hounds, the hounds!"

Syagrius did not flinch to see the thing done. He had intended himself to have the traitor crucified, a death equally dreadful and longer drawn out. He saw only justice. Not without pleasure, he watched Sigebert die.

They found Lucanor in one of the upper chambers. He was unmistakably dead, shriveled as if by fire though neither charred nor blistered. Had his neck been cut, as by a tight-drawn chain, all round? None could be sure.

So, then. King Veremund would be glad to learn that death had been done on the mage who had destroyed his queen, body and mind and soul. Cormac and Wulfhere cared but little. The man who had died at the head of the marble stair had been more dangerous than forty such as the mage, for all Lucanor's powers of sorcery.

Count Bicrus's body they discovered below. It was wrapped, with cynical pretense at respect, in a shroud.

"It is over then," Syagrius said wearily. "Poor Bicrus was the last hope left me. I might as well have fled south at once. I have achieved little save to spend lives and burn a part of the city."

"Blame Sigebert for that, not yourself," Wulfhere said gruffly. Almost he clapped the Roman on the shoulder, but remembered the man's freshly splinted arm. "Let the city—and Gaul— take care of itself, as it will. I and Cormac mean to go away from here and get mightily drunk until dawn, and it's my counsel that ye do the same. What say ye?"

Consul-King said to pirate. "I say lead on!"

24

The Dark Huntsman

The long dusty road shimmered in summer's haze. At its end lay the town of Vannes, and the enclosed stretch of water known as the Morbihan, with the open sea behind it. There waited the lean pirate ship named *Raven*. Other ships lay in there too, to carry a deposed king and his followers into exile.

The death birds had flown. The *Raven* of the sea and the ravens of war; the owl had flown and fallen to a better huntsman, and the eagle of Rome and at last the stern eagle of the northlands. Now there was only *Raven*.

Big Gothic war-horses paced steadily toward the waiting ships. Their hooves clopped, lifting dust in yellowish puffs.

Three men rode at the cavalcade's head, mail-shirted and helmed. One carried his arm in a sling and yet sat his horse as if born to the saddle. His two fellows rode more clumsily. One, dark and grim with a scarred face, trailed from his helm a horsehair crest as white as the Roman's was red. Nor looked he happy in the saddle. The third man, whose horse laboured most, was a giant in a mail corselet and a northron's casque on his head.

Behind them, awkwardly, rode a round score of Danes, shifting their buttocks in the saddles and wishing for oar-benches instead. After them paced fourscore and two Gothic horsemen. Silent they were, not even grinning at the sight the Danish pirates made ahorse. All showed signs of hard travel and harder fighting. Dusty they were, and sweaty, and with wounds on them.

Cormac glanced back. He knew this tired procession represented history amaking. The Vandals misruled Carthage; between them the Visigoths and Sueves held Hispania; Odovacar the German was master of Italy and Rome itself; and from Britain the last legions had been withdrawn threescore years agone. The splendours of southern Gaul belonged to the Goth and to the Burgund. Gaul's western peninsula was become again what it had been before Rome's first Caesar; wholly a land of Celts. Syagrius had been the last consul in Gaul. The "Roman Kingdom" of Soissons had been the last, the very last fragment of the Western Empire.

Now it too was gone, fallen to red-handed barbarians. Rome had conquered and occupied Gaul; Rome rode away at Cormac's side.

Was naught to mac Art, true. Still, the mood of the man with whom he rode communicated itself to him. Gone, all gone. He fell suddenly prey to the inborn, irrational nostalgia of the Gael. A sense of evanescence was on him, and of things passing away. Blood fertilized soil and only Time conquered.

Wulfhere drew him back with a grunt and an indicative nod. By the roadside up ahead, a small group tarried. Cormac recognized the woman; tiny she was with broad hips and erect, graceful carriage, with strands of grey in her flowing black hair, despite her youth. What, he mused, should Morfydd be doing out here at this time?

To Syagrius he said quietly, "Do give the halt by yon people, will ye?"

The Roman did not question, but gave the order. Danes sawed and tugged without competence at their horses' mouths so that the animals milled even while the Goths smoothly drew rein. With exchanged glances and no words, they aided the Danes in quieting their mounts.

"Good hail, Cormac," Morfydd said. "I foresaw we should meet here."

"Give you good day, Morfydd. It's news you bring?"

"I traveled hither in hopes of preventing it." She indicated a litter on the roadside grass at her feet. It bore a motionless shape covered by a cloak. "Cathula would not listen. She ran away, Cormac. Not from her enemies this time, but from her friends. By the time I learned she was gone, she had too long a start. Child, child!" Morfydd shook her head. "She walked to the standing stones in Broceliande, to do what I forbade. You remember?"

"Aye," Cormac answered, his mouth going dry. "A thousand years agone it seems . . . but I remember. And the rest of it happed? That which you warned of?"

"You guess aright." Morfydd's voice was sorrowful. With respect, she drew the cloak from Sigebert One-ear's last victim.

Cormac looked. A wind from the outer gulfs seemed to blow past him and chill his flesh. Only a girl! None would have believed that Cathula had died such, a young girl. The wind-stirred hair framing her face had gone white. Her body was shrunken as with great age; her open eyes were opaquely filmed as with cataract. Tough-souled though mac Art was, his thin lips writhed involuntarily back from his teeth. He sucked a short breath between them. Aye. Sigebert's last victim, drained of its soul.

"She tried to summon the Wild Hunt, herself alone?" he said, asking for confirmation, not because he doubted. "This was the result?"

"Yes."

"Sigebert!" Cormac said it as if it were a curse. "Are there no bounds to the destruction that evil dog has wrought?"

"He is dead," Morfydd said. Was not a question, the way she uttered it.

Cormac nodded. "I and Wulfhere and this man saw to that, in Nantes. Ye have knowledge of this?"

"In essence, as I know who it is you ride with. Cathula failed then, poor child . . . she did what she did to no purpose, and gave all she had."

"I cannot say," Cormac said thoughtfully. Sigebert One-ear's last shrieked words came ominously back to him. "It's in my mind that she just may not have failed, Morfydd. If so, he suffers . . . forever."

The hounds!—aahhhh, mercy, no, no, the hounds, the hounds . . .

The seeress replaced the cloak over Cathula's body. "Tell me of it ere you do depart for Danemark, an you will, Cormac. For now, there is naught here to delay you. I will see Cathula fittingly buried, and give her soul such repose as I can. I'll follow in your tracks when that is done."

Cormac only nodded. Solemn and silent as a funeral cortege, they passed by, one hundred men

and five. The deposed Roman king and the out-
lawed Gaelic descendant of kings led them. Their
hooves drummed a slow dust-muffled tattoo that
was as a dirge on the ancient road. They vanished
slowly, into the green distances of the forest. Morfydd gazed at the litter with its covered burden.

"A short life, and cruelly wasted," she murmured, "and a terrible end thereto. The gods do
not care, little Cathula. I tried to warn you. Now
you must go as you came, a shadeflower fast fad-
ing and soon forgotten."

She lifted her head. The strange, far-seeing eyes
gazed after the riders.

"And what of you? The living, and the dead?
Cormac, Wulfhere, Syagrius, Bicrus, Sigebert?
When the stars have turned but a little way farther
in the sky, who will remember you? Or the names
of the kingdoms you strove for?"

The echoes of a hunting horn jewelled with
black stars seemed still to ring through the glades
of Broceliande.

ALL TWELVE TITLES AVAILABLE FROM ACE
$1.95 EACH

11671	**Conan, #1**
11672	**Conan of Cimmeria, #2**
11673	**Conan the Freebooter, #3**
11674	**Conan the Wanderer, #4**
11675	**Conan the Adventurer, #5**
11676	**Conan the Buccaneer, #6**
11677	**Conan the Warrior, #7**
11678	**Conan the Usurper, #8**
11679	**Conan the Conqueror, #9**
11680	**Conan the Avenger, #10**
11682	**Conan of Aquilonia, #11**
11681	**Conan of the Isles, #12**

Available wherever paperbacks are sold or use this coupon.

Ace Science Fiction, Book Mailing Service,
SF Box 690, Rockville Centre, N.Y. 11571

Please send me titles checked above.

I enclose $ . . . . Add 50¢ handling fee per copy.

Name . . . .

Address . . . .

City . . . . State . . . . Zip . . . .

FRITZ LEIBER

FAFHRD AND THE GRAY MOUSER SAGA

79175	SWORDS AND DEVILTRY	$1.95
79155	SWORDS AGAINST DEATH	$1.95
79184	SWORDS IN THE MIST	$1.95
79164	SWORDS AGAINST WIZARDRY	$1.95
79223	THE SWORDS OF LANKHMAR	$1.95
79168	SWORDS AND ICE MAGIC	$1.95